THE VAMPIRE IN THE ORCHARD

A Monstrous New York Novel

E.M. SAUBER

Editing & Proofreading - Nice Girl, Naughty Edits

Cover Design - Impyeu

Orchard Map - Amberclopedia

To all the overstimulated, tired moms out there who wished for a hot vampire nanny to do the laundry and the dishes...

and you.

You're welcome.

NOTE FROM THE AUTHOR

Dearest reader,

Welcome to Monstrous New York! This series is set in an alternate version of New York City, where monsters and humans live together in harmony… usually. I have taken creative liberties with some of the setting, as well as Maggie and Viktor's occupations. So use your imagination and allow me to bend reality within the confines of these pages.

This is a sweet monster romance, but that doesn't mean we can forgo some warnings. If any of the following make you uncomfortable, please consider choosing a different book or proceed with caution.

- Death of a spouse (not on page)
- Mentions of grief and depression
- Mentions of pregnancy, childbirth & chosen sterilization
- Detailed depictions of sex between consenting adults
- Use of profane language
- Prejudice and misogynist ideations (not by either MC)
- Blood play and biting
- Degradation
- Anal sex

CONTENTS

1. Maggie   1

2. Maggie   11

3. Maggie   21

4. Viktor   27

5. Viktor   41

6. Maggie   49

7. Viktor   61

8. Maggie   73

9. Viktor   89

10. Maggie   107

11. Viktor   113

12. Maggie   123

13. Viktor   131

14. Maggie   141

15. Viktor   151

16. Maggie   157

17. Viktor   173

18. Maggie   191

19. Viktor   201

20. Maggie   213

21. Viktor   223

22. Viktor   235

23. Maggie   243

24. Viktor   255

25. Maggie   263

26. Viktor   275

27. Maggie   283

28. Maggie   291

Epilogue   303

Chapter 1

Maggie

The envelope crinkles, rough against my trembling hands. I should have stuck it behind the cookie jar with the rest. Instead, I chose to start the morning under a black storm cloud, no doubt setting a precedent for the rest of this miserable Monday.

Final Notice taunts me, emblazoned across the clean white paper in bold red ink.

I tear it open, only to find another mortgage payment that I don't have the money to pay for.

Cyrus, my brother-in-law, would front me the money if I asked, but— I swallow around the lump in my throat and swipe at the tears gathering in my eyes. Shoving the bill in the growing pile behind the ceramic bear-shaped cookie jar, I force out a breath. "We'll be fine, Mags. You'll find a way like you have for the past four years."

Roman would know what to do. A gusted breath passes my lips.

He *always* knew what to do.

Roman wouldn't have let our finances get this bad in the first place. Nausea churns in my stomach, the same way it does every time I think of him.

My husband.

My first love.

If only he was still alive.

It'll be fine. *It has to be.*

Spinning, I brace my hands on the edge of the kitchen sink, and my eyes wander to the rows of trees outside the window. Nearly ripe apples peek from behind the green leaves. Bright red and just waiting to be picked.

It's almost harvest season. Pretty soon, people will be lining up at the orchard gates to select their own bushel and enjoy a hayride around the grounds. At least, I hope they will. After last year, I'm not so sure.

If we can just make it through the remainder of summer, then the cash should start flowing again.

Busying my hands to distract myself from my chaotic thoughts, I focus on the dishes in the sink. The pink plastic plate adorned with rainbows and unicorns has a smile tugging at my lips.

At least I have Lily. Everything I do is for her now. I pulled myself out of that dark pit four years ago... for *her*.

Turning my head, my eyes cut across the room to the kitchen table, landing on my five-year-old daughter.

Her tiny legs swing beneath her chair, eyebrows pinched while her little tongue pokes out of her mouth. Intense green gaze focused on the purple crayon in her hand, she scribbles a path along the paper.

Uncapped markers and glitter paints litter the worn wood of the tabletop like an explosion of creativity.

"What are you working on, Lily bug?" Setting the final plate on the drying rack, I flip off the water and dry my hands on the dish towel before wandering over to where she sits.

As I peer over her shoulder at the paper, I stroke a hand through her curly blonde ponytail and spot—

"A buttfly!" Shimmering light eyes peek up at me as she bounces in her seat.

I stifle my laugh and smile. "And what a beautiful butterfly it is. What colors did you use?"

"All my favorites, Momma!"

Sure enough, the butterfly's wings are decked out in every shade of purple and pink in her art box. Bright, bold, and sparkling, just like her vibrant personality. "It's perfect, Lil. Should we hang it on the fridge when you're done?"

Chubby cheeks smudged with purple marker scrunch when she smiles, showcasing a missing bottom tooth. The first of many to come.

She's not my little baby anymore. In a few weeks, she'll be starting kindergarten and making new friends. My heart squeezes with every sign of her getting older.

It squeezes to the point of pain when I remember all the milestones Roman's missed. Clutching at my chest, I wipe that thought away. *It's too early in the morning for a pity party, Mags.*

A clipped knock at the front door has my head swinging up. "I'm going to get the door. Let me know when you're all done."

"Okay!" Oblivious to the second round of knocks, Lily picks up her crayon and turns her attention back to her masterpiece.

With my daughter sufficiently occupied, I head down the hall as *another* knock rings through the air. "Impatient much?"

I'm about ready to read this person the riot act, but the breath stalls in my lungs when I swing the door wide and am met by the most handsome man I've ever seen—besides Roman.

Striking rich crimson eyes meet mine, and my brain goes blank. "C-Can I help you?" I manage to choke out. *Smooth, Maggie.*

"Mrs. Maggie Wilcox?" His dark eyebrows rise, a direct contrast to his nearly translucent white hair. The long strands are neatly combed back into a sleek ponytail, fastened at the base of his skull, and leaving his sharp jaw on display for my wandering eyes. A jaw that's been carved from marble, surely, like one of those famous statues you'd see in a museum.

Is it hot in here, or is it just me? Every inch of my skin heats, and I swallow the saliva pooling in my mouth before continuing my perusal.

He really must be carved from marble; his skin is so pale, it's unnatural, and he nearly glows where the morning sun beats against the side of his face.

Based on his appearance alone, I'd wager he's something otherworldly, but I know it's rude to ask.

Humans and monsters live in symbiosis for the most part, so I try to treat them like I would anyone else.

In fact, several of my harvest employees are monsters. Wings make it surprisingly easy to reach the apples at the tippy-tops of the trees that would otherwise go unpicked.

A throat clearing pulls me back to the oddly attractive stranger on my doorstep. His full lips curl up in a grin, revealing glinting sharp fangs.

Definitely *not* human.

My cheeks burn as I extend my hand and try to recover from my blatant ogling. "Yes, actually it's Ms. Wilcox. I'm no longer married." I'm not sure why I clarify the status of my love life. "How can I help you?"

He nods, gripping my hand in a firm shake.

Goosebumps race up my arm at the contact. He's so *cold*. My mind wanders to what it would be like to have his chilly hands running up the outsides of my thighs while he pinned me to the wall.

I shiver, yanking my hand from his and instantly missing the icy kiss against my palm. *What's wrong with you, Mags? Lusting after a man you've literally just met. He could be a serial killer, for crying out loud!*

"Right. *Ms.* I'm Viktor Bielski. I was sent by Bottles and Babes Nanny Co. to care for one Liliana."

So, probably not a serial killer.

Once his words register, my jaw drops. *But*— "I didn't hire a nanny. There must be some kind of mistake. Are you sure you're at the right house?"

Long fingers slip into the breast pocket of his peacock-blue suit jacket, drawing my gaze when he pulls out a thick stack of folded papers.

As he unfolds them, I catch the official company letterhead at the top. *Seems legit.* Still doesn't explain who hired him.

"Is this your address?" He turns the papers to face me, and I scan the address listed under my name.

"Yes."

"And we've already established you're Maggie Wilcox."

Okay, so he's probably in the right place.

Viktor flips through the papers, skimming the lines with a slender finger before tapping a spot. "A Mr. Cyrus Wilcox paid the contract in full... for the rest of August and first months of autumn. Three months total." His eyes swing up from the papers, and I'm dumbfounded, mouth gaping like a damn fish.

Of course Cyrus is behind this. Never one to let me refuse his help, he's taken matters into his own hands this time. He knows I've been struggling to keep up with running the orchard while Lily is home on summer break.

And fall is harvest season, our busiest time of year.

Oh, he's about to get an earful. Once I figure out what the hell is going on.

Crossing my arms over my chest, I lean against the door-frame. I don't miss the quick downward flick of Viktor's eyes. They land on my chest before slowly skimming back up to my face.

My spine straightens under his perusal, pushing my small breasts out farther. Let the man look. It's been years since I've been checked out.

"You don't *look* like a nanny," I say, gaze sliding over his brightly patterned silk shirt and blue three-piece suit. The fabric is molded to his tall, lightly muscled frame like it was sewn onto him. A chain dangles from the small pocket of his vest, probably attached to a fancy old-fashioned watch. He seems the type—stuffy and uptight. "You look more like a flamboyant chocolatier from a children's movie." I can't help the giggle that slips out.

Clearing his throat, Viktor tugs at the burgundy tie wrapped around his neck. "And what *should* a nanny look like?"

"First of all, you're a man," I retort. I don't think I've ever heard of a male nanny, not that I have much experience with childcare. Before Roman died, I stayed home with Lily. Since then, I've been fortunate enough to work from the small office space off the kitchen while Lily plays in the kitchen or living room.

"Does being a man make me ill-equipped to care for a child?"

My face flames. As a single woman running a business, I should know better than to judge someone based on their anatomy alone. "Um, well, no. But—"

"Who were you expecting? Mary Poppins?" Those damn fangs peek out when he flashes a mirthful smile my way.

My eyebrows dip together, and I chew on my lower lip, trying not to think about what it would be like to have those fangs scrape against my flesh.

Shit. Where did that thought come from?

Schooling my features, I recover quickly and throw a retort his way. "No. Although, you are dressed like her." Viktor's smile widens, making my lips curve into a devilish grin. "How are you going to chase after a rambunctious five-year-old in *that*?" One finger points to his stuffy outfit. Still a strange choice for a supposed nanny, if you ask me.

The smile dissolves from his face, and he fidgets under my gaze, fiddling with the chain of his pocket watch before straightening the hem of his vest. "I'll manage just fine, Ms. Wilcox. I haven't met a child I couldn't corral in all my years of service."

"If you say so," I sing-song, stepping back from the door and letting him into the house. "I suppose we could do a trial run today to see if Lily likes you. But this isn't the Upper East Side. This is the country... We're not afraid to get dirty around here, city boy."

Oh my god, am I flirting? Where are these brash words coming from?

"I bet you know all about getting dirty, country girl." He returns my remark tenfold, thirsty eyes perusing from the tips of my toes to the messy pile of blonde curls tied in a bun on the top of my head.

Once he's done eye-fucking me, he has the sheer audacity to wink.

I didn't think I could possibly blush any harder, but my skin must be close to the color of a ripe apple, and sweat dampens the armpits of my shirt. I'm so out of practice with how to act around an attractive member of the opposite sex.

Luckily, I have a daughter with zero filter and the inability to judge a situation before she interrupts.

"Whoa! Are you a vampire?"

Ladies and gentlemen, there she is... right on cue.

Heads turning at the same time, Viktor and I find Lily standing in the entryway hall, mouth hanging open and eyes as wide as saucers.

"Lily," I grit out through clenched teeth. "We talked about this. You can't just ask someone what kind of monster they are." Swinging back toward Viktor, I wince. "Sorry."

His expression softens, warming when he lowers to one knee and extends a hand to my daughter.

Even bent down, Viktor is a large, looming figure as she comes to stand in front of him. Damn, he's gotta be well over six-feet tall.

"Quite alright, little one. I'm Viktor. And you must be Liliana."

Lily eyes his outstretched hand with a furrowed brow before finally taking it in her little hand. The size difference is adorable and has my ovaries perking up. *What the hell?*

Four years of grieving and being alone, not once has my body been interested in anyone—man, woman, monster, or anything in between. Why is this vampire suddenly getting my blood pumping?

"And you are correct. I am a vampire." A smile has his fangs poking out to dig into his plump lower lip. My insides turn to goo when Lily takes a step closer, a grin lighting up her face. "I'm here to play with you today. Would you like that?"

Lily peers up at me, eyebrows lifted in question.

"It's okay, Lily bug. Viktor is a friend. He's going to take care of you while I work for a few hours." I point down the hall behind her, where my office is. "I'll be right in my office if you need me. Sound good?"

My words spark confidence in her eyes. For as long as she can remember, it's just been the two of us. So I'm not sure how she'll take to a stranger, but I'll keep an eye on them until I'm assured Viktor's as qualified as he claims.

"Can we play dolls?" Lily bounces on her toes, vibrating with energy.

"I would be honored to play dolls with you, little one." Straightening to a stand, Viktor tips his chin down to me and winks once more.

He really needs to stop with the subtle flirtations. I'm not sure I like the flutters he's awoken between my thighs.

My phone buzzes in the back pocket of my jeans, saving me from trying to flirt with Viktor. Pulling it out, Cyrus's name lights up the display. *Sneaky asshole.* "I've got to take this," I say, but Lily has already dragged Viktor down the hall, her tiny hand clutched in his giant one.

"My dragon doll is my favorite. Annie gave it to me! She's a real dragon. Have you ever met a dragon?" Lily chatters away as I follow behind them. To say she's obsessed with Cyrus's mate is the understatement of the century.

We part ways in the kitchen. Lily and Viktor head to the family room, while I head into my office, listening to her happy voice as it filters into the room behind me. Viktor assured me he's qualified. He was hired through a nanny agency, so he must be trustworthy. Right?

Plopping into my desk chair, I swipe my thumb across the screen of my still ringing phone and press it to my ear. "Oh, you're in trouble!"

CHAPTER 2

Maggie

"Hello to you, too, Mags." My brother-in-law's deep voice filters down the line as I settle into the leather desk chair. From here, I still have a line of sight to the family room, where Viktor sits on the floor with Lily.

Seems a shame for his beautiful suit to get wrinkled and dirtied up by my daughter. Oh, well. If he stays, he'll learn to dress for the job. He's lost his suit jacket and rolled his sleeves to expose the veiny flesh of his forearms. Drool.

Lily shoves a doll into his hands. The thing looks puny in his massive grip.

"A nanny, Cyrus? Really?" I hiss, turning my attention to my computer screen. *Am I mad?* Not really. Since Roman died, I've been drowning in motherhood and keeping the orchard afloat.

I *could* use the help.

If anything, my pride is bruised. I'm hurt he didn't tell me before he swooped in and saved the day... again.

Cyrus has a habit of playing the knight in shining armor. He can't help it; it's how he shows his love.

He's three years older than Roman and me, and had to step in when their parents died. His intentions may be well placed, but he could work on his execution. "Lily and I have managed just fine all summer—"

"Come on, Mags. Cut the bullshit. I've been there almost every Sunday for dinner. You think I don't see the bags under your eyes, the stacks of papers on your desk, or the laundry piled high next to the washer? You're burning the candle at both ends. How much longer do you think you can keep this up? Let me help. Please."

"You overstepped, Cy," I snap. Tears well in my eyes, all the inadequacy of being a young widow and single mom bubbling to the surface. The bills piling up in the kitchen are a constant reminder of my failures. It's never enough.

I'm never enough.

It's been four years of constant juggling, and I think I've finally dropped the ball.

Actually, I've dropped all of them.

"I'm sorry. I'm just overwhelmed with the upcoming harvest season and Lily starting school again."

Cy blows out a breath, voice softening when he speaks. "Don't apologize, Mags. That's my job. I'm sorry I overstepped, but I'm just trying to help."

"I know."

"By no means did I mean to imply you're a bad mom or anything. Because you're not. Fuck, you're one of the strongest people I know. Lily is thriving because of you."

Is she? For the first few months of summer vacation, she's been stuck in the house, mostly entertaining herself while I work. She deserves better. Ugh, maybe I do need some help.

"Thanks, Cy." One tear slips free, trekking down my cheek before I can brush it away.

"Viktor is the top nanny at the agency. He's been taking care of kids longer than either of us has been alive." *How old is this guy?* "Just give him a chance."

Lily's shrill laughter floats in from the other room, followed by a deep, soul-warming chuckle. It's a sound I want to bathe in, like it would heal all my wounds and take away the years of pain after losing Roman. My heart clenches, and I push that thought away. Lily's happiness is my priority, not this weird interest in a vampire—no matter how handsome he might be.

"He's already paid for," Cy continues.

Closing my eyes, I rub at the bridge of my nose. Viktor would be able to get Lily out of the house. Get her brain and her body moving, instead of wasting the rest of her summer break on the couch.

With Lily out of my hair for a little while, I could finally catch up on all the work I've been shoving to the side. For once, I could get ahead and maybe find some spare money to cover the endless debt. "Fine, but next time... ask first."

"I will. Promise."

"Likely story. How's Annie?"

His voice fills with so much love when he talks about his mate. She's a dragon shifter who used to hate Cyrus, but they overcame their differences and went into business together. "Good. Great, actually. We're set to open the warehouse remodel in a few months. It's amazing to see Antoinette living out her dreams."

"I'm glad you finally found someone to put up with you, Cy." I laugh, soon joined by Cyrus's gruff chuckle. "Tell her I said hi. Will we see you for Sunday dinner this week?"

"Wouldn't miss it for the world, Mags."

A soft knock on the door to my office drags my attention away from Cyrus.

One of the first things Roman did after dedicating this room of the house as the office was add an exterior door that opens onto the wraparound porch. That way, no workers would track dirt all over the main house when they needed something. And we could separate the business from our private lives.

Two glacial eyes peer through the half window at me. Jean-Luc, my foreman.

"I've gotta run. Duty calls. We'll see you Sunday." Standing from my desk, I cross the small office and unlock the door.

"Talk soon. Love you, Mags."

"Love you, Cy."

I stuff my phone into the back pocket of my jeans and swing the door open. "Morning, Jean-Luc. What can I do for you?"

Tipping his head to the side, he maneuvers his wide horns through the doorway, hooves clicking against the hardwood when he ambles toward the extra chair in my office.

The minotaur sighs, his massive frame dwarfing the chair as he settles his weight into the seat. I should probably invest in a larger chair, since Jean-Luc seems to be my most frequent visitor.

His nostrils flare with a snort, the ring bisecting them wiggling with the force. An angry red lump on the tip of his nose catches my attention.

Oh, no. Not again.

"You're in a fine mood this morning. What happened?" Before I can stop it, a giggle slips out of my mouth.

If anything, my laughter adds to his already sour mood and the big bull snorts again. "*Ça me fait chier.* Damn bees. I was trimming the dead branches, and *le bâtard* got me."

His nose twitches, and I lose it. Clapping a hand over my mouth, I try to calm my runaway giggles, but it's no use. He levels me with a glare, and I laugh harder.

On a normal day, Jean-Luc is a surly asshole, but he seems to be extra grumpy this morning.

"It's not funny, Maggie," he clips in a rough voice. But one corner of his mouth tips into a slight smile.

Got him.

"I'm sorry." I wheeze and wipe a finger under my eyes. "It's not funny, but this is the third time in a week. Maybe we need to get you a custom beekeeper suit or something."

"*Ostie!* I'd look ridiculous."

"You would!" I giggle again, imagining his massive body crammed into the white fabric, before sobering. "Is that why you came to visit me? Or is there something important?"

Jean-Luc has been an integral part of the mild success we've had with the orchard. Originally from Quebec, he was the foreman for the last owner, so Roman and I begged him to stay and show us the ropes when we bought the place.

Lucky for us, he took pity on a couple of city slickers who knew nothing about running an orchard.

He leans back in the chair, crossing his arms over his barrel chest. I'm surprised the flannel of his shirt doesn't tear under the flex of his huge biceps. Towering over me, he may be intimidating, but he's a big softie once you get through his tough exterior. "*Oui*. Harvest will be here in another month. I wanted your approval to call back the team from last year. They were hard workers. A good crew."

Last year, we hired a mix of pixies, trolls, and humans to pick and process the apples. They worked hard, even though our numbers were down due to the massive drought.

A pit forms in my stomach. Bringing back the crew from last year means spending money I don't have in order to pay them. But I can't very well pick all the apples myself.

No.

The golden ticket out of this financial mess is a successful harvest.

Realizing I'm still awkwardly standing by my desk, I plunk down into my chair and nod. "Yes. Of course. Please hire back the same crew from last year. We're expecting a bigger harvest this year, right?"

One massive hand runs over the brown fur bursting over the neckline of Jean-Luc's red flannel. It's like he walked off the set of a documentary about lumberjacks. Thick, fur-covered forearms strain the rolled fabric of his sleeves. "*Oui*. Should be the best harvest yet."

Butterflies startle in my stomach. This is good. This is what I need.

A boisterous, deep chuckle echoes in from the family room, followed by a high-pitched squeal.

On the sides of his head, Jean-Luc's fuzzy ears twitch. *"C'est qui?"* His eyes widen, and he asks again in English. "Who is that?"

I blow out a harsh breath. "Ugh. Cyrus took it upon himself to hire a nanny for the next few months. He thinks I have too much on my plate—"

"You do." Jean-Luc leans forward, bracing his elbows on his knees and giving me the full weight of his stare.

"Thanks for the vote of confidence," I respond, tone dry as the desert.

"*C'est la vérité*. Mags, you've gone through more heartbreak and grief in the past few years than most people do in their entire lives."

Jean-Luc was one of the few people I leaned on after Roman died. He's seen me at my worst and stuck around. Something I'm forever grateful for.

Dipping my head, I sniffle as my finger runs along the top of a notepad lying on my desk. "I know." My voice thickens with a sudden wave of sadness. "I just miss him so much. Sometimes it's easier to drown myself in work and Lily, because if it's too quiet... that's when the darkness creeps back in. And I can't go back there."

I barely survived losing my husband—my best friend. Without Jean-Luc, this place wouldn't have survived my grief either. He stepped up in ways I'll never be able to repay him for.

The chair legs scrape along the wooden floor, and two big hands engulf mine, stopping my nervous fiddling with the notepad. "I know, Mags. I won't let you." When I tip my head up, I'm met by deep pools of ocean blue radiating with concern. "I miss him, too. So much."

Swallowing, I blink away the stupid tears that have formed on my lash line. Sometimes, it feels like all I've done for the past four years is cry, and I'm tired of it. I just want to be happy and whole, like I was when Roman was alive. "You're probably tired of hearing this by now, but thank you for sticking around through everything."

"No thanks needed, Mags. Roman was like a brother to me. I would never abandon his family. *Ma famille.*"

After we bought the orchard, Roman was glued to Jean-Luc's side for months, learning the ins and outs of running the place. Roman didn't want to sit behind a desk and be in charge. No, he wanted to get his hands dirty and be involved in every part of the process, no matter how minute.

He and Jean-Luc became unlikely friends. My sunny, golden retriever husband matched with a surly, brooding minotaur. But they were brilliant together. Making so many plans for the future of the orchard.

Now it's up to me to see those plans to fruition.

"He'd be proud of you, Maggie." Jean-Luc squeezes my hand again.

I swallow down the fresh wave of emotions clogging my throat. "I'd like to think so."

On the desk, my phone pings. A calendar notification lights up the screen: grocery calls.

"Sorry." Pulling my hand from his grip, I fumble for my phone, nearly dropping it on the floor when I swipe the notification away. "I have another call. But bring in the old crew, get prepped for harvest. This is our year, Jean-Luc. I can feel it," I say, thumping a hand over my heart. I have to, because the harsh reality of losing this place, and the last memories of Roman, isn't an option.

Jean-Luc grunts, standing and peeking into the family room. "A vampire? Hmm?"

"That easy to tell?" I stand next to him, head barely level with his shoulder.

He huffs, then turns and saunters toward the back door of my office, tail swishing behind him. Hand poised on the doorknob, he peers over his broad shoulder. "Keep the nanny, Mags. You deserve a break. *Salut.*" Another snort, and he's out the door.

Seems everyone—but me—knew I was in over my head. Guess all the coffee and concealer in the world aren't hiding the bags under my eyes quite as well as I thought.

CHAPTER 3

Maggie

R enewed resolve flooded my body after Jean-Luc left, so I threw myself into my work. A good harvest this year will mean plenty of product to sell.

We fell into a harsh drought last year, plus low customer numbers. It was the perfect storm for a losing year.

This year, I planned ahead.

I used my graphic design background to revamp our website, hopefully attracting a larger customer base. I shelled out any spare dollars I could for advertising on social media.

With Viktor watching Lily, I can focus solely on one task at a time. I spent the morning on the phone with every local grocer in the area, setting up meetings for the rest of the week with the managers.

Getting contracts with even a few of these stores could bring in a huge profit. Better yet, it's a guaranteed amount of cash, not unpredictable like the money we make from people coming to pick their own apples.

Put a "locally grown organic" sticker on anything, and people snap it up—no matter the cost.

As I'm ticking off the last name on my list, the most divine aroma wafts through the crack in my office door. On cue, my stomach rumbles, reminding me I've been holed up in here for—I glance at the clock on my computer screen—four hours!

How is it already one o'clock?

I was so engrossed in my work that I completely forgot about Viktor and Lily in the other room.

Springing to my feet, I race to the door. Lily must be starving. We usually make lunch around noon, then she spends a few hours in her room for "quiet time."

"I'm so sorry, Viktor. I lost track of—" The words die on my lips when I barrel into the kitchen and find my new nanny at the stove, flipping a grilled sandwich while Lily watches from her step stool.

"Momma!" My daughter hops down, running over to hug me.

On instinct, I scoop her into my arms and nuzzle the top of her head, the distinct soapy scent of her shampoo filling my nose. This, right here, is why I carry the weight of the world on my shoulders. All the Lily hugs, kisses, and snuggles make it worth the stress.

Lifting my head, my gaze locks with ruby red irises. Viktor's eyes crinkle slightly at the corners, one fang poking out from behind his smiling lips.

"Sorry. I got caught up with work. I meant to check in sooner." Lily's sticky fingers tangle in the stray curls that have fallen loose from my messy bun. I wince as pain radiates from my scalp.

This Adonis is standing in my kitchen, and I look like a hot mess. But when I get engrossed in work, everything else fades into the background, ceasing to exist.

Like a damn professional chef, Viktor flicks his wrist, jostling the frying pan ever-so-slightly and sending the grilled sandwich into the air. His arm muscles bunch under the thin fabric of his dress shirt, and I can't seem to peel my eyes away. Even as the sandwich lands gracefully back in the pan, on the untoasted side.

"It's not a problem." The rich, smooth baritone of his voice pulls my attention from the defined muscle of his arms to his face. Flames flicker in his beautiful eyes, like he caught me drooling over him... and he *liked* it. "Miss Lily was hungry, so we decided to make some lunch. This one's for you."

And there go my cheeks again. I'm blushing like a damn nun in a brothel. Viktor's kindness is disarming after being on my own for the past few years. I'm not used to someone putting my needs first.

"And look, Momma! My grilled cheese isn't burned!"

My cheeks heat further at the rise in Viktor's eyebrows. Clearing my throat, I set Lily on the ground. She scampers back to her step stool, eager eyes taking in all of Viktor's movements as he plates the grilled sandwich. "I've only burned one—"

"Or five," Lily chimes in.

"In my defense, I'm usually trying to do ten things at once," I say, leaning a hip against the counter.

"Even the best chefs burn things on occasion." Viktor chuckles. "Lunch is ready. Would you like to join us?"

By his side, Lily bounces on her toes.

"I would love to. Thank you for cooking." As he passes by with the plates of food balanced in his hands, I catch a whiff of his earthy sandalwood scent.

Damn, he smells good.

When did I become so easily distracted by a man's existence?

Shaking my head, I focus back on Lily. "Bug, can you pick some cups for us?"

She nods with enthusiasm before pushing her step stool to the other side of the kitchen. Climbing up and opening the cupboard, she taps a tiny finger on her chin while contemplating the choices.

Lily is at an age where she craves independence. But I've found giving her small, manageable tasks throughout the day keeps her from getting into trouble on her own... like finding the permanent markers in my office and coloring on the wall of the kitchen.

Her masterpiece still adorns the wall by the fridge. Two stick figures holding hands beneath a shining sun with an apple tree in the background. It's clear by the matching smiles and curly hair, it's me and her.

I haven't had the heart to paint over it yet. Instead, I run my fingers over the happy faces whenever I walk by. It's a reminder of why I'm working my ass off to save this place.

This orchard is Roman's legacy, and I hope to pass it on to Lily someday.

"Unicorns?" She turns toward me, with three bright pink plastic cups with unicorns printed on them in her hands.

I raise my hand and give her a thumbs-up. "Perfect choice, bug. Why don't you go sit with Viktor? I'll bring the water over to the table." Smiling, my eyes follow her as she runs to the old wooden table and hops into the chair right next to Viktor.

It's clear she's smitten with him already. Maybe he arrived at the perfect time—right when I needed someone the most.

CHAPTER 4

Viktor

Maggie Wilcox is beautiful. That's the first thought I had when the cherry-red farmhouse door swung open this morning.

My father's threat loomed over me with every mile I drove north from New York City, souring my already shitty mood. Give up my career and join him, or be cut off from my trust fund—and my family.

Losing his financial support would hinder my current lifestyle, yes. But I'd manage on the meager salary I make as a nanny. It would mean giving up my luxurious clothes and my apartment in a prime part of the city...

However, the thought of losing my mother and sister is like a knife being plunged into my heart.

I love what I do, shaping and nurturing young minds. And I'm fucking good at it.

But he's blind to anything other than his bigwig investment clients, so I'm caught in an impossible situation. According to him, this is my last nanny contract. We'll see about that.

Usually, the agency places me with wealthy families on New York City's Upper East Side, but the fresh air and endless blue sky of Maple Ridge Hollow are a welcome change.

The city, a place I've called home my entire life, is suffocating as of late, and I'm eager for the change of environment. Most importantly, somewhere I can avoid my father for a little while.

All the harsh emotions melted away, like snow under the warm spring sun, the minute I laid eyes on *her*—the beautiful angel with golden hair and stunning sea-glass green eyes.

Being a vampire, my skin is usually icy to the touch, but her lingering gaze had it heating beyond belief.

As she saunters to the kitchen table, I can't peel my eyes off the sway of her wide hips, and her thick thighs have my cock taking notice, too. She's sexy, with an innocence I wouldn't mind sinking my fangs into.

"Do you really turn into a bat? Can you fly?" Lily's voice draws my attention back to her before my thoughts can run rampant with what her mother's skin would look like when she...

Clearing my throat, I run a hand over my mouth and turn toward the vivacious little girl sitting next to me. Eyes wide and glittering with hope, the same striking pale green as her mother's, she tilts her chin and smiles up at me.

"No, little one." I tap a finger on the tip of her button nose, and she scrunches it. "Unfortunately, I'm stuck with this ugly mug for eternity. Such a shame."

Her tiny eyebrows furrow over narrowed eyes as they linger on my face. "I don't know. You're not *that* ugly."

Hopefully, her mother agrees.

Maggie joins us at the table, three plastic unicorn cups filled with water in her hands.

"So what *can* you do?"

"Lily bug, remember? It's rude to pry. Eat your lunch." Maggie slides the plate in front of her daughter, who scowls, but picks up the grilled cheese sandwich and takes a big bite.

Maggie's gaze turns to me. "Sorry. She's very curious about monsters. She does the same thing to Cyrus's mate."

"She's a dragon!" Lily proclaims around a mouthful of gooey cheese and bread. "It's so awesome!"

I stifle a laugh and take a bite of my own sandwich. The cheese slides down my throat as I contemplate what to say next. Reaching into the pocket of my trousers, I grab what I need. "I may not be as cool as a dragon, but—" Quicker than she can blink, I lift my hand to Lily's ear and pull it back, revealing a shiny foil wrapped chocolate coin. "I do have a few tricks up my sleeve."

Lily's mouth drops open on a soft "whoa," eyes nearly doubling in size. "You're really fast!"

"Indeed." When I lift my gaze to Maggie, I find her eyes already on me. The pink flush to her cheeks is giving me all kinds of inappropriate thoughts.

The last thing I need is to explain why my cock is hard to a five-year-old... and her mother.

Taking another bite of my sandwich, I focus on the warm, melted cheese and perfectly crispy buttered bread.

Cooking is another passion of mine that my father despises. *Feminine hobbies aren't fit for vampire males of our caliber*, he used to tell me any time he caught me in the kitchen with Mother.

Instead of arousal, irritation fills my veins, instantly wilting my inappropriate boner.

Shaking my head, I lock his hurtful comments in the box where they belong, tucking it away in the far corner of my mind to collect cobwebs.

Once the runaway train of my mind is back on its tracks, I turn to Lily. "I'm not only fast. I can see really, really well in the dark, and I can hear and smell things that are far away. And I'll live forever."

Clutching the chocolate coin in her hand, she brings it to her chest. Voice filled with awe, she whispers, "You might be cooler than Annie."

Maggie's laughter bubbles from her throat, and I wish I could bottle the sound for later. When I'm alone. It's crisp and lyrical, filling my empty soul like nothing else ever has. "No one is cooler than Annie. Coming from Lily, you should consider that a huge compliment."

Her smile is radiant, and for the first time, I notice a slight gap between her top front teeth.

Fuck, it makes her even more gorgeous.

In all my years on this planet, I've never been so instantly enamored by a creature before—human, monster, or otherwise. This could pose a problem since she's a client.

"I'm honored," I say, placing a hand over my chest, my smile growing until my fangs are on display.

I don't miss how Maggie's eyes dip to the sharp teeth. Chest growing flush, she quickly snaps her gaze to her plate and takes another bite of her sandwich.

Interesting.

"Momma, can I eat this now?" Lily holds up the chocolate coin.

Swallowing a mouthful of food, Maggie shakes her head. "Eat your lunch first. You didn't eat very much for breakfast."

Grumbling, Lily sets the coin on her plate and takes another bite of her grilled cheese.

Since Lily is occupied, I work on getting more information out of Maggie. "So did I pass your test?"

Maggie's lips twist to the side, and silence stretches between us. "It was refreshing to be able to focus on my work in a quiet, uninterrupted environment. And I really appreciate you cooking lunch. You didn't have to do that."

My brow dips. "Isn't feeding Lily part of taking care of her?"

"Yes. Of course. I just didn't expect to lose track of time like I did."

I reach my hand across the table, but stop myself from grabbing hers at the last second. Is it appropriate for me to touch her? Even though I'm fucking dying to find out if her skin is as soft as it appears. My fingers itch to trace the freckles dotting her tan flesh.

There goes my cock again, threatening to tear a hole in my slacks, when a wave of her sweet apple scent crashes over me.

Closing my eyes, I hold my breath until the urge passes.

I've never had such a visceral reaction to anyone. Granted, I've been celibate for decades—in more ways than one.

"Lily is an easy child. It was really no bother cooking with her around. That *is* part of the job description, after all."

More of that ethereal laughter fills the air, making me smile.

"I suppose you're right. And to answer your question... Lily seems to like you, and there weren't any tears. I guess you'll do, city boy." She flashes me a cheeky wink. The gesture has my heart ramping up its rhythm, pounding harder.

Why does she have to be so adorably sexy? And why do I want to find out how dirty I can make her?

"There's a guest house at the edge of the property. You're welcome to stay there for the remainder of your contract."

"That would be greatly appreciated." I give her a lopsided smile that, once again, has pink creeping up from the neckline of her shirt. I want to play with her more and see how far down this beautiful shade paints her skin.

Later. Much later.

It would be entirely inappropriate to cross that boundary with a client...

Unless she makes the first move.

"Great. After lunch, we'll give you a tour. Lily and I can take the four-wheeler—

"Four-wheeler ride!" Lily's scream has my eardrums ringing. I'd been so caught up in every little reaction from Maggie, I almost completely forgot about her daughter.

S omehow, I managed to keep my dick under control for the rest of lunch. Lily chattered away about starting kindergarten in a few weeks, while Maggie asked questions that prompted Lily to open up more.

It's clear as day how much Maggie loves her daughter, simply based on the way her eyes shine when she watches an animated Lily explain why the middle swing is the best on their backyard playground.

Once the dishes from lunch are cleaned up, I trail behind Maggie and Lily to the garage.

"Got your helmet, Lily bug?" Maggie grabs a set of keys from a hook on the wall.

Tucked under Lily's arm is a bright pink helmet. "Got it, Momma!" She turns toward me, extending her little hand in a thumbs-up. "Safety first!"

I laugh. But when Maggie swings one luscious leg over the seat of a red four-wheeler, my laughter cuts off on a choked groan, all the saliva pooling in my mouth and my blood pumping south.

Down, boy. Not the time. She's your boss.

I've been a city dweller all my life, but the sight of this woman on a dirt-crusted motorized vehicle is doing strange things to my insides.

Am I jealous of a damn four-wheeler? Wishing Maggie would ride me instead?

I can't let my thoughts go there with a woman I've known for mere hours and know nothing about.

"You catching flies over there, city boy? Or are you ready for a tour?"

Maggie's humored voice has my jaw snapping shut and my thumb skimming under my bottom lip to make sure there isn't any drool. "I'm ready," I croak, tugging my car keys from my pocket and jingling them in the air.

We'd agreed earlier that I'd follow behind in my car so I'll know how to get to the guest house. "Lead the way." I sweep a hand toward the open garage door, where my black SUV sits in the large cement driveway.

Once Lily has her helmet on and is safely tucked in front of her, Maggie fires up the ATV and rolls out of the garage at a slow speed. Safety first.

Getting into my car, I crank the key in the ignition and follow Maggie along a narrow dirt trail that runs between the rows of trees to the back of the property.

The sun beats down through the full branches. Each limb weighed down by juicy red apples. They look good enough to eat.

A short drive later, a small cabin comes into view, nestled in between vibrant evergreen trees. Their crisp, woodsy aroma hits my nose without even rolling my windows down. It's refreshing with a hint of sweetness.

Nothing like the damp, exhaust and garbage scents that assault my nostrils in the heart of New York City.

The constant noise of the city is usually overwhelming to my sensitive ears, but out here, it's quiet. Serene. Only the soft twitter of songbirds and the whoosh of the gentle breeze.

Maybe being in the middle of nowhere for the next few months won't be so bad. Maybe I'll even like it.

Especially if I get to drool over Maggie on a daily basis.

Pulling up next to the four-wheeler, I shift into park, grab my overnight bag from the backseat, and get out of my car. "This place is really beautiful."

Maggie smiles, helping Lily off the ATV and removing her helmet. "The previous owner told us this was the original building on the property. They had it restored when they built the new farmhouse." She points through the trees in the direction we came from. Her white two-story home is barely visible from the guest house, giving it a feeling of privacy and solitude. "Annie and Cyrus stay here occasionally, but it's clean and fully stocked with linens. It's all yours for the next few months." Slipping a key into the doorknob, she unlocks it before opening the wooden door.

Lily zooms past us, making a beeline for the bed.

"Uh-ah, Lil. No jumping on Viktor's bed. This is his space now."

With a huff, Lily plops on her butt and scoots off the bed.

I can't help but chuckle at the utter disdain for her mother written on her face.

"It's not much." Maggie walks past me, and I'm hit by her intoxicating aroma again. Following her, I suck in a lungful. I can only hope the sweet smell lingers in the air even after she leaves.

She's completely oblivious as she brushes a hand over the narrow kitchen counter. "But you'll be close to the main house. I expect you to at least stay here Monday through Friday. The weekends will be your time, so you can come and go as you please."

The cabin is one large room, divided into a kitchen, living space, and bedroom by the furniture. A bathroom adorned in modern fixtures is the only walled-in space.

"You should have everything you need except laundry, so feel free to use the main house for that. I usually aim to start work at eight, but it's been hit or miss without childcare."

I nod. "I'll be at the main house by 7:45 each morning."

"Thank you. Lily has summer camp at the elementary school on Wednesday mornings. And swim lessons at the Community Center on Thursday afternoons. You'll have to take her to those."

I nod again. "Of course." So far, their schedule seems pretty basic compared to what I'm used to. Many of the children I've nannied in the past were so booked with activities, they hardly had time to be children. To be wild and impulsive. Making mistakes and learning life lessons through experience.

Sometimes it felt like I was simply there to shuttle the children from place to place, while the parents avoided all responsibility. Based on my first impression, Maggie seems to be much more involved in her child's life.

"You can either take my car or grab the booster seat out of it for your car."

Scratching the back of my neck, I glance at Maggie. "I actually have a booster seat in my car already. Based on Lily's age, I anticipated she still needed one."

Maggie's eyebrows rise. "Oh."

"It's the best money can buy. Safety first, right?" I chuckle when her jaw falls slack.

Clearing her throat, her mouth tips into a crooked grin, showcasing my new favorite thing... the gap between her otherwise perfectly straight teeth. "Well, you really are Mary Poppins. Aren't you?"

I match her smile with one of my own, puffing my chest out a little when her cheeks darken and her pulse visibly hastens in her delicate neck.

A dull ache, like I've never experienced before, fills my fangs. *Strange.* It takes all my restraint to keep my feet planted on the ground. Foreign need rushes through me; the need to sink my fangs into her perfect flesh and taste her sweet nectar.

Before my thoughts turn too debauched, I shake my head and spin to examine the room further. "Like I said before, I've been doing this for a long time. Liliana is safe under my care."

The slender column of Maggie's throat ripples with a swallow, her tone soft when she speaks. "I believe you."

Lily zooms around us, a stuffed unicorn she magically produced from somewhere held in her hand. Keeping my voice quiet, I pry for a little more information. "What about Lily's father? Is there anything I should know? The agency only listed you on the file."

Suddenly, Maggie's whole demeanor shifts, and my heart clenches. Gone is our playful back-and-forth. Shoulders rolling in, she crosses her arms protectively around her stomach. "Lily's father passed away a few years ago." Tears shimmer in her eyes when she finally meets my gaze, grief evident in her green irises.

Fuck, I want to hug her, pull her tight to my chest and bury her in my scent. Drown her sorrows in me.

Somehow, I resist that urge. I must be a fucking saint—more like a glutton for punishment. The heartbreak in her eyes tears a shred off my own heart.

Instead, I play it safe and opt for words I hope are comforting. "My condolences, Maggie. I didn't mean to bring up anything painful."

A few blonde curls tumble free, framing her face when she shakes her head. "You would have found out sooner or later. Better to get it out of the way now." There's pain in the slight wobble of her voice. Pain I'd do anything to take away.

Fuck it. Hastily, I step closer, deciding to cross the line I drew earlier, and set a hand on her shoulder. To my surprise, she leans in, her warmth cascading up my arm and spreading through my chest. "You know, I'm not just here for Lily. If you ever need a night off or some time to yourself, I'm happy to step in so you can have a break. Just say the word."

As the full weight of her stare lifts to mine, I get lost in her beautiful eyes. "Thank you, Viktor. I really appreciate the offer."

"Of course. And I'm also a really good listener... if you ever want to talk about anything."

Her lips tip into a sad smile as she sniffles. "I just might take you up on that." Glancing at her smartwatch, she suggests, "Why don't you spend the rest of the day getting settled? Lily and I have some errands to run, so we'll see you in the morning. 7:45?"

I nod, setting my bag by my feet. "I'll be there with bells on."

She places the key in my hand, and my fingers curl around the cool metal. Once again, I relish her soft touch, soaking it in before she pulls away and walks to the door. "Great. Come on, Lily bug. Time to go grocery shopping."

Lily sprints to the door, hugging her mother's legs. "Can I get a gumball?"

Maggie nods, but her attention is on me. Her eyes stay trained on my face as she looks over her shoulder. I'm graced with one more shy smile before she and Lily head back to the four-wheeler.

The subtle glances. The flushed cheeks and flirty banter. If I was a gambling man, I'd wager this attraction between us is mutual.

Except, there's rawness in the glimpse of sorrow she displayed earlier. What's the story behind the death of her husband? Maggie must be in her mid-thirties, making me think her husband's death was unexpected and possibly tragic. How deep does her heartache go?

And how do I help her heal?

CHAPTER 5

Viktor

With a plate of freshly baked muffins balanced on one hand, I poise the other to knock on Maggie's front door. I woke up around four-thirty this morning, restless energy surging through my body.

And when I get restless or stressed, I bake.

When I'm happy, I bake.

When I'm sad, I bake.

Really, any emotion can be worked out with baking. A skill I acquired thanks to my mother, and something all my previous clients took full advantage of when I would stock their kitchens with homemade muffins, cookies, and breads—pretty much all things carby and delicious.

Every time I closed my eyes and willed sleep to fill my body, I was met with visions of striking light-green eyes, coils of dark-blonde hair, and the cutest spray of freckles dusting an even cuter button nose.

In less than twenty-four hours, Maggie Wilcox has consumed all my thoughts, especially in my sleep.

But I can't act on this invisible force pulling me to her until I know more about her past.

Oh, and she's my boss.

One problem at a time, though.

Eventually, I gave up on catching some shut-eye and whipped up a batch of chocolate chip muffins. If I've learned one thing over a lifetime of taking care of children, it's that chocolate is the best way into even the most stubborn child's heart.

Luckily, I had the foresight to explore the little town of Maple Ridge Hollow last night, making a pitstop at the local grocery store to stock my new home with food and any other necessities.

Before I have a chance to knock on the door, my ears perk up to tiny feet padding against the floor on the other side, followed by a soft giggle. The door swings in, and a wisp of a child collides with my legs.

"Oomph." I manage to brace the plate with both hands before it can drop to the ground. Taking a step back, I stop Lily from sending me sprawling to the ground as well.

Good thing I'm a vampire with fast reflexes.

"Good morning, little one." My voice is filled with laughter at her excitement. Now that the muffins are safe, I stroke one hand down the back of Lily's curly hair, which is wrangled into a low ponytail.

She pulls back, releasing her death grip on my waist. A sunny smile lights up her whole face. "You're here!"

"I'm here," I confirm. Taking her hand in mine, she leads me into the house as Maggie comes down the hallway from the kitchen.

She smiles, wiping her hands on the dish towel she's carrying. "She's been waiting by the window since she finished her breakfast."

My heart sings at Maggie's words. Based on our first encounter, Lily seems to be a very outgoing and intelligent child. I'm not surprised she's taken to me so quickly. Now, if I could only gauge her mother a bit more.

"What do you have there?" Maggie's curious tone breaks me out of my thoughts, the eyes I've been dreaming about locked on the plate in my hands.

"Chocolate chip muffins. One of my specialties." I pass the plate to her, and we venture farther into the house.

In the kitchen, Lily grabs one of the muffins, scampering off to the kitchen table, leaving me and Maggie standing awkwardly on opposite sides of the island. "You didn't have to bake us anything, but thank you." She picks up a muffin and takes a generous bite. A moan slips out as her eyes flutter closed, and I nearly pop an ill-timed boner in front of my new employer—again.

That moan, sultry and smooth, will be on repeat in my brain for the rest of eternity.

Not the time, Viktor.

Totally oblivious to my lustful thoughts, Maggie runs her tongue over her bottom lip, chasing a rogue crumb, before sucking one finger into her mouth and licking it clean of chocolate.

How do I tell her I had to bake these muffins in order to distract myself from my thoughts of her? If I'm not careful, I'll end up jerking off on a nightly basis to visions of her plump lips wrapped around my cock instead of her finger.

Clearing my throat, I turn so my rapidly hardening cock is wedged against the counter and out of sight. "It's no bother. Baking is somewhat of a hobby of mine." I plaster on a wide smile in hopes of covering up the hunger that's raging beneath my skin.

"Well, these are amazing. And chocolate chip is my favorite."

I tuck that little nugget of information away for later. "Thank you. So what's on the agenda today?" Switching to a safe subject will surely get me thinking a little more with my brain and less with my dick.

Maggie slides the plate of muffins to the side before brushing her hands on the dish towel again. "I know it's your first full day with Lily, but I need to go out for some meetings today. Will you be okay? I should be back after lunchtime."

"This isn't my first rodeo, country girl." My wink sends a brilliant pink flush up Maggie's chest and neck until it spreads across her supple cheeks. "You have nothing to worry about. Lily is in good hands."

I've dealt with my fair share of parents being apprehensive... and some who had no qualms at all leaving their child with a stranger. "Here," I say, tugging my phone from the pocket of my slacks. "I know you have a landline." I nod toward the old, corded phone mounted on the wall across from us. "But direct contact may ease your nerves. Put your number in here."

When she reaches for the phone, her fingers brush mine. I'm almost too caught up in the heat of her skin that I nearly miss the soft gasp that falls from her lips.

Almost.

But I don't.

I also don't miss the flare in her pupils as her eyes linger on our hands.

Or how she doesn't flinch or pull away.

No. If anything, she leans a fraction of an inch closer, her hand seeking mine when I break contact.

My normally cool fingers tingle; it's a sensation I want to experience over every inch of my body.

And there goes my dick again—springing to life and fighting against the zipper of my pants. Fisting my hand in front of my mouth, I fake a cough and angle my body away from hers.

From over my shoulder, Maggie snaps her mouth shut as her thumbs tap against the screen of my phone. "Okay, I put my cell number in here, along with Jean-Luc's. He's the orchard foreman, and you can use him as an emergency contact. Call me if you need *anything*."

I nod as I take the phone back from her. Much to my dismay, Maggie plops it into my outstretched palm, avoiding any more physical contact. "I will."

After a quick goodbye with Lily and grabbing her purse, Maggie heads out the garage door, an almost forlorn look pinching her features. The expression sours my gut, and I want nothing more than to tell her to stay here with Lily. With *me*.

But I'm not here to be Maggie's white knight. I'm here to be her nanny.

Swallowing back the lump in my throat, I turn toward my little companion, who's busy coloring a picture at the kitchen table. Chocolate smudges adorn her cheeks, and I can't help but chuckle. We'll be just fine today.

An hour, and a wash of Lily's face, later, we're headed out the backdoor of the farmhouse. A pink backpack filled with snacks and drawing supplies is strapped to Lily's back.

I need to get the lay of the land if I'm going to be here for the next few months, and what better way to do that than with a "nature hike." At least, that's how I explained it to Lily.

"Okay, little one. I want you to find a yellow flower. Then we'll stop and draw it in your notebook. Sound good?" On my walk to the main house this morning, I passed by a patch of vibrant yellow wildflowers.

Her feet pound on the dirt path when she takes off toward the guest house.

Puffy white clouds float across the big blue sky overhead. They provide the perfect amount of shade for my sensitive skin.

Vampire lore has been skewed, thanks to Hollywood. We don't burn to a crisp in the sun, but it isn't exactly comfortable either. It's a bit like how an extreme sunburn feels for humans. Unbearably itchy and painful.

Long sleeves, long pants, and a hat are necessary when venturing outside during daylight hours.

Pushing my sunglasses up the bridge of my nose, I wince when a stray ray of sun beats down on me. Unfortunately, I forgot my hat at my apartment in the city. I'll have to make due until I go home this weekend.

We spend the better part of the morning on our exploration of the orchard. Me giving Lily random items to find on the grounds. Her scampering ahead to capture them and add them to her sketchbook.

Along the way, I snap pictures on my phone and send them to Maggie in hopes of easing her nerves. She responds to each one with a heart emoji or a thumbs-up.

By midday, Lily has devoured all the snacks we packed, and her pace has slowed. It's time to head back to the house for lunch.

"My feet hurt," Lily whines from my side, stumbling a step.

Stopping in my tracks, I tap my chin. "How about a piggyback ride?"

She giggles, but the sound cuts short, her eyebrows pinching together. "But I'll get dirt on your fancy clothes."

Glancing down, I brush a hand over my vest. I left the tie at home today, going for a more relaxed vibe. Shrugging, I kneel in front of Lily. "A little dirt never hurt anyone."

Her eyes widen, ponytail brushing side to side with the shake of her head.

"Hop on, little one." I hook a thumb toward my back. "Just don't pull my hair."

With a squeal, she climbs onto my back, wrapping her slender arms around my neck.

"Hang on tight!" Then, we're zooming through the rows of trees, past the few workers checking on the apples. A trail of Lily's laughter bounces through the air behind us until we reach the deck on the back of Maggie's house.

Chapter 6

Maggie

I'm so late. Shit.

Way to look like an incompetent adult to your nanny on his first full day, Mags. I rub my fingers against my temple to ease the growing headache. It's been a long day, and all I want is to get home and cuddle Lily.

Her sweet hugs make even the worst day better.

The clock on the dash reads five-fifteen as I careen out of town. I told Viktor I would be home by late afternoon, not dinnertime. "Ugh. I hope everything is still okay."

He'd been texting me updates all morning while they went on a nature walk. At least, that's what Viktor called it.

To me, it looked like an excellent way to burn off Lily's endless amounts of energy.

My phone sits in the cupholder, with no new texts since lunchtime. "No news is good news."

Truth is, I've been busy running from one meeting to the next with several local grocers that I barely had time to react to any of Viktor's messages. But each little glimpse of my daughter beaming at the camera—or so engrossed in her drawing that she didn't even notice her picture being taken—warmed my heart and calmed the wiggling nerves in my belly.

Each new picture was more proof that she's in good hands with Viktor.

Viktor.

While I drive toward the orchard, my mind wanders to the oddly striking vampire who showed up at my door only a day ago.

He already seems to fit into our routine and our home. Making Lily laugh and smile. Making my stomach flutter with butterflies like it hasn't since—

"Since Roman," I whisper, eyes burning with tears as I navigate the familiar country roads.

Too bad my life is a mess. I'm drowning in debt, and my heart is still in pieces after losing Roman. I'm better off focusing on Lily, instead of opening myself up to more heartache.

Heartache that only happens from letting another man into my life.

Plus, Viktor is my employee. He's off limits... No matter how gorgeous he is, with his tall, muscled stature. Or his pale, almost luminous skin and penetrating red gaze.

...And his hair.

The man could walk onto the set of any shampoo commercial, and they'd probably beg him to model.

Hell, I'm even jealous of his flowing, silky white locks.

This morning, those shiny strands were fastened into a sleek ponytail at the base of his skull, matching the rest of his polished exterior. Like yesterday, he was dressed in slacks, a button-up shirt, and that infuriatingly sexy vest. All tailored to perfection to fit his lanky body.

For some reason, I want nothing more than to tarnish Viktor's perfectly manicured exterior.

Something lurks deep in his crimson gaze, telling me there's a wildness hidden beneath the professional side.

I caught flashes of it yesterday when he thought I wasn't looking.

Would he let me see that wild side?

The old wooden sign on the side of the road brings me back to the present. Scrawled in red paint, the name *Sweet Orchard Dreams* is barely legible on the worn wood planks.

When Roman and I bought this place, we'd talked about renaming the orchard, but we couldn't come up with anything we liked better. It only made sense to keep the name and avoid unnecessary paperwork and fees to change it. Plus, we had a few diehard patrons come back during our first harvest. Even with the new ownership, they were all too happy to support us during our learning phase.

I sigh, scratching at the skin over my heart. The all-too-familiar ache builds in my chest like it does every time I think of Roman.

Now the name is a remembrance. A legacy. And I can't bear the thought of changing it without Roman being here.

So *Sweet Orchard Dreams* we'll remain.

But a new sign is a must this season. A rundown, barely legible sign won't attract hordes of happy harvesters, which we need in order to turn a profit this year. A new sign is an expense I can't really afford, but one I'll have to grin and bear.

If luck is on my side—which it doesn't seem to be lately—Cyrus can help me DIY a new sign to save money.

The melancholy washes away, like waves heading out to tide, when the two-story white farmhouse comes into view. Our bright red front door always has my lips stretching into a smile. It was one of the first things I changed when we moved in.

Moisture springs to my lash line at the thought of losing this place.

It holds the last memories I have of Roman, so I'll do everything in my power to keep it.

Pulling into the garage, I turn off my car—and shut down my thoughts of my dead husband. After drying my eyes, I grab the to-go bag from the passenger seat and head inside.

"Hel—" The greeting dies on my lips at the scene waiting for me when I walk through the door.

Viktor's back is to me, broad muscles stretching the fabric of his dress shirt. A tabletop ironing board is set up on the island with a light-blue dress shirt draped across it.

One large hand wraps around the handle of the iron, gliding it across the fabric. Like everything else, Viktor is meticulous, not missing a single wrinkle and creasing the collar and cuffs to perfection.

Without making a sound, I place my purse and the food I picked up for dinner on the counter. I lean against the wall as my eyes wander over the muscles flexing in Viktor's forearm with each swipe of the iron.

The man seems to make anything he does look sexy.

Sometime while I was gone, he seems to have lost a little bit of his stuffy outfit. His vest is absent and his shirtsleeves are rolled to expose the thick sinews of muscle lining his glorious forearms.

What if I could come home to this scenario every day?

I shake my head, dismissing the silly thought. He's your nanny, not your boyfriend or husband. He's here to do a job.

"And how many apples will you have if you pick two more?" The dark timbre of his voice has me taking a step closer, and a shiver rushes down my spine.

I hear soft shuffling, then Lily's little voice answering from the kitchen table. "Four!"

Tipping his chin over his shoulder, I gasp when Viktor's eyes meet mine, a grin curling up one corner of his mouth. *Shit, I've been caught red-handed.*

Heat rises on my cheeks, and I open my mouth to apologize, but Viktor places a finger to his lips and tips his head toward Lily.

Stepping next to him, his calming presence surrounds me. My daughter sits at the kitchen table, squirming in her seat. Her gaze is focused on a line of apples placed in a neat row in front of her.

"Enhanced hearing, remember? Can't sneak up on me, country girl." He taps his ear, and his smile grows wider.

Right. I gulp. Definitely forgot about his *special qualities*.

"I hope you don't mind, but we picked a few that looked ripe this afternoon." Warm breath fans the side of my face when Viktor leans close, whispering into my ear. He's so close, the sweet notes of his cologne fill my nose with each greedy inhale I take.

And I take plenty, wanting his scent to overtake my lungs.

Turning toward him, I realize just how close we are when I notice the dark-brown and burgundy flecks scattered among the crimson of his irises. There's so much dimension there. So much emotion.

Right now, they seem to glitter with adoration for Lily as they dart between me and her. "I figured it would make a good learning opportunity without her realizing it. That's one of my favorite ways to teach at this age. Play can be such a vital tool when it comes to learning."

My gaze drops to his lips, watching them curve and twist with each word he speaks, his fangs peeking out ever-so-slightly. Dumbfounded, I nod along with what he's saying, like I'm paying attention to every word and not imagining what it would be like to have those fangs scrape across my skin.

Or, better yet, would it hurt if he sunk them into me and fed on my blood?

Unbidden, goosebumps trail up my arms, and I shiver.

"Momma! You're home!"

Tiny arms wrap around my waist, and I tear my attention away from lusting after *my nanny*, focusing on my daughter.

I kneel and pull her in for a hug. "I missed you, Lily bug. Did you have fun with Viktor?"

When we separate, her head bobs up and down, a wide grin stretching across her face. "He gave me a piggy bank ride!"

Eyebrows furrowed, I peer up at Viktor, mouthing *piggy bank*?

"Piggyback," he clarifies as I straighten to a stand. Lily runs back to the table and puts the apples into the basket like a centerpiece. "She was too tired to walk back to the house this afternoon, so I may have had her climb on my back and used my enhanced speed to get us here faster." Color grows on his cheeks, his usual pale skin flushing a light pink. *Cute.* "I hope you don't mind. I wanted to get us back quickly since she was hungry and starting to get crabby."

I shake my head. "You don't need my permission, Viktor. I think you've more than proven to know what you're doing. If anything, I'm the one who owes you an apology." I wince. "I'm sorry I'm so late. My meetings took longer than expected today."

"Good news, I hope."

Stepping around him, I grab the takeout bag before making my way to the table. "Amazing news! I landed contracts with three local grocers to start distributing our apples as soon as we have the first harvest."

Cool, comforting arms snake around me, and I'm pulled into a hard chest. "That's amazing, sweetheart! Congratulations!"

Sweetheart. Why do I like Viktor calling me that? Maybe even more than him calling me *country girl*. And why do I like the feel of his arms wrapped around me?

I let myself sink into the embrace for a second longer than I probably should before we both stiffen.

Viktor steps back. Clearing his throat, his eyes linger on the wall just above my head. "I should get going. I'll let you two enjoy your celebratory dinner. See you in the morning."

"You know—" Wiping my clammy hand on my jeans, I reach out and wrap my fingers around Viktor's, halting his retreat. "There's more than enough food... if you'd like to stay."

Already having dug into the food containers, Lily stops mid-chew to beg, giving him a face I know all too well. With her lower lip pushed out, her eyes grow wide and glassy. Classic puppy dog look. "Please stay, Viktor!"

Hook, line, and sinker, Viktor nods.

"Since you said 'please.'" He winks at Lily, who seems to be the only one in the room immune to his charms. Grabbing some plates and silverware from the kitchen, Viktor joins us, and we settle in for what's sure to be an awkward dinner.

Thanks to Lily, dinner is neither quiet nor awkward. In fact, it's... *nice*.

Apart from our Sunday dinners with Cyrus and Antoinette, it's usually just the two of us scarfing down a quick meal I manage to throw together in my perpetually exhausted state.

Not tonight.

Tonight, the table is filled with Lily's chatter about all the things she found on their earlier nature hike. Viktor coaxes her to really think, her little face scrunching up as she searches for each answer to his gentle questions. It's clear he has a knack for getting kids to fall in love with learning, something I can already see rubbing off on Lily.

As I wash our dishes in the sink, their conversation continues at the table. Viktor's deep, rumbling laughter is a welcome addition to our household. "Very good, little one. Should we try to find some different insects tomorrow after camp?"

"Insects?" Lily asks, and I smile, shaking my head as I set a plate on the drying rack.

"Bugs, Lil. Insect is another word for bugs," I call out from my place at the sink.

Her reply is drowned out by blood whirring in my ears when I spot an envelope with bright red lettering scrawled across it sitting on the counter. Another bill I've been dreading.

It's Lily's job to get the mail, so she probably dragged Viktor along today.

Snagging the envelope, I shove it behind the cookie jar near the fridge. The stack is getting thick. I really need to find a better place to keep all my overdue bills. The marks of my failure.

Hopefully, Viktor didn't look too closely. I don't need his pity or help. One of the contracts I landed today came with an advance that should keep us afloat for another month or so.

It won't make a dent in the back payments I owe on the mortgage, but I can keep the lights on, keep us fed, and pay my workers.

"Can I do anything to help?" Hands braced on the countertop behind him, Viktor leans back, a larger-than-life presence in my suddenly small kitchen.

Don't ogle the nanny, Mags.

Huffing a breath, I shut off the water and dry my hands on the dish towel, using the extra seconds to muster the courage to face Viktor. If this arrangement is going to work, I've got to get my raging hormones under control.

In the years since I lost Roman, I haven't once found myself as infatuated with anyone like I am with Viktor. And it's only been a little over a day.

What happens when he's been here for a week? A month?

What happens when I get to know the man behind the pristine suits and sleek ponytail?

By now, Lily has lost interest in the conversation with Viktor and is playing on the family room floor with her dolls.

"That was the last of the dishes. I just have to fold some laundry and get Lily to bed, so you're off duty for the night." I flash him a smile.

One long finger points at a laundry basket tucked on one of the kitchen chairs. Neat piles of perfectly folded clothes fill the cracked plastic bin to the brim. I've been so distracted by Viktor's presence and making sure Lily ate her dinner, I hadn't even noticed. "That laundry?"

"Viktor!" I huff. Somehow, I refrain from stomping my foot in indignation. "You're not here to be our maid!" Softening my voice—and my expression—I add, "You didn't have to do our laundry."

Like it's no big deal, he shrugs. "I don't mind. All my shirts were wrinkled from the trip here, so I had to iron them anyway. When I was looking for the iron in the laundry room, I saw your full dryer. Figured then you'd have one less thing to worry about later."

"Thank you." My voice cracks... And, damnit, are these tears? I sniffle, not letting them fall.

"You're welcome. More time to focus on Lily, right?"

I nod, unable to find my voice. This one act of kindness should not be turning me into a blubbering mess, but I've been doing life virtually on my own for years.

Suddenly, he's in my space, one big hand engulfing my shoulder. He makes me feel so tiny, so fragile. For some reason, I don't hate it.

It's refreshing.

With a gentle squeeze to my shoulder, he draws my eyes to his. "I'm here to make your life easier, not harder—remember? If you know you'll be late, send me a text, and I'd be happy to cook dinner."

Swoon.

"Thank you, Viktor. I think having you here is going to be good for all of us."

Leaning closer, his hand slides up to the side of my neck. His thumb rubs icy circles against the skin, sending my heart into a frenzy. My gaze flits to his lips before returning to his eyes.

He does the same, and when we lock eyes again, there's a flame blooming in his that I want to bathe in, letting it warm my broken soul. "I sure hope so, country girl." His voice drops an octave, deep and alluring.

Fuck, that nickname has my thighs clenching and my brain conjuring images of him purring those two words while I ride him. In fact, my brain is so riddled with horny thoughts of Viktor, I don't think I'd stop him if he closed the gap between us and kissed me.

Part of me actually hopes he does.

It's been so long since anyone has touched me in an intimate manner, and Viktor has unlocked a craving deep inside me that's been dormant for years.

Before either of us makes a move, Viktor's eyes close and his nostrils flare wide. When his lids open again, the fire in his eyes is gone.

He steps back, a hand going to the front of his pants when he turns away from me. "I'll get out of your hair." His words are choked, feet blurring to carry him to the back door in the blink of an eye. With his hand braced on the handle, he turns to flash a smirk over his shoulder. "Goodnight, country girl."

"Goodnight, city boy."

In another blink, he's gone, leaving me reeling.

Before I can replay whatever the fuck just happened, an all too familiar emotion swirls in my stomach. *Guilt*. It weighs me down like a block of cement. Unshakable, even after four years.

The guilt of surviving when Roman didn't.

The guilt of letting myself move on, and potentially forgetting him.

The guilt of not being a good enough parent for Lily.

The guilt of being on the brink of losing the orchard and Roman's dream.

The guilt of what letting Viktor into my heart will mean.

Sliding down to the kitchen floor, my butt hits the hardwood as the first tear falls. I can't lose sight of what's important: Lily and the orchard. There's no room for anything—or *anyone* else right now.

CHAPTER 7

Viktor

My first week at the Wilcox residence passes in a flash between carting Lily to camp and swim lessons, and keeping her out of Maggie's hair for the remainder of the time. We've done everything, from more nature walks (which Lily seems to love), coloring for hours, a variety of simple learning activities, and, of course, playing with her coveted dolls.

It's Friday, and I thought I'd let Lily show me around Maple Ridge Hollow, the nearest town to Maggie's orchard. It's also home to the elementary school and community center, two places I've become familiar with already.

"Does Momma have to work late again tonight?" Lily's voice fills the quiet space of my SUV.

Adjusting the rear-view mirror with one hand, I take in the crease between her eyebrows and her pursed lips. Clearly, she doesn't like all the extra hours Maggie has been putting in, staying locked in her office most of the day and into the evening for the past few days. I'm not sure what their routine was like before I showed up, but the change seems to be taking a toll on both Maggie and Lily.

"I hope not, little one. But how about we do something nice for her. Yeah?"

Her eyebrows rise. "Like what?"

This morning, dark circles marred the flesh under Maggie's eyes, and her beautiful curls lacked their usual luster. Every fiber of my being wants to swoop in and take away whatever is causing her so much stress, but since our almost kiss in the kitchen, she's kept her distance.

Not knowing the full extent of her past, the last thing I want to do is come on too strong.

Okay, that ship may have sailed... far away, lost at sea.

I'll admit, I got a little carried away that night. But she smelled so fucking good. And when her pulse raced under the soft caress of my thumb, my vampire instincts took over. Every fiber of my being wanted to lean in and taste her, sink my fangs into those luscious pink lips and drink her down.

Even now, the mere memory has a low ache growing in my fangs. I bite back a groan, eyes flashing to the child in the back seat.

Somehow, I stopped myself from kissing her at the last minute, and I've been a good boy the past few days, taking Maggie's cues and giving her the room she needs.

That doesn't mean I can't still do nice things for her, which is my plan for tonight.

"It *is* Friday. How about we make something special for dinner to surprise her? Sound good, little one?"

That idea gets a smile of approval as Lily's head bobs in agreement. No one wants to be stuck working late on the gateway to the weekend. Not when you could be spending time with a child as sweet as Lily. Tonight, I'm determined to get Maggie to quit work early to have a much-needed relaxing evening with her daughter.

Gripping the steering wheel, I turn out of the library parking lot, heading down Main Street toward the quaint little grocery store in town. "What does she like to eat?"

My gaze flits between the road in front of me and Lily's contemplative face in the mirror.

She hums, tapping one small finger on her chin. I chuckle. Over the past few days, I've come to find Lily can be a little dramatic, but it's all part of her charm.

In all truth, she's one of the easiest children I've ever cared for. Her exuberance is contagious, and she's eager to learn, scarfing down every morsel I teach her, then asking for more.

It's one thing to be enamored with her mother, but Lily has easily stolen my heart, too.

Mind finally made up, Lily proclaims, "Chocolate and vegetables!"

Okay, not my first choice, but I can make it work.

Before I can respond, she sticks out her tongue, nose wrinkled in disgust. "I don't like vegetables. But Momma makes me eat them."

I'm chuckling again as I pull into the store's parking lot and find a spot close to the cart return. "Duly noted. No veggies for Lily. As scrumptious as chocolate and vegetables sound, I think we'll need a few more ingredients. Ready to go shopping?"

A half hour later, we have a cart full of everything I'll need to make a special dinner for Maggie. Since we're short on time, I opted for pre-marinated chicken breasts from the store's butcher counter. Lily managed to sneak a few unnecessary items into the cart, too, but I figure a week of big changes warrants a few treats... after some vegetables, of course.

After paying the cashier, I push the cart out to my car with Lily riding on the back. Little fingers curled around the metal bars, she squeals. "Faster, Viktor! Faster!"

I give in to her enthusiasm, using a tiny fraction of my supernatural speed to zoom us the rest of the way to the car. It's worth potentially looking ridiculous to any passersby just to have Lily's contagious giggles surrounding me. Each new burst of laughter fills my heart like I've never experienced.

The almost-instant attachment I have to this child—and her mother—should be frightening.

Father wants me back in the city and settled down with a "nice vampire girl," but that's the last thing I want.

After only a week, I can easily envision a life with Maggie and Lily. Waking up early to cook them breakfast. Enjoying my morning blood coffee with their chatter as the soundtrack, before spending the day in the orchard. Even though I'm not quite sure what that entails, it still sounds pretty good to me.

Much better than being stuck in some stuffy office, pouring over meaningless numbers and trying to make the rich even richer.

No, thank you.

I just haven't figured out how to make it blatantly clear to my father that the future he wants for me isn't the life I want for myself.

Before the cart collides with the side of my shiny black SUV, I slow us to a stop. With it, I slow my racing thoughts of the future.

It's too soon.

I'm sure to send Maggie screaming and running to the peaks of the Appalachians if I confess my overwhelming infatuation with her so soon. "Give her time to warm up to you," I murmur while loading the bags into the trunk.

"Who are you talking to?"

So observant. I huff a laugh at Lily's question, loading the last bag and closing the trunk.

"No one, little one." I boop her on the nose, making another giggle bubble from her throat, before returning our cart. "Ready to head home?"

With an enthusiastic nod, she hops into her booster seat once I open the car door. After securing her seat belt, I can't help myself, and I bend to place a kiss on the top of her head.

The journey home is a quiet one, with Lily engrossed in her library book, and me lost in my thoughts of Maggie.

I'm so distracted that I almost forget where to turn, but the rundown *Sweet Orchard Dreams* sign on the side of the road signals the entrance to the long driveway to Maggie's house. It's become a landmark for me over the past week, but it could use a little TLC.

Parking, I notice the garage is open and Maggie's truck is inside. *Good, she's home.*

Lily and I spent most of our day in town, exploring and having a picnic lunch at the park, before checking out the library. I'm still not familiar with Maggie's daily schedule, but my nerves settle for some reason at the knowledge that she's just inside... waiting for our return.

"Lily, why don't you go inside and play while I unload the groceries? Okay?" I help her unbuckle and get out of the back seat before she runs to the door. Hopefully, she doesn't interrupt her mom and spill the beans about our dinner surprise. I smile at the thought.

The smile stays firmly in place as I zip in and out of the house, unloading the bags of groceries onto the kitchen counters.

Continuing to speed around the kitchen, I gather bowls and pans, getting everything I need to prepare our feast. Cooking for others is one of my favorite things. Knowing a dish I made brings someone I care about even a flicker of joy brings *me* joy.

And it's become abundantly obvious in the past week that I care about Maggie and Lily, even if we still have a lot to learn about each other.

Eventually, Lily comes to investigate, crawling onto one of the stools tucked under the kitchen island. Leaning her elbows on the counter, she props her chin on her hands. Eyes wide, she tracks each flash and swish of my hands as they blur between various dishes.

"Do you think she'll like it?"

Stopping mid-stir, I lift my head from the large mixing bowl to meet the question lingering in her green eyes. "Everyone loves my double chocolate raspberry cheesecake." I wink.

Lily giggles, snagging a runaway chocolate chip from the counter and popping it into her mouth.

"Hand me the rest of those, will you?" I tip my chin to the open bag of chocolate chips in front of her. "Actually, why don't you dump them in while I stir?"

Her eyes grow to the size of dinner plates. "The whole bag?"

"The whole bag," I confirm. *Because Maggie loves chocolate chips.* And this is for her.

An avalanche of sweet morsels fall onto the dark-brown batter, and I fold them together with gentle turns of my rubber spatula. The rich aroma fills my nostrils with each flick of my wrist until, finally, everything is combined. "Perfect. You're such a great helper, little one."

Lily beams at my praise.

Transferring the mixture into the graham cracker crust—chocolate, of course, because you can never have too much—I prepared earlier, I set it in the pre-heated oven to bake.

Five o'clock rolls around before Maggie's office door finally creaks open. My heart picks up speed at the sight of the messy blonde bun bobbing on top of her head and the smile lighting up her face. She still has dark rings under her eyes, giving away how tired she truly is, but at least she's smiling.

Sniffing the air, she steps into the kitchen. It's clean now. I like to wash and dry dishes as I go, so I'm not left with a mess once I'm done. That way, I get to enjoy the food with the people I made it for.

"It smells divine in here. What have you two been up to?" Pulling Lily in for a hug, Maggie's eyes sweep across the covered dishes scattered across the countertop.

I scratch the back of my head, my cheeks heating. *Why am I embarrassed?* She's going to love this. I get the feeling Maggie isn't used to others taking care of and pampering her. "It's been a long week, so we made you dinner."

Lily puffs out her chest as she pulls out of her mother's arms, like *she's* the one who did all the cooking... not me. "Yeah, chocolate and vegetables. Your favorite!"

Biting my lip, I try to hold in the laughter clawing up my throat, but I fail, a booming chuckle ringing through the kitchen.

"You have a great laugh," Maggie says, a soft smile on her lips.

Lips I can't stop dreaming about every damn night. Are they soft and sweet like her personality? Does she taste as good as she smells? Like crisp, succulent apples.

Right on cue, her intoxicating apple scent swirls around me, clouding my senses for a second before I blink and push those thoughts away. Far away... for now. "Thank you. Are you done with work for the day?"

"All done." She wipes her hands on her jeans, drawing my eyes to the wide set of her hips and her thick thighs. Saliva pools in my mouth, fangs aching to sink into her supple curves.

"Sorry I've been putting in long hours this week. We're gearing up for harvest, so I need to make sure everything is in place."

Turning away from her lingering gaze, I busy my hands in the cupboard, grabbing a stack of plates. "I get it. This place doesn't run by itself."

Maggie grabs silverware and napkins from one of the drawers. "It's such a beautiful evening. We should eat outside. You're staying? Right, Viktor?"

"Pleeeeeeease," Lily adds with her bottom lip pushed out. No one could say no to those big eyes and cute face.

"Yes, of course. I wouldn't miss such a wonderful feast."

Maggie's eyes heat at the word *feast*, but she clears her throat. Dropping her gaze to her plate, she fills it with grilled chicken breast, sauteed veggies, and creamy fettuccine alfredo.

"That was amazing! I don't think I've ever had chocolate raspberry cheesecake." Maggie dabs her mouth with a paper napkin before setting it on her plate.

"*Double* chocolate raspberry cheesecake," I correct, following suit.

She laughs, the lyrical sound floating on the evening breeze. "Nothing like death by chocolate. Thank you for cooking. You enjoy it, don't you?"

Smiling, I lace my fingers together and rest my hands on the table. "I do. It helps me express my emotions. If I'm sad, I cook. If I'm happy, I cook. If I'm stressed... I cook. You get the idea."

When I'm trying to impress someone, I cook. But I keep that part to myself.

"I suppose there are worse habits to have. I certainly won't say no to more delicious desserts." Her wink catches me off guard.

"Momma, watch me!" Lily calls out from the trampoline. Like most children, she ate a few bites of her dinner, declared she was full, and ran off to the play set and trampoline while Maggie and I finished eating. However, when I brought dessert out, she suddenly had more room in her belly.

Sufficiently sugared up, she's been bouncing on the trampoline for the past fifteen minutes or so.

"I'm watching!" Maggie yells, head turned toward her daughter. Lily falls back onto the trampoline, letting it spring her up onto her feet again.

With Maggie working long hours this week, I haven't gotten many opportunities to have an adult conversation with her. I want to know everything about her. Where did she grow up? How did she end up the owner of an orchard? Most importantly, how did she end up a widow?

Curiosity gets the better of me, and I blurt, "How did your husband pass?"

Smooth, Viktor. I wince, removing my foot from my mouth—metaphorically speaking.

Wide-eyed, Maggie's gaze slides from Lily to me, and I'm unable to decipher the emotion that flits behind her pale-green irises.

"I'm sorry. I shouldn't have asked that. It's just... I'd like to get to know you better."

Her throat works, but she nods. "It's okay. I-I'm used to people asking. It's been over four years, for crying out loud, and Maple Ridge Hollow is kind of a small town."

"I noticed."

Reaching onto the table, she fiddles with the edge of her balled-up napkin. "Roman and I were high school sweethearts. We grew up in the same town a few hours north of here. My parents actually still live there. Anyway, after college, we got married and lived in the city for a while. But we were miserable—especially Roman." She smiles at me, eyes watery. "He hated the noise of the city. The smells. All the people. And he especially hated working inside all day."

He sounds a lot like me.

"When I found out I was pregnant with Lily, the decision kind of made itself."

"What do you mean?"

"We didn't want to raise our kids in the city, so knowing we had a baby on the way forced us into action. This place was up for auction. It needed a lot of work. And I mean *a lot*. But Roman was determined." With her eyes focused on Lily, she releases a content sigh.

I turn, watching the little girl run after a firefly as the sun's last rays fade along the horizon.

"Hindsight, we were *idiots*." She chuckles. "We didn't know the first thing about running an orchard, two thirty-year-olds who grew up in the suburbs. Who were we kidding?"

My eyebrows scrunch. The abundance of apples on the trees would prove otherwise. "It seems like the trees are thriving."

"All thanks to Jean-Luc. I don't think you've met him yet. He's a grumpy bastard, but he took Roman under his wing and taught him everything. He was the foreman for the previous owners and graciously agreed to work for us once we took over."

Silence falls over us, only interrupted by the crickets chirping and Lily's distant laughter.

"Jean-Luc is the one who found him."

Before I can second guess myself, I reach across the table to squeeze her hand. "I-I can't even imagine the pain you've been through, Maggie. I'm so sorry. I shouldn't have brought it up. You don't have to tell me anything else if it's too hard."

Chapter 8

Maggie

Twisting my hand, I weave my fingers through Viktor's. After our almost kiss the other night in the kitchen, I've been fighting the urge to touch him again. But it's time to put on my big girl panties and face the facts: not touching Viktor is a losing battle.

Friends touch, right?

It doesn't mean anything else is going to happen. He can be my nanny and my friend. Totally platonic. At least that's what I keep telling myself.

Viktor is calming and comforting, and right now, I need a little bit of that comfort.

Closing my eyes, I let the coolness of his flesh ease my racing heart. Along with his stoic presence, it gives me the strength to go back to the hardest fucking day of my life.

The day I lost everything.

The day I almost didn't survive.

"I'm okay. Promise." I flash him a small smile, even though my voice shakes.

He squeezes my fingers tighter. "As long as you're sure.""I am." Nodding, I swallow past the lump in my throat. My voice is hoarse when I continue. "Lily had just turned one, so I don't know how much she remembers Roman. She asks about him sometimes when she sees the pictures around the house. I owe it to Roman to keep his memory alive for her." My eyes flit to my daughter. "Roman was very hands on, always going out into the fields to shoot the shit with workers. They loved him so much. Everyone did. He got up that morning like normal. Got dressed, had breakfast with me and Lily, and went about his day. If I'd known that kiss was the last one I'd ever get from him, I would have held on to him for just a little bit longer."

That's when the tears start, my heart cracking when they roll down my cheeks. With my free hand, I swipe them away. Unable to bear Viktor's beautiful crimson gaze right, I focus on our hands. His pale skin nearly glows in the fading sunlight, a direct contrast to my tanned flesh.

"He never came home that day," I whisper, biting my tongue to hold back the sob that wants to escape.

My hand trembles in his grip, but Viktor is there, wrapping his other hand around it to calm the tremors.

"Maggie. Sweetheart."

Throat thick with emotion, I shake my head. "Please, just let me finish." For some reason, I want him to know my darkest day, and the hole I had to crawl out of to get where I am today. I want him to shoulder some of my pain, like he shoulders the menial tasks around here. "A brain aneurysm ruptured while he was making his rounds. The doctors said h-he died instantly." I choke on another sob, but don't stop, forcing the words out. "Roman was the epitome of health. He worked out every day. He had the occasional beer with Jean-Luc or Cyrus. H-He never smoked. There were no signs that anything was wrong. It was all just a terrible accident."

My vision blurs with tears and, suddenly, I'm pressed against a hard presence. *Viktor.* He's cool like the first snowfall, but comforting, like my favorite blanket. I sink into the embrace and let the tears flow.

"I'm so sorry, Maggie. No one should have to go through that." His fingers card through my hair, and I focus on the soothing rhythm of his other palm on my back, rubbing in circular motions. Combined, the sensations have my hiccupped breaths settling back to normal.

I'm not sure how much time passes with me cocooned in the safety of Viktor's arms.

Eventually, I gather the courage to leave the embrace. I don't want to pull away from the shelter of his body, but it feels like we're crossing a line.

I wipe my face with the sleeve of my sweater and blow out a breath, blinking back my remaining tears. "I'm sorry, I shouldn't have dumped all that on you so soon. You're just really easy to talk to. It's only been a week, and here I am, burdening you with my trauma." I laugh, but it's more from embarrassment than anything.

Those same cool fingers hook under my chin, bringing my gaze back to his. Deep red, like two beautiful rubies. "You're not a burden, sweetheart. Never. Not with me. Do you understand?" Sincerity oozes from his smooth voice.

Awestruck, I say nothing as his fingers continue up to my cheekbone. They twirl in a lock of stray hair that hangs by my face. The one stubborn curl that's always escaping from my bun.

Viktor leans closer, soft breaths fanning over my face when he tucks the curl behind my ear.

I like his hands on me. His touch is soft, yet there's an underlying possessiveness that I crave.

I finally nod.

Somewhere in the haze of my emotions, Viktor scooted his chair next to mine. His sweet masculine scent wraps around me like the hug he just gave me.

In the fading rays of the sun, he's cast in a golden glow. Mix in his stark-white hair and pale skin, and he appears ethereal, every bit the supernatural being he is.

Damn, he's gorgeous.

Why does my nanny have to be gorgeous—and off limits?

Viktor is like Roman, on so many levels that I could easily see myself falling for him. He's kind, generous, smart, and hard-working. But he's an employee. A temporary one at that.

And, right now, I need a nanny more than I need a quick fuck, which is all I could give him with the current state of my heart.

Clearing my throat, I sit back in my chair, scooting it away from Viktor's. Hurt flashes across his eyes before they leave mine. *Fuck.*

"Momma, I'm tired." Lily runs across the deck and crawls into my lap, snuggling her head against my neck. Saved from the awkwardness by my child.

My watch shows it's only six forty-five. A little early for bedtime, but it has been a long week. Lots of new changes and adjustments with Viktor being here and me being locked away in my office, so the extra sleep might do her some good.

Viktor finally looks at me again, eyes warming when they land on Lily cuddled in my arms.

"I'm going to put her to bed, but... will you stay? I'd really like to hear how your first week went. Make sure we haven't scared you away, city boy." Adding the nickname, I wink and settle back into our comfortable banter. No heavy sadness, and certainly no sexual tension.

He smiles. "Of course. I'll finish cleaning up the kitchen while you tuck her in."

Even though I asked him to stay, I'm surprised to find Viktor still in the kitchen when I come back downstairs. There's a lot of baggage in my past, I know this, and I just dumped a heaping portion onto him. But the fact that he's still here has my heart beating a little faster... because I need a nanny for Lily.

There's absolutely no other reason why I'd be excited to have a hot vampire standing in my kitchen. Absolutely not.

"Hey," I rasp, coming to stand on the opposite side of the island from Viktor.

He hangs the dish towel on the hook by the sink and turns toward me. "Did she go to bed okay?"

"She asked me to read a few more books than normal, but I think she just wanted some extra cuddles. Something I'll never say no to. This week was the first time in her life that she wasn't with me all the time. I think she took the adjustment pretty hard." Mom guilt churns in my gut. You're damned if you do and you're damned if you don't as a mom. "I probably shouldn't have worked so much this week. I'm still figuring out how to balance Lily's needs and the needs of the orchard."

Society shames us for going back to work after having kids but, on the other hand, you lose all respect if you choose to stay home with your kids. It's a lose-lose situation. Even more so as a single parent who has to fill both roles.

Viktor must sense the negative shift in my mood. He squeezes my forearm and says, "You're an incredible mom, Maggie. Not many individuals in your situation would be thriving like you are."

I huff. "I most definitely am not thriving. I don't know what I would have done without you this week. You've been a godsend. I just wish I'd spent more time with Lily."

"Well, tomorrow is a new day. A new opportunity to get it right. You'll have the whole day to shower our girl with affection."

Our girl.

"I like the sound of that," I say, unsure if I'm talking about his claiming of my daughter or the chance to spend all day with her.

Spinning to the fridge, Viktor rummages around before pulling out a bottle of wine. "I figured you might need this after the week you've had."

I can't help but smile. "Making me dinner—and dessert. Now wine. A girl could get used to this."

"I hope so." He winks. "Girl like you deserves to be pampered."

Cheeks burning from his words, my jaw drops when, instead of using a wine opener like a normal person, one of Viktor's nails lengthens to a claw. He shoves it into the cork of the bottle and pops it free before pouring a healthy glass full of light-pink liquid.

"Hot," I murmur before I can stop myself. "I-I mean, it's hot in here." I fan my face. "Why don't we go back outside?" Smooth, Mags. Real smooth.

Viktor pours another glass of wine, handing the first to me, and we head back out into the summer night. The sky is dark now, tiny flickers of starlight along with beams of moonlight illuminating the black canvas when I settle onto the porch swing. It's wide enough for two, so I pat the spot next to me until Viktor takes the hint and sits down, too.

I sigh, taking a sip of the sweet, fruity wine. "This is my favorite time of day. Everything is quiet except for the frogs and the crickets. The world is at peace."

"It's beautiful here. We don't get stars like this in the city."

When I glance over, Viktor's head is resting on the back of the swing, tipped up toward the constellations above us. Under the moon's glow, the strong slope of his nose, full lips, and sharp chin are visible. A jaw cut from stone and equally carved cheekbones.

The man is gorgeous. There's no denying it, even if I am fighting the urge to give in to this invisible thread pulling me to him. "It sure is beautiful," I whisper, never taking my eyes off his profile.

Letting the buzz of the wine relax my tired body, my gaze wanders back to the stars overhead.

We glide gently in silence for a while, Viktor's long legs propelling the swing back and forth. Back and forth. The rhythm is soothing after a hectic week.

At least I can sleep a little easier with the first grocery store payment safe and sound in my bank account.

"Does Lily like to paint?" Viktor finally breaks the silence.

His question is a little out of left field, catching me off guard, but I indulge him with an answer. "She does, but *I* don't enjoy the mess. I usually save it for an outdoor activity on a nice day. Are you already out of ideas to keep her busy?"

A slow smile spreads across his face, fangs glinting in the moonlight. "On the contrary. I may have noticed the poor excuse for a sign hanging near the entrance to the orchard."

"Oh... *that*." I bite my lip. "It's on my mile-long to-do list, but it's not a priority. What does that have to do with Lily and paint?" I raise an eyebrow at the handsome vampire.

Viktor's smile widens at my prying question. "What if Lily and I made a new sign? It'd keep her busy, get her outside, and be a sort of heirloom for this place."

My chest tightens, eyes burning. He's so perceptive, so thoughtful. I'll have to thank Cyrus for finding the perfect nanny when I needed him most. Even if I didn't realize it until this moment. "I think that's an amazing idea. But... are you prepared to help her paint unicorns and rainbows?"

His answering chuckle has me nearly melting off the bench. It's so dark, yet smooth and intoxicating.

I shake my head, clearing the haze of lust.

"Unicorns at an apple orchard. Could be a good selling point." He winks.

Those damn flirty winks. They get my heart fluttering and my stomach swooping. He really needs to quit it.

Does he, though? You like the way he flirts with you. Even if you're too scared to act on it.

"Perfect." Viktor stops my runaway train of thoughts. "I'll get started on the new sign next week."

"Thank you. I really appreciate it. One less thing I have to worry about." With another sigh, I drain the contents of my wineglass.

Cool fingers wrap around my other hand, where it rests on the wooden swing between us. "Like I said before, I'm here to make your life easier, not harder."

What Viktor doesn't know is that he's doing just that. Making my life both easier and harder at the same time.

His presence during the day is amazing, easing the burden of looking after Lily so I can give the orchard one hundred percent of my energy.

But at night, when he's tucked in his own bed, my mind is stuck on him. The only remedy has been my fingers between my thighs until I'm whimpering his name into my pillow. Yet every time I bring myself to orgasm with thoughts of this sweet vampire, guilt swoops in and ruins any euphoric high.

It's like I'm cheating on Roman, even though he's gone. And never coming back.

So for now, I need to keep Viktor at arm's length. I need him to be a friend—and nothing more.

Instead of dwelling on the lust I feel for my vampire nanny, I lock those thoughts into a cage in the back of my mind and throw the key as far away as possible.

Better yet, I flush the damn thing down the drain.

No naughty thoughts about the nanny, Mags.

Setting my wineglass on the ground, I clear my throat—and my mind. "Are you going back to the city this weekend?" It's a safe question, but it will hopefully lead to Viktor telling me more about himself. So far, he's a big ol' mystery.

A gusted breath leaves Viktor, chest deflating. "Yeah. Tomorrow."

"You don't sound too excited."

He sighs again. "It's not that. I'm excited to see my sister."

"Are you two close?"

His mouth curves into a wide smile. "You could say that. We're twins."

My mind conjures up images of a female version of Viktor. The same snowy hair, only longer. The same luminous pale skin. And the same elegant features. I bet she's stunning. "What's she like?"

"Ness? She's the wild one of the family." His soft laughter fills the air, a welcome addition to the symphony of crickets and frogs. "She's independent and strong, but she has this gentle, calming way about her. We did everything together growing up in the city."

It dawns on me then that I still have no idea how old Viktor is. From my little knowledge of vampires, I'm aware they can live for centuries. "And, umm, how old are you?"

His smile turns wolfish at my question, and I drop my eyes to my lap, cheeks scorching.

"I'll turn 100 this year."

Before I can stop it, a gasp flies from my mouth.

"Does that surprise you, country girl?"

Mustering the courage to look over at him, Viktor's smile somehow turns even more smug.

"Well, you certainly don't look a day over thirty."

Booming laughter surrounds us, bringing a smile to my lips.

"I'll take that compliment." Suddenly, his voice shifts to a serious tone. "In all honesty, I'm dreading my birthday."

"Why?"

One hand grips the arm of the swing, his knuckles turning white, and I swear the wood creaks under his death grip. "My father doesn't agree with my life choices."

Life choices? From what I've witnessed this week, Viktor is punctual, considerate, and hard-working. What's not to agree with?

"What do you mean?"

A harsh breath leaves his lips before he gulps down the rest of his wine. "My father has always been a hard man. Growing up, Ness and I didn't want for anything. Father sent us to the best prep schools in New York City. The best colleges. We had fancy clothes, cars... you name it, we probably had it. But the one thing I craved most, Father kept locked away."

My eyebrows pinch. Sounds like a pretty charmed life. "What's that?"

"His love. All my life, I've done everything to please him. To toe the line. But when I chose to work as a nanny, he made his opinion very clear. 'Women's work,' he called it."

I scoff. "Asshole."

He flashes a sad smile at me. "He gave me an ultimatum. When I turn 100, I claim my rightful place as his heir and work for him, or he cuts me out of the family."

Like it has a mind of its own, my hand settles on his, our fingers lacing with a gentle squeeze. "He would do that to his only son?"

Viktor nods. "My father is a very wealthy man, Maggie. He's spent years—decades building an investment banking firm that caters to only the richest of the rich. Since I'm the only male child, I'm expected to follow in his footsteps and take over when he retires. But I have no desire to spend my life in a stuffy office, hunched over a computer screen full of numbers all day. As it stands, my sister and I receive payments from a trust fund every month... as long as we follow his rules."

My eyebrows rise. "Rules? What kind of rules?"

"For me: quit nannying and work for him, then find a nice vampire female to settle down with. For my sister: give up her career and become the perfect vampire wife to a suitor of his choosing."

Anger whirrs in my veins, leaking into my voice when I say, "It's not the 1950s anymore! Doesn't he know his path may not be what's best for you both?"

Squeezing my hand, Viktor shakes his head. "He doesn't care. All he cares about is money and continuing our family bloodline."

"What about your mom?"

"Mother is a gentle soul. She loves me and Ness, but she's never stood up to him in all the years I can remember. If he cut me off, I'm afraid she'd side with him."

"Don't they see what they're doing to their children?" My throat thickens. I can't imagine sacrificing my relationship with my child for money.

Viktor clicks his tongue. "He doesn't care. We have family dinner once a month and the entire time, he's on my case. I'm sure tomorrow will be no different."

He waves a hand, clearly done talking about himself. "Enough about my tumultuous relationship with my father. This week with Lily was the reminder I needed as to why I love this job. Why I can't give it up."

He's smiling again. All because of my daughter.

"Most of the contracts I get through the agency are for wealthy families in the Upper East Side or the Hamptons. The parents are nowhere near as involved as you are, Maggie. Most times, I'm the only source of love those children receive. It's sad, really."

My heart drops, agreeing with his words.

Crimson eyes are on me again, scorching up my body until they settle on my face. "It's different with you. You love your daughter more than life itself. This—" One big hand flits from me to him. "Everything feels different with you."

The damn organ inside my chest is galloping now, threatening to break out of its cage.

But I open my big mouth and ruin it. "Ye-yeah. Like we could both use a friend."

Next to me, his stature deflates, gaze dropping to his lap.

As much as my body might light up under Viktor's subtle glances, I'm not ready to jump into a relationship. *Plus, he's your nanny.*

"Umm... anyway, like my daughter, I don't really know the proper monster to human etiquette here. Can I ask you a question?"

A smirk tugs at the corners of his lips. "Sure, sweetheart."

There's that nickname again. *Sweetheart.* It does *things* to me.

I shuffle across the bench, giving myself a little space, and clench my thighs together. "I understand the basics of vampires... I think. All week, you've eaten meals with me or Lily. And, umm, well..." I wince. "Do vampires really drink blood, or is that a myth?"

Scratching a hand across the back of his neck, I swear his cheeks pinken, but my vision is shit in the darkness. "I haven't fed on a living creature in a long time... And they were always willing participants when I did," he quickly adds, answering my next question before I can even ask.

"What do you do if you don't feed? And how come you still eat normal food?"

"So curious." He chuckles.

I flush at his husky tone.

"I enjoy the flavor and experience of eating normal food, so I still let myself indulge. But vampires require specific nutrients we can only get from blood. Luckily, there are synthetic blood powders on the market now. Similar to how you would take protein powder or other supplements. I prefer to mix it into warm milk. That's really the only way it tastes authentic."

"That must be awful, never feeding like you're meant to."

"It's not so bad. And for those who do want to feed on living creatures, there are blood clinics in the city. For a fee, vampires can feed on willing participants. Everyone is vetted by the clinic and there are rules in place to protect both parties."

Now I'm more curious. The option to feed in a safe environment exists, so why does Viktor choose a manufactured substitute? "Why don't you use the clinics?"

Those damn hypnotic eyes peer over at me again, trapping me like one of the frogs Lily catches and puts in a glass jar. The intensity behind them sucks all the air from my lungs until I'm panting, nearly gasping for breath.

Never breaking eye contact, Viktor finally speaks, and his voice drips with seduction. "Feeding for a vampire is intimate.

Sensual. I don't want to do that with a stranger. Next time I feed on someone, it will be someone I have a special connection with. Someone I *love*."

His declaration hangs between us, thickening the already humid summer air. Why does it feel like that someone is *me*?

CHAPTER 9

Viktor

Last night, the conversation between Maggie and I took a different turn than I was expecting. In fact, the whole evening took a different turn.

I didn't expect her to open up so soon about losing Roman. It was clear how much the events of that day hurt to relive. The pain in her beautiful eyes. Fuck, I wanted to tug her into my lap and take it all away. Instead, I settled for a hug.

I was so tempted to lean in and kiss her. The hungry vampire within me begged for a taste of her lips. But I resisted... somehow.

Even now, boundless hunger claws at my gut, looking for anything to satiate the urge for blood.

Sure, if I was a lesser man, I'd go to one of the blood clinics to take the edge off. Or better yet, one of the underground sex clubs I conveniently left out of my conversation with Maggie.

The idea of fucking anyone else sours my stomach, and I gag. For the first time, I realize, if I can't have Maggie, then I don't want anyone else.

My fangs won't sink into anyone's skin except hers.

"Oh, good. You're finally here." Vanessa's voice cuts off my spiraling thoughts. The fabric of her light-blue sundress swirls around her ankles in the summer breeze. She crosses her arms and leans against the brick front of my parents' brownstone.

When our father first amassed his fortune, he bought this one and the one next door, knocking down the walls and renovating to create the perfect ostentatious dwelling. Since most of my childhood was spent in boarding schools, it's far from home, unless my mother is around.

And if she is, we're usually holed up in the one room in the whole house that *does* feel like home—the kitchen. Trying new recipes is our thing, and it's something I've cherished since I was a small child.

Last night, I told Maggie I thought my mother would side with my father if I didn't meet his ultimatum, but I'm actually not so sure. She loves me and Ness, and I don't know if she would let Father tear her only children from her life.

"Hey, Ness." I pull my twin sister in for a hug. "It's good to see you, but why are you out here?"

She rolls her burgundy eyes. Several shades darker than mine, Ness had an easier time passing as human before monsters were "out." I was forced to cover the bright crimson of my irises behind dark glasses to keep people from staring. Ness's eyes, on the other hand, could pass for a deep, rare shade of brown.

"Dad's in a mood again." Tossing her wavy hair over her shoulders, she sits on the top step of the stairs leading to the front door.

Not ready to face my father quite yet, I take a seat next to her.

"He's already asked me twice when I'm going to 'get my head out of the clouds and find a nice vampire male to marry.' *As if.* Did you know he emailed me a list of eligible bachelors last week?"

We both scoff before breaking into a round of laughter.

I lean over, bumping her shoulder with mine. Ness is tall and willowy. Gorgeous in an ethereal way, with her waist-length white hair and porcelain skin. "The thought of you married is laughable. Downright ridiculous."

She bumps my shoulder back as a smile plays on her lips. They're painted with a shimmering pink gloss today, matching the rest of her subtle makeup. "Try telling that to Dad. Why is he such an elitist asshole, Viki?"

Wrapping an arm around her, I bring her closer to me, and she rests her head on my shoulder. "The only reason you get to call me Viki is because I love you."

Her melodic laughter fills the air around us, soothing the ache in my chest at seeing my father.

"As for Father... I wish I knew, Ness. I really do. How long have you been here?"

Her sigh ruffles the stray hairs around her face. "Too fucking long."

"Where's Mother?"

"Take a wild guess."

In unison, we utter, "Kitchen."

"Come on. Let's get this over with," she says, standing and brushing the back of her dress. She extends a hand to me and pulls me up. "At least I have you as a buffer now. Mom can only do so much."

"Gee, thanks. How's the spa doing, anyway?" I ask as I open the front door for her.

With the flip of a switch, my sister's whole body lights up, the energy palpable when a wide smile spreads across her lips. "Amazing! I just hired a new masseuse, and we're almost booked solid for the rest of the summer."

Vanessa runs an upscale spa in the heart of the city. Monsters and humans are invited to relax in the tranquil environment she's created in the middle of the bustling concrete jungle.

"That's amazing, Ness! You've worked hard for your success. You deserve it."

She deflates as we round the corner to the kitchen. "I wish Dad shared your sentiment. He just sees me as a way to keep the Bielski bloodline alive."

I grab her hand, hoping to slow her, but she spins out of my grasp and plasters a smile on her face.

"Look who I found," Ness sing-songs as we enter the kitchen.

The room is large and airy. Sage-green wooden cabinets climb the walls up to the ceiling. Above the farmhouse-style sink, a row of windows lets in the afternoon sunshine. Butcher block lines the countertops, and a tall waif of a woman stands at the island.

Her long white hair is tied into a sleek bun at the base of her skull, a few loose strands framing her face. A stained apron covers the crisp red dress she's wearing underneath. When she turns to face us, a smudge of flour on the tip of her pert nose has the tension melting from my muscles.

Evelina Bielski, my mother, doesn't look a day over forty, even though she is, in fact, centuries old. Her eyes light up when she spots me. She stops pouring cake batter into a round pan and opens her arms to me. "Viktor! Come here, darling!"

Rounding the counter, I oblige her. Long arms wrap around me, tugging me into a tight hug. The scent of strawberries and sugar invades my nostrils and warms my soul.

When we part, she cups my cheeks, tipping my face from side to side while her deep burgundy eyes examine me.

Ness and I share a lot of physical similarities with our mother. From our snowy-white hair to our long, lean body types. Being a vampire male, I'm packed with a little more muscle than they are, but nowhere near as much as Father.

We also inherited her calm and nurturing demeanor, which is probably why I ended up working with children. A fact my father never forgets to remind me of.

Her eyebrows furrow, eyes narrowing. "There's something different about you."

My heart picks up speed. Is it that obvious that I'm falling for Maggie?

Taking a step back, she hums and taps a slender finger on her chin. "But I can't put my finger on it."

"I have been spending a lot of time outside with my new job. Maybe I'm finally getting a tan," I joke with a nervous laugh.

We don't have enough melanin in our skin for it to tan, even if spending time in the sun wasn't painful.

Lily loves being outside, so I've had to adapt quickly since working for Maggie. I've managed to find all the shady nooks on the property to protect me from the sun.

Mother laughs, but her eyes continue to scan me. "That's not it. You seem lighter somehow. I'm probably just being silly." She waves the thought away with a flick of her wrist. "Anyway, how is the new job?"

I release a breath, thankful when her attention turns to putting the cake in the oven and chopping strawberries. Her hand moves faster than humanly possible, cutting up two containers in mere seconds. "It's a single mother—""Oooo, scandalous. Don't go falling in love, Viki," Ness interrupts, ever-so-helpfully. She steals one of the strawberries and pops it into her mouth. Mother smacks her hand away when she goes to steal a second one.

Choosing to ignore her childish remarks, I continue. "It was a last-minute contract just north of the city, and I couldn't turn it down." What I don't mention is how I felt called to take the position by a presence I don't completely understand. Maybe it was fate that led me to Maggie and Lily, or maybe it was a coincidence. Either way, I thank my lucky stars for whatever brought me to that orchard earlier this week. "The mother, Maggie, is newly widowed and owns an apple orchard. She's been juggling her daughter's needs and the orchard for the past few years. I'm just glad I can help."

"Oh, poor woman. I can't imagine losing your father. And how's the little girl? What's her name?" Mother's eyes lift from the bowl of fluffy whipped cream in front of her.

Snapping out a hand, the movement blurs as I dip a finger into the cream and bring it to my mouth. It melts across my tongue, smooth and sweet.

"Viktor!" Mother scolds, like always, and I smile. So many of my childhood memories involve helping her in the kitchen. Every time I came home from boarding school for breaks, I'd practically live in the kitchen, watching her whirl around making home-cooked meals and sweet treats.

For a while, I contemplated becoming a chef, but there was no way in hell Father would support that dream. Instead, I opted for a double major of finance and child psychology, giving Father the false hope I would join his firm someday.

I chuckle, snagging another scoop of fresh whipped cream before she pulls the bowl away, and I answer her question. "Her name is Lily. She's amazing. So intelligent and curious."

"Sounds like you're smitten," Ness chirps from her seat at the counter.

You have no idea.

A few hours later, the aroma of my mother's cooking surrounds us as we sit around the dining room table, passing dishes and filling our plates. Father is an imposing figure at the head of the table.

He's the opposite of my mother in every way. The darkness to her light. Styled to perfection, his jet-black hair shines under the fading rays of sunlight spilling through the windows behind him. The corners of his mouth purse downward. Assessing onyx eyes track every movement around the table. Calculating. Cold.

Body so broad, the chair strains under his weight each time he leans forward to grab a dish. His crisp white dress shirt is nearly bursting at the seams, trying to hold in his bulky muscles.

The one thing I did inherit from my father is my sense of style.

Except, where he chooses harsh, boring colors—blacks and grays—I prefer to use my style as a form of creativity, evident today with my eggplant slacks and vest. I tug at the brightly patterned blue tie around my neck and fiddle with the cuffs of my light-green dress shirt.

I chose it specifically because it reminded me of Maggie's beautiful eyes.

"Viktor." *Even his voice is commanding.* "Will we see you at the annual charity gala this year?" Father scrutinizes me over the rim of his wineglass, the blood inside sloshing as he brings it to his lips.

Like an ant under a magnifying glass, my skin flames beneath the laser focus of his dark eyes. "I hadn't thought that far ahead. I'll have to check with—"

"See that you're there. It's important for you to network now in preparation for when you join Bielski Investments after your birthday." The dreaded birthday that's less than six months away. "No son of mine will spend his life *babysitting*. It's time to accept your rightful place." And there it is... the jab that I've been waiting for.

Holding back my retort, I bite my tongue. No matter how many times I protest, my words go in one ear and out the other.

"There will also be several beautiful females there. Any one of whom would make the perfect wife. When's the last time you were with someone? You—and your sister—need to start thinking about the future of our family." His eyes shoot across the table to Ness. Her nose wrinkles, and she sticks her tongue out once Father turns to our mother.

Asshole.

I don't know if my father believes in love. It seems like all he cares about is a strong vampire bloodline and money. Hell, I don't even know why my mother is still with him. Growing up, he was noticeably absent. If we weren't at boarding school, Mother was the one taking care of us. Tending to any scrapes and cuts. Tucking us in at night. Loving us like a parent should.

"Kas," my mother coos, lacing her fingers with his on the table. "Can't we enjoy one family dinner without fighting?"

"No, Evie. It's time the boy faced the hard facts. *Nannying* is woman's work." His lip curls into a sneer. "It's beneath him. I've held my tongue for the past half-century, letting him live in the clouds, but it's time to face reality. After the gala, Viktor, I expect you to start working for me."

"You know what?" I crumple my napkin into a ball and throw it on my plate, ready to flee.

Kasmir Bielski is a ruthless businessman. He has to be to get where he is—one of the top financial investment firms in New York City. His clients are A-listers with deep pockets.

But that's not the life I want.

"The only reason I'm even here today is because of Mother and Ness." The chair legs scrape against the floor as I stand. "If you can't accept my career choice, then maybe I don't need to be part of this family." With those parting words, I make a beeline out of the room.

Stumbling into the kitchen, I brace my hands on the counter, harsh breaths sawing in and out of my chest.

I can't believe I said all that. If he takes Mother and Ness from me, then he might as well drive a stake through my heart and end it all.

My legs buckle, forcing me to lean against the counter. I've never stood up to him before. Usually, I take his barbed words in silence.

"Viktor." A cool hand brushes up my back. Soothing. Gentle.

Mother.

"Why is he like this?" I ask, turning to face her.

Sighing, she squeezes my hand. "Your father has been through a lot in his long life. He was raised with different beliefs. He came from nothing and, in his own way, he just wants you to have the same success as him. And to continue our family line." She holds up a hand when I open my mouth. "I know. That doesn't excuse his hurtful words toward you or your sister. Please don't write him off yet, darling. For me?"

As much as I hate it, I nod. My mother is the soft one. The kind one. Without her, I wouldn't be who I am.

She smiles, eyes sparkling. "If it's any consolation, I'm proud of you, Viktor. You're shaping the minds of the future, one child at a time."

"Thank you, Mother. That means a lot."

"And I hope you'll still come to the gala. I'd love to see you. Maybe you could bring Maggie. It sounds like she could use a night out in the city."

Averting my gaze, I scratch the back of my neck. Throwing a human into the pits with my father seems like the worst idea ever. "I don't know if that's really appropriate. She's my boss."

"Just think about it. And don't worry about your father. I'll handle him." There's a glint of mischief in her eyes that I've never seen before. Maybe she does have the gall to stand up to him after all.

I chuckle, pulling her in for a hug and placing a kiss on the top of her head. Even though Mother is tall, I still stand at least a head taller than her. "I love you. Tell Ness I'll see her at breakfast tomorrow.

"I will. Get home safe."

The entire walk back to my apartment, I try to put my father's comments out of my head. Instead, I focus on curly dark-blonde hair, enchanting green eyes, and a body built for sin.

My heart sinks when I open the door to my apartment and I'm met by silence.

It's quiet. *Too quiet.*

Over the last week, I've gotten used to Lily's constant chatter. She always has questions to ask or something to say. It's amazing the random facts that come out of her little mouth.

Suddenly, the familiar cozy environment I've created for myself in the city feels wrong. I miss Lily's giggles and Maggie's warm smiles.

Once I've gone through the motions of my nighttime routine, I draw the curtains and put on some sweatpants before slipping into bed to read for a few hours.

Getting lost in the pages of a fantastical world seems like a good distraction.

But it doesn't work. My eyes skim the same passage over and over for what must be an hour, not registering a single word.

Giving up, I sigh and set the book on my nightstand. A certain green-eyed beauty keeps stealing my attention.

I settle back against the pillows and close my eyes. Images of her lips wrapped around her fingers flash behind my lids. The way she moaned as she cleaned the chocolate from them. Fuck, that sound is seared into my brain for eternity.

Electricity buzzes under my skin as I let my mind wander.

Maggie doesn't even know she's the perfect mix of sexy and adorable—and it's driving me crazy. There's an innocence to her that I yearn to corrupt with my cock and fangs until she's dripping my cum and her blood fills my mouth.

My hand trails beneath the covers and into the front of my sweatpants, where my cock is aching to be touched. To be licked and sucked. To be inside Maggie's warm heat.

I bet her pussy is spectacular.

Groaning, I fist my cock and glide my hand up the piercings that line the underside. The cool metal of each one brushes across my skin as I stroke up to the tip.

Five in total; one for each time I found myself at the door of the local underground sex club in a haze of lust and hunger. Each time, I managed to drag myself away, chug some synthetic blood, and add a rung to the ladder.

For decades, I've been saving myself for the perfect partner. The one I'll keep forever.

"Maggie," I moan, hips bucking to meet my fist as pleasure spikes at the base of my spine. My balls tighten with each stroke, imagining it's Maggie's soaking wet cunt instead.

The icy skin of my hand on my hard cock kills the fantasy. Instead, I bring it to my mouth, sinking my fangs into my palm until the coppery tang of blood fills my mouth. Warm and wet.

Wrapping my bloodied hand around my throbbing shaft, I stroke faster, using the dripping crimson liquid as lube. My fingers squelch along the piercings, blood leaking between them like Maggie's arousal would.

"Yes," I growl, and stroke faster, tightening my grip until a pinch of pain has my balls drawing up to my body.

Her sultry moan echoes in my head, then her whispering voice flutters in my ear. *"Come for me, Viktor."*

The soft command is my undoing, and my eyes slam shut as I explode. Hot ropes of cum splatter across my lower stomach and fist, where it squeezes the tip of my cock. There's a piercing there, too, a single hoop bisecting the head. They're all for her pleasure, something I hope to be able to show her soon.

After jerking off before bed last night, I crashed hard, only to awake this morning with another raging boner. I took care of it in the shower before dressing and walking to meet my sister for breakfast. This constant thinking about Maggie thing is becoming a problem.

"I ordered you a blood coffee and cinnamon roll," Ness says as I slide into the bright pink booth across from her.

The diner, Cream Me Up, is a hub for all things monster here in the city. Their menu has standard human dishes, along with more niche items, like blood coffee and shakes for vampire clientele.

"Thanks, Ness. How was dinner after I left?" Waiting for the worst, I curl my lips over my teeth. I shouldn't have talked back to Father, and I certainly shouldn't have left Ness there to deal with the aftermath.

She blows out a breath, cupping the sides of her mug. Steam wafts up from the red-tinged liquid inside. Probably a raspberry mocha with a shot of synthetic blood, her favorite. "It wasn't so bad. Dad got a business call, so he locked himself away in his office while Mom and I cleaned up. I left after that. I don't know why she stays with him."

I shrug. "He must have been different when they met."

A heavy hand clamps down on my shoulder before I can dive deeper into my parents' issues. Phil, the orc who owns the diner, stands next to our booth, tusks and teeth on display in a cordial grin. "Viktor, good to see you. It's been a while."

I nod as he slides a steaming mug of blood coffee in front of me, followed by one of his signature cinnamon rolls. It's the size of a dinner plate and covered in a thick smear of the best frosting I've ever tasted. A family recipe that Phil guards with his life. I've attempted to recreate it in my own kitchen countless times, failing miserably. "Good to see you, too. I started a job out of the city, so this is the first time I've been back all week."

"Good for you. Hope the kids aren't too monstrous." His thick belly bounces with a deep chuckle.

"Trust me." I wink. "It's nothing I can't handle."

He laughs again, turning to help another customer. Waving over his shoulder, he shouts, "Enjoy your food. Don't be a stranger."

When I turn back to my sister, her narrowed eyes are scrutinizing my face. "What?"

"Mom's right. There's something different about you lately." *Oh, shit.* "How is the new gig, anyway? You were kind of vague yesterday." She's pressing for more information.

Ness is my best friend, but usually, she's the one bragging about her latest conquest, while I live vicariously through her.

Taking a sip of my coffee, I let the hint of blood soothe the ever-present ache in my fangs—and cock. Over the past week, I've been trying to ignore this need to sink my fangs into something. "The first week was amazing, Ness. Maggie is—" I groan. "She's beautiful. And smart. And so motivated. She's been running the orchard virtually on her own since her husband died."

Ness smirks over the lip of her mug. "You're attracted to her, aren't you? That's why you seem different."

Dropping my gaze to the table, I swallow. I don't want to lie to my sister, and maybe she can help me work through the developing feelings for Maggie. Finally, I nod and look up. Her smile widens until her fangs are on full display.

"Yeah," I croak.

"I knew it! Oh! I can't wait to meet her!"

"Ness, *slow down*. She doesn't even know yet. It's only been a week, and she's still grieving her husband. Plus, all the stuff with Father. Could you imagine if I brought home a *human* woman? He'd lose his fucking mind."

She reaches for my hand and gives it a squeeze. "Don't let that old asshole dictate your life, Viki. You know he can't keep us apart. And he damn well doesn't get a say in who we date. Don't give up on her. Okay?"

My eyes stay on my mug. "I'm not giving up. I-I think she might be the one."

When I look up again, Ness's burgundy eyes widen, and she coughs, choking on a sip of her coffee. "It's serious, then?"

I nod. "But she doesn't know any of this."

"You've always been the patient one out of the two of us. Give her space to heal, and I'm sure she'll love you back. But tell me about the little girl. What's her name again?"

The mention of Lily has me smiling, her sweet little face popping into my head. "Lily. She's so full of life and exuberant. And she has this hunger for knowledge."

Ness leans her elbows on the table, smiling as I regale the past week I spent with Lily.

"You're staring at me again, Ness." I smooth a hand over my hair before fiddling with my cufflinks. "You're making me nervous."

"I just love the way you light up when you talk about the kids you take care of. You have such a passion for nurturing them."

"Beats being stuck in an office with Father." I chuckle when she scrunches her nose and grimaces.

Ness rolls her deep burgundy eyes. "Ugh. Don't remind me. The only reason I got out of the family business is because I don't have a dick and balls filling the space between my legs."

I almost choke on a bite of cinnamon roll at her words. "Like you'd want to work in investment management anyway."

She scoffs. "No, I much prefer my spa. Thank you very much!"

This is why I love spending time with Ness. We have this easy back-and-forth; plus, I can tell her anything without fear of being judged.

She fills me in on the nitty-gritty of the spa while we finish eating and order a second round of coffee. By the time I leave the diner, I'm ready for a new week with Maggie and Lily. I'm resolved to give Maggie the space she needs to heal, while still being there for her in a friend capacity. Even if it means shoving this all-consuming attraction deep down inside me for the time being.

CHAPTER 10

Maggie

This is the time of day I hate most. Pacing around the kitchen, I put the last of the clean dishes away. My brother-in-law, Cyrus, and his mate, Annie, came for dinner, but they've since gone back to the city. Lily is tucked into her bed upstairs. The house is eerily silent.

It's these quiet moments when grief rears its ugly head.

This is when sadness engulfs me, shrouding me in its inky black embrace until I'm left to wallow in my own thoughts until morning. This is when I remember all the things I'm missing without Roman.

From the boring conversations about retirement savings and who's taking Lily to school the next day. To the cozy nights, with him watching the sports channel while I read, my feet in his lap.

His eyes would linger on me from the opposite side of the couch, never ashamed of still finding his wife attractive after countless years of marriage.

Soon enough, I'd end up under him, his hard body pressing mine into the soft couch. His usually steady hands would turn frantic, shoving my nightgown up and pulling my panties to the side so he could slide inside me. The heat between us never died, and I crave it more than ever since his passing.

I'm touch starved, but I'm terrified of finding someone else.

Earlier, Annie asked me if I was ready to start dating. Like always, bile crept up my throat, and I wanted to vomit.

Dating means moving on, replacing Roman. And my heart can't bear someone else in this house, someone else raising Lily.

Beams of light shine in the front windows, snapping me back to the present. To the utter silence that makes it hard to breathe.

A car door slams. Seconds later, there's a soft knock on the front door.

When I open it, Viktor is standing on the other side, a pink box clutched in his hands. "Did I wake you?" His voice is quiet, likely not wanting to wake Lily since it's a little after nine.

Brilliant crimson eyes scan me from head to toe, taking in the oversized t-shirt hanging off one shoulder. It's Roman's shirt from college, when he was on the football team. After he died, I kept it and wore it for weeks until his scent faded and it began to smell like me. I still don't have the heart to throw it away, even though it's riddled with holes and the fabric is threadbare.

My skin prickles under his perusal, nipples pebbling against the worn cotton and reminding me I'm *not* wearing a bra.

Crossing my arms, I attempt to hide the arousal coming to life in my traitorous body.

How does the simple presence of this vampire take me from melancholy to horny in the blink of his beautiful eyes?

Shaking my head, I will my body to calm the fuck down. "I was awake. Couldn't sleep. Seems to be a regular problem since Roman died."

The corners of Viktor's mouth twitch down. "I have something that might help." Lifting the pink box between us, he opens the lid to reveal a dozen giant chocolate chip cookies. "Fresh from my favorite bakery in the city."

"Cream Me Up?" The familiar flying saucer logo catches my eye.

A smile spreads across his face. "You know the place?"

I nod, beckoning him into the house. "It's Antoinette's favorite."

His answering chuckle has goosebumps dancing across my arms. "Right. The dragon. What do you say, country girl? You up for a late-night snack?"

I can't help but smile when his broadens, flashing his fangs. "I'll get the milk, city boy."

As we head to the kitchen, I notice the cloud of grief has dissipated and the uneasy silence is replaced by the soothing baritone of Viktor's voice. Maybe the reason moving on makes me physically ill is because my body has been waiting for the right person.

Maybe I've been waiting for Viktor?

He's only here temporarily. Do you really want to get involved with someone who's set on leaving in a few months? My conscience pipes up, joining the party of emotions currently plaguing my body. Plus, he makes Lily happy, which is more important than my sexual needs. Who's to say we'd even be compatible in that department?

An orgasm isn't worth fucking up the good thing I have going with Viktor as the nanny. Nope, I'll just continue to take care of myself with the help of my trusty vibrator.

"How was your weekend?" I ask, pouring two glasses of milk while Viktor takes a seat on one of the stools. With me standing on the other side of the counter, there's a barrier between us, so I don't do something stupid like climb him like a tree and kiss his lush mouth.

Viktor rolls his eyes. It's the first hint of attitude I've witnessed from his otherwise polished behavior. I clap a hand over my mouth to stifle my laughter. "About as good as expected. I stood up to my father, though."

"Good for you!" I raise my glass of milk in a salute.

His answering chuckle has my belly somersaulting. Like I told him before, he really does have a great laugh. Smooth and rich, like a perfectly aged whiskey.

As quickly as his laughter started, it stops, his mouth dropping into a frown. His Adam's apple bobs with a swallow. "I wish I understood why he doesn't respect my job. He thinks I'm just a babysitter."

Around a mouthful of cookie, I ask, "Have you ever explained to him what you do? How you're not a glorified babysitter?"

"No." His eyes drop to the rim of his glass, long fingers tracing the edge. His hands, much like the rest of him, are so elegant.

"Maybe you should try. You're already having an impact on Lily after only a week. She demanded to go for another nature walk yesterday, and I had to look up every bug and flower we came across so we would know the correct names."

That gets a smile back on his face. A smile I'm starting to see in my dreams.

"What about you? Besides becoming an encyclopedia of insects and flowers, how was your weekend?"

"The weather was beautiful, so we went to the pool in town. Lily got to see some of her friends who were in her preschool class last year. But we both got a little sunburned." In fact, my skin is still itchy and red. "And we had dinner with Cyrus and Annie tonight."

Viktor chews a bite of cookie while I talk. He's such a good listener. His eyebrows rise at the mention of Cy. "Cyrus is your brother-in-law, right?"

Before I can think better of it, I reach a hand across the counter and brush the crumbs clinging to the corner of Viktor's mouth. At the same time, his tongue swipes across his bottom lip, skimming my thumb. Eyes flaring, I swear his tongue lingers on my skin for longer than is appropriate.

Sucking in a gasp, I snap my hand back.

Why did I do that? Stupid hormones!

"S-Sorry. You had some crumbs." I wave a hand at him as my cheeks flame. "Umm, Cyrus. Yes. He's Roman's older brother. He pitches in a lot around here when he can. But he and his mate, Annie, just opened their own commercial real estate firm, so they're a lot busier now. We try to have Sunday dinner at least once a month. You're more than welcome to join us next time."

"I'd really like that."

Finishing the rest of his milk, Viktor stands and pulls his car keys from his pocket. "It's getting late. I should let you get some rest."

I wish you wouldn't, I want to scream. But my mouth splits open on a yawn instead, the full belly of cookie and milk taking hold. "I'll see you tomorrow, city boy."

He smiles. "Goodnight, country girl."

CHAPTER 11

Viktor

Over the next few weeks, I fall into a comfortable rhythm with Lily, between camp, swim lessons, and trips to the library, all while Maggie works tirelessly to prepare for harvest. I've also gotten into the habit of cooking, cleaning, and taking care of the laundry. Anything to shoulder some of the load for her.

We're approaching the end of August now, and autumn is right around the corner, bringing with it shorter days and cooler weather. Lush, heavy fruit hangs from the trees surrounding the main house, waiting to be harvested. Workers flit around the orchard grounds, picking apples from some areas and monitoring the growth in others.

Clouds drift across the sky above, and a breeze rustles my hair. Taking full advantage of the weather, I've spread a tarp on the ground and laid out supplies.

"What is it?" Lily asks, standing next to me with her little hands balled on her hips.

It's taken more hours than I care to admit and several trips to the local hardware store, but I finally finished sanding down and prepping the old orchard sign for its facelift. "This, little one, is the sign that hangs at the entrance to the orchard. It needs some love."

"Why?" Her face scrunches, and I bite my cheek to hold in a laugh.

"The sign is the most important part. Without a sign, no one would be able to find the orchard. And they wouldn't be able to enjoy all the delicious apples."

Lily's eyebrows climb up her forehead. "So we have to make it pretty again?"

"Exactly. Do you want to help?"

Her lips purse. "Momma doesn't like it when I paint. She says it's too *messy*."

This time, my laughter spills free as I recall my conversation with Maggie from my first week. "That's why we're outside, little one. The next time it rains, the paint will get washed away if we make a mess. So, what do you say? Wanna help?"

I extend a paintbrush toward her.

Kneeling next to me, she grabs the brush. "Okay!"

Before we came outside, I had Lily change into some old clothes that already had stains, just in case she *did* get messy.

Over the next hour or so, the sign comes back to life before my eyes. Using a steady hand, my brush trails vibrant red paint along the final flourish of the 'S'. *Sweet Orchard Dreams* spelled out in big block letters.

"Done. There's no way anyone will miss the sign now. What do you think, little one?" Laying my brush on a paint-smudged towel, I turn toward Lily.

Just like the sign, a rainbow of color dots her clothes and hands. Her little tongue pokes out of her mouth, eyes focused on her hand as it forms the final arch of the rainbow she's been working on for the past few minutes. "Can we do another rainbow?"

"I have a better idea." Wiping my brush clean on the towel, I load it up with red paint. "Can I see your hand?"

Lily creeps closer and sets her hand in mine. Her precious giggle floats along the breeze when I drag my brush over her thumb. "That tickles! And it's cold!"

Working quickly, I paint the rest of her fingers in orange, yellow, green, and blue, finishing by painting her palm purple. "Now, turn your hand over and press it here." With a gentle touch, I guide her palm down to the corner of the wooden sign, pressing against the back of her hand before pulling it away to reveal a perfect rainbow handprint.

Maggie wanted a new sign, but I'm going to give her an heirloom. Something to make customers feel like they're right at home when they drive through the front gates.

"Your turn!" Using her paint-stained hand, Lily snatches at the paintbrush in my grasp. Her hand slides onto the sleeve of my crisp blue shirt, leaving a trail of mixed paint behind. She gasps, eyes wide and bulging. "Oh, no," she whispers, mouth gaping.

Never one to get mad at a child, my booming chuckle fills the air. "I guess I should have chosen a different outfit for such a messy task. Right, little one?" My wink has a smile creeping back onto her face.

She finishes painting my fingers and palm. Together, we add my handprint next to hers. The only thing missing is Maggie's.

"Let's get cleaned up. Your mom should be home soon." Thankfully, I had the foresight to bring an old towel out from the laundry room, so I wipe our hands as clean as I can. "Can you go wash up in the laundry room sink while I finish cleaning up?"

Lily doesn't move, her eyes fixed on a car coming up the driveway. It's a luxury sports car, flashy and red, clashing with our current surroundings. "Who's that?"

My stomach twists. Maggie never has visitors, and something about the tall man stepping out of the fancy vehicle has my hackles rising. "I don't know," I say, bracing a hand on Lily's back. "Go inside and wash up in the laundry room. I'll be in soon."

With her gaze locked on the stranger, Lily sprints into the garage. A moment later, the door to the house slams shut.

"You lost?" I call out to the man as he rounds the hood of his car, a smarmy grin on his face.

I recognize the designer brand of his suit. It's one of my father's favorite labels and costs a pretty penny. My best guess: this asshole is in the financial world. But why the fuck is he here?

The man approaches, sneering when dirt scuffs the tops of his shiny brown loafers. Probably designer, too. "Is Ms. Wilcox available?"

Maggie had a meeting in a neighboring town with one of the local grocers today. She seemed genuinely excited this morning at the prospect of another sales deal.

A growl rumbles in my chest with every step the man takes toward me. His presence feels wrong. "Why?" My upper lip curls back, revealing my fangs when the overpowering stench of his expensive cologne hits my sensitive nose.

Ignoring me, his eyes skim past me to the rows and rows of ripe trees. Tucking his hands in his pockets, he rocks onto his toes and lets out a harsh whistle.

Wincing at the sound, I rub one of my ears, but I don't miss his next statement. "This place really is a goldmine. It's a shame she's gonna lose it." *Lose it.* What the fuck is he talking about?

"What do you mean?"

A lecherous smirk crawls across his face, and he smooths a hand over the strands of his slicked-back golden hair. "Ms. Wilcox hasn't paid her mortgage in four months. I'm here to issue her final notice before we seize the property." There's a hint of glee in his voice as he spews the words.

The world tilts around me, stomach nearly dropping out of my ass. Maggie's broke? Why didn't she tell me?

Why would she? You're the nanny—nothing else.

I thought we'd reached a point where we were friends. Where she felt she could tell me if she was in trouble.

"There must be some kind of mistake—"

"No mistake. We've issued several warnings. Unless she pays the outstanding balance in thirty days, we'll be forced to evict her."

No. Maggie can't lose this place. It means everything to her.

I won't let that happen. Opening my mouth, I'm ready to offer to pay the money owed when screeching tires draw my attention. Maggie's truck barrels down the driveway, squealing to a stop next to the banker's sports car. The engine is barely off before she's out the door and charging toward us.

"Mr. Fletcher," she greets, extending a hand to the man.

A low, menacing growl rips from my chest when he grips her dainty hand in his big mitt. I don't like his hands on her. No one should be touching her, except me.

Wide-eyed, Maggie turns those beautiful green eyes on me, hurt radiating from them in waves. "Viktor, please go inside and check on Lily."

No is on the tip of my tongue. I don't want her alone with this man. Every instinct inside me vibrates to life as I approach her. Bending, I whisper in her ear, voice rougher than it should be. "I can stay. I can help."

Her eyes meet mine when I pull back, burning with anger. Is she mad at me?

She shakes her head. "No. I don't need a white knight, Viktor. I can handle this. I'll explain everything later."

My gaze flits over my shoulder to the sleazy banker—a wolf in an overpriced suit. "You sure?" I swing my eyes back to hers, hoping mine convey how I'd chase this asshole back to the city if she asked me.

Throat bobbing, she nods.

Maggie is a strong, capable woman. She doesn't need me to fight her battles for her, but I sure as fuck want to.

From my place at the front window, I peer through the curtains, eyes locked on Maggie and the man from the bank. Pulling my pocket watch from my vest, I flip it open again.

Ten minutes.

My woman—*not yours*—has been out there alone with him for ten whole minutes. I should be out there with her.

But she doesn't see you like that. You're just the nanny.

Closing my eyes, I let the cool weight of the metal pocket watch in my hand ground me. I can see her, and if he tries anything, I'll be outside faster than he can blink.

Finally, Maggie hands the man an envelope. His lips move. "Pleasure as always, Ms. Wilcox." My sensitive ears pick up the faint echo of his voice. Then he's in his car and speeding away.

Maggie's whole body deflates, shoulders sagging as her heavy sigh flutters to my ears.

When she turns toward the house, her eyes shimmer with fresh tears. *Fuck*. I hate that she's in pain. My heart breaks as the first tear rolls down her flushed cheek.

She wipes it away, going back to her truck and grabbing her bags before coming to the front door.

Her eyes widen when she opens the door and finds me standing on the other side. "What was that, sweetheart?" I keep my voice soft, opting for a pet name in hopes of calming her. My gaze drifts to her neck, the rapid pounding of her pulse not slowing in the slightest. "Why didn't you tell me you were in trouble?"

"Later, Viktor. *Please*. I signed over the advance I got from the grocery store today. I bought myself a little breathing room."

"I can—"

She holds a hand up, silencing me. "This isn't your problem, city boy." One corner of her mouth tips into a sad smile, but it doesn't reach her gorgeous eyes. "Can you get Lily some dinner? I need to go talk with Jean-Luc. I'll be back in a little while."

Not giving me a chance to respond, she's out the door again, disappearing toward the storefront building near the main road.

"Is Momma coming home soon?" Lily asks from across the kitchen table.

My focus has been divided since the unwanted bank visit this afternoon, but I managed to make a simple dinner of macaroni and cheese with hot dogs for Lily. It's one of her favorites, and I'd hoped it would distract her from Maggie's absence.

Ever since my first week, Maggie has made it a point to quit working at four every day so she can have dinner with Lily. Usually, I cook and end up joining them, too, feeding this sick fantasy in my brain that we're some kind of family.

"I'm sure she'll be back soon. She had to talk to Jean-Luc." I had the pleasure of meeting the grumpy minotaur foreman the other day while Lily and I were catching frogs. He is surly, that's for sure, but he'll warm up to me.

When? You're only here for two more months.

I push the thought away and focus on something else, like how to ease some of Maggie's stress. "We should do something nice for your mom." The words tumble out before I can stop them.

Lily bounces in her seat, cheeks puffed out with hot dog and noodles. "Like what?" she mumbles around her food.

"Chew and swallow, please."

Rolling her eyes, she makes a show of swallowing down the food, then repeats her question. "Like what?"

"Well..." An idea springs to the front of my mind. "She does a lot to take care of you. She cooks for you. Cleans up after you. Makes sure you're happy and safe. Don't you think she'd like a day of someone taking care of her?"

Lily's nose scrunches. "Like a doctor? I don't like the doctor."

I chuckle. This is good. This is the distraction I need so I don't dwell on the fact that Maggie is in debt and seems to be avoiding me. "Not quite, little one. Like someone pampering her and making her feel special. My sister owns a spa in the city. Do you think your mom would like to spend a day there?"

"What's a spa?"

Right, I doubt a five-year-old has ever been to one. "Umm, well, it's a quiet place where adults can go to relax."

Her eyes light up and, suddenly, she's scampering from the table. Little feet pitter-patter up the stairs and down the hall.

The hinges of her bedroom door squeak before a faint jingle floats down the stairs.

Bounding down the steps, Lily hops right over the bottom one, and her socked feet slide on the wood floors as she skids back to the table. Clutched in her tiny hands is a plastic unicorn piggy bank.

"Clever child," I praise, running a finger under her chin once she's settled in her chair again.

Unscrewing the bottom of the bank, she shakes the container vigorously, coins of various sizes clattering to the wooden table-top. "Is this enough to buy Momma a spa day?"

If my eyes are correct, she only has a few dollars, and I don't plan on letting her use a single cent for Maggie's spa day. I have plenty of savings to foot the bill, but Lily doesn't need to know that. "It's more than enough, but let's count it to make sure."

We spend the rest of the evening counting and recounting her money. All the while, my gut churns, waiting for Maggie to get home safe.

CHAPTER 12

Maggie

"And you're sure these numbers are correct?" My eyes scan over the latest profit projections, relief washing over me.

"*Oui*. Five acres for pickers and five for the stores." Jean-Luc leans back in his chair, crossing his arms over his chest. We're in his small office at the back of the storefront building.

It's already stocked with jams, jelly, and honey from some of the locals. They sell their goods here every year in exchange for working the registers for me. It's a win-win situation.

I nod along as he speaks, but all I can focus on is the total estimated revenue. It's the highest number we've had in the past four years. After paying my crew, it'll be close, but I'll be able to get my head above water.

The visit from Mr. Fletcher this afternoon was a shock I didn't need. I nearly had a heart attack when he called me to say he was pulling into my driveway. Luckily, I'd just passed the Maple Ridge Hollow town limits and was almost home.

But now, Viktor knows about the debt.

And, like a dog with a bone, I'm sure he's going to want to swoop in and fix it.

Over the past few weeks, Viktor has shown himself to be a true caretaker and problem solver. But this isn't his problem to solve. I'm not his to fix.

You could be.

I sigh, closing the ledger and handing it to Jean-Luc. How easy it would be to let Viktor swoop in and fix everything. But after Roman passed, I vowed to do this on my own. I don't need a man to save me.

It would be nice to have one to give me a few orgasms and do the laundry and dishes, but that's it.

Viktor already does two out of three. Why not add orgasms?

Shaking my head, I clear the muddled mess in my brain.

"Everything okay, Mags?"

My throat bobs with a harsh swallow. His soulful blue eyes meet mine, and I'm *fucked*. I can't lie to Jean-Luc anymore. "No," I whisper, plopping into the seat across from him. "Remember the drought last year?"

Ears twitching, he nods. "*Oui*, somehow, we still managed to turn a small profit. *C'était un miracle.*"

Bile climbs up my throat. "No, we didn't. I dipped into my personal savings to make sure you and the crew got paid. The rest of the money went to keeping Lily and I fed and warm through the winter, but I fell behind on the mortgage payment."

"Mags, why didn't you tell me?" I hate the underlying pity in his tone. This is exactly why I *didn't* tell him.

I don't want pity. I don't want a savior.

I can save myself. And I will—if this year's harvest goes off without a hitch.

"It's not your problem, Jean-Luc. I've got it under control. "With a snort, he shakes his head. "Maggie, you're family. The crew and I... we know how important this place is to you. We would have done something to help."

"I don't want to be a burden to anyone. I'm supposed to be the boss." A sad smile ghosts across my lips.

"Well, now that I know, tell me how I can help."

"Keep this to yourself. I don't need anyone else worrying, okay?"

He nods.

"And make sure the crew morale stays up. By the end of September, we'll be busy, and I need all hands on deck.""You got it, Mags."

"Oh, and when you give hayrides this year, make sure you smile real pretty for all the kids."

The barked laugh that comes from his chest has the fist around my heart loosening. We'll be okay. We have to be.

"You're lucky I like you," he says. Reaching into the bottom drawer of his desk, he produces two glasses and a bottle of whiskey. "Drink?"

"Not tonight, but thank you. I need to get Lily to bed."

"Ah, yes. How is *mon petit bug*?"

I smile at his nickname for my daughter. Even though he might not show it much, Jean-Luc has a big heart. "Good. She starts kindergarten soon."

"*Crisse!* I remember when she was just a babe." His eyes twinkle, a smile tugging at his dark lips. "And the nanny?"

Pressing my hands to my cheeks, I will them not to turn bright pink, but my palms are met by warmth. I clear my throat and murmur, "Good. He's good."

Jean-Luc's deep chuckle takes me by surprise. Getting him to laugh twice in one conversation is a rarity. "You're smitten, aren't you, Mags?"

"It's not like that. He's kind and generous. And I'll admit, he's *very* attractive. But I'm not ready for anything like that. Plus, wouldn't that be unethical?"

He winks. "Not if no one knows. Now get home to that girl. Apples will still be there in the morning."

"Goodnight, Jean-Luc. Get home safe."

The minotaur owns the property next to mine. He may work for me, but he also taps the trees on his property for maple syrup.

"Goodnight, Mags. You could use some more good in your life. Maybe the vampire is the answer."

As I walk to the main house, Jean-Luc's words play on repeat in my head, echoing and bouncing around. Could Viktor and I be together if no one knew? If we kept it a secret?

I clench my thighs and hold in a whimper at the idea of sneaking around with the handsome vampire. Stolen kisses. A quick fuck on the couch after Lily goes to bed.

Sounds pretty fucking hot.

And maybe that's exactly what I need. No feelings involved, just orgasms. Lots of orgasms.

My body lights up like a Christmas tree at the idea alone.

The sky glows a fiery red, reminding me of Viktor's eyes, as I approach the house, the sun sinking low on the horizon. Sobering from my horny thoughts, my stomach drops.

Who knows how much that idiot Fletcher told Viktor about my debt before I showed up. Blowing out a breath, I wrap my hand around the front door handle, steeling my spine for an awkward conversation.

As I walk into the house, I'm met by a chorus of the sweetest giggles and the slap of tiny feet on the hardwood floor. "Hide, Momma! He's coming!" Bare feet squeaking on the floor, Lily comes to a stop in front of me.

She grabs my hand and tugs me with her into the coat closet in our front entryway. "Bug, what—"

"Shhh," she hisses, pressing a hand over my mouth.

Viktor's muffled voice comes from the other side of the door. "Eight, nine, ten. Ready or not, here I come!"

Hide and seek. I should have known. This has been Lily's favorite game since she was about three. She knows all the best hiding spots around the house.

Smiling, I tug her to the back of the closet, positioning our winter coats in front of us.

Shuffling feet sound on the other side of the door, then silence.

"I think we fooled him," I whisper, right as the door flies open, revealing Viktor. There's a smug grin on his face that showcases his fangs.

Fangs that have been making an appearance in my dreams on a nightly basis.

"Found you!" Wrapping his arms around Lily, he pulls her from the closet. Laughter spills from her lips when he spins them in a circle, her little body clutched in his strong arms.

Moments like this make my heart leap. He's so good with her. In fact, before Viktor, Lily didn't laugh or smile nearly as much.

Part of me wishes I could keep him forever. But I know we're limited on time.

My watch beeps, letting me know it's time to get Lily ready for bed. I missed the whole evening, spending longer than I thought down in Jean-Luc's office, double checking my harvest projections.

"Time for bed, Lily bug. Say goodnight to Viktor."

Her laughter dies, bottom lip sticking out in a pout when he sets her on her feet. "Do I have to?"

"Yes, bug. School starts next week, so we need to get you back on a normal sleep schedule. That means early bedtime so you can get up early."

As Viktor kneels in front of her, my chest warms. "Goodnight, little one. I had so much fun with you today. Should we do it again tomorrow?"

"And the next day?" Lily wraps her little arms around his neck. Okay, now I'm officially a puddle of goo on the floor. It's cuteness overload between these two.

"And the next day," Viktor echoes as my daughter pulls him in for a hug.

Lily tips her head up, lips close to his ear. The whispered words are too soft for me to hear, but it must be something good with the way a slow, easy smile spreads across Viktor's face.

She smacks a loud kiss on his cheek before running over to where I wait at the bottom of the stairs.

Hands tucked in his pockets, Viktor trails toward us.

"Thank you for staying later tonight," I say, scooping Lily into my arms. She yawns and nuzzles her nose against my neck. Always one to pretend she doesn't want to go to bed, even when she's actually tired.

Viktor shrugs. "Not a problem. That's what I'm here for."

On any other night, I would invite him to stay for a glass of wine, and we'd chat on the porch swing, taking in the peacefulness and the stars. But my mind is a mess, between Fletcher's unexpected visit and my growing attraction to Viktor. Right now, I need a minute to catch my breath and sort through my feelings. "I'll see you in the morning."

Before I can change my mind, I rush up the stairs, putting all my focus on getting Lily ready for bed.

CHAPTER 13

Viktor

The window to Lily's room goes dark, and I start counting in my head. Thirty minutes.

I'm giving Maggie thirty minutes before I charge through the trees to the back door of the house. Anticipation and dread swirl through my veins. I had to tamp the emotions down and take care of Lily for the evening, but now my mind whirls with the worst-case scenario.

Which is me marching down to the bank and buying this place.

My gut tells me Maggie would hate me if I did that. *I don't need a white knight, Viktor.*

Maggie is strong and independent. The last thing she needs is me playing the hero.

But there has to be a way to help her without crushing her pride.

I peer through the trees outside my window, squinting until my eyes lock on their kitchen window. It's hard to see from this distance, but that's one of the perks of vampire night vision.

A breath later, a soft glow filters through the sheer curtains.

I've given her space and time to process, so now it's time for her to tell me what the fuck is going on. Snatching my thermos off the kitchen table, I leave the guest house and zip through the trees toward the main house.

One unexpected addition to our routine over the past few weeks is regular chats with Maggie after Lily is in bed. I savor every moment I get to be in her presence, and every bit of information she shares with me only feeds the hunger I have for her.

Like how she studied graphic design in college. Or that her favorite flowers are purple freesias.

Every drop she gives me, I lap up like a thirsty puppy. Starved for attention.

The wooden steps of the deck creak under my feet as I ascend. "Fancy meeting you here, country girl."

Swaying gently, my eyes are drawn to the porch swing. Maggie's favorite spot.

"V-Viktor." Her voice cracks around my name. "I don't know that I'll be very good company tonight."

"I thought you might want to talk about what happened earlier, but I can go..." I hook a thumb over my shoulder.

Maggie shakes her head. "Stay. I thought I wanted to be alone, b-but I changed my mind." Shifting her weight, she makes room for me next to her. "What concoction do you have tonight?" She tips her head to my thermos as I settle onto the swing beside her.

After that first night, and explaining how I don't consume real blood, I've opted for various beverages featuring one common ingredient: synthetic blood powder.

"This, country girl, is my specialty—blood hot cocoa." I turn to face her, chest swelling at the flush that my pet name sends spreading from her cheeks down to the neck of her pajama top.

As much as I've fought the urge to kiss Maggie during every one of these nightly chats, I've resisted, keeping things platonic. Although, with what she's wearing tonight, I doubt my restraint will last much longer.

It's one of the last warm, muggy nights of summer, so she's opted for a wide-strapped, figure-hugging tank top and baggy sweatshorts. And my mouth is watering at the subtle peaks of her nipples through the thin cotton of her top.

But once again, Maggie seems more than oblivious to the effect she has on me.

Do not get hard, Viktor. I'm still in my dress slacks, so any movement in my pants would be more than noticeable. Changing into a t-shirt was a must after the paint dried into my silk dress shirt. I doubt I'll be able to get the stain out, but it was worth it to see the pure joy on Lily's face while we added our handprints to the sign.

"I see you got rid of the paint stains." Her laughter calms the beast inside me. The one clawing at my skin, screaming for me to sink my fangs into her beautiful skin and feast. "What was it from anyway?"

"Let me show you." Placing my thermos on the deck boards, I fetch the wooden sign from where it's been drying since this afternoon. "Lily and I worked on this today. What do you think?"

Maggie's hand flies to her mouth, covering a gasp. "Viktor. It's perfect." Her voice is soft, wobbling with emotion.

Lit by streaming beams of moonlight, moisture wells in her green eyes.

"Actually—" Setting the sign down, I jet around to the garage. Thankfully, the side door is unlocked. I grab what I need and sprint back to the deck.

Maggie traces over the letters with a single finger, then lays her hand over Lily's rainbow handprint. A smile plays on her lips, making my heart sing.

"It is missing one thing." Holding up the paintbrush, I tip my chin toward the sign.

When I extend my free hand to her, she places her small hand in mine, palm up. Zero hesitation in her actions.

A few moments later, her giggles fill the night sky when I drag the paintbrush across her palm. "You're just like your daughter." I chuckle, remembering how Lily had the same reaction when I coated her skin with the cold paint.

"What did you expect? It tickles!" Maggie's top teeth sink into her bottom lip, stifling my favorite sound.

Second favorite. Although, I haven't heard what she sounds like when she orgasms... yet.

"*Now* it's perfect," I proclaim, pressing her hand against the wood. Together, we pull our hands away to reveal a perfect rainbow handprint on the other side of mine. Lily's tiny hand nestled between ours.

There's a reason Maggie is my last nanny assignment. This is where I'm meant to be forever. Father be damned, I'm never leaving this woman, especially not if she lets me into her heart.

She already holds half of mine. The other half belongs to her daughter.

I'm so fucked.

Clearing her throat, Maggie pulls her hand away. She wipes it on the cloth I brought from the garage, then takes a seat on the swing again.

I place the sign on the table to dry before joining her. "Now no one will miss the orchard when they drive by."

Her hand lands on my thigh, squeezing gently before pulling away. "Thank you, Viktor. You created something I'll cherish forever."

And me? Hopefully, you'll cherish me forever. I hold the words inside until my fangs sink into my tongue, and the warm, coppery tang of blood fills my mouth.

Maggie flashes me a tight smile before her eyes fall to her lap. She twists her hands together, gripping until her knuckles are white. Silence stretches between us, unbearable and awkward.

Finally, I can't take it any longer. The need to speak vibrates through my body, and I blurt out the question. "Are we going to address the elephant in the room, sweetheart?"

A whooshed sigh gusts from Maggie's lips, her eyes still locked on where her hands fidget in her lap. "You mean what happened earlier? With Fletcher."

I nod. "That slimy asshole said you owe the bank money. Are you in trouble, sweetheart? Did Roman leave you in debt?"

The instant the question is out of my mouth, regret swarms me like a nest of angry hornets.

Tears shimmer in Maggie's breathtaking eyes when she finally tilts her head up to meet my gaze.

"I-It's my fault," she croaks, voice breaking right along with my heart.

"I find that hard to believe, Maggie. You spend every second working when you're not taking care of Lily."

She shakes her head, and a few strands of frizzy golden hair slip from her messy bun. "After Roman died, I-I could barely function. This dark pit of grief and depression swallowed me whole. I was so lost. I wished I'd died right along with him." A hiccupped sob racks her chest. "What kind of horrible mother does that make me? I couldn't even take care of myself, let alone Lily and the orchard. I let everything fall apart around me."

My arm shoots out, wrapping around her shoulder and bringing her warm body to mine. "Sweetheart, none of this is your fault. You went through something no one should have to experience, and you made it out the other side."

Sniffling, her nose brushes against my neck and sends a wave of tingles down my spine.

Maggie's lips graze the sensitive skin when she speaks, her breath heating my flesh. "My mom and Cyrus stepped up to help with Lily. Jean-Luc kept the trees alive, but I didn't have the heart to open the orchard for harvest. It felt wrong without Roman. And after the drought last year—"

I hold her tighter to me, hoping my presence takes away some of her pain. Right now, her grief and anguish are tangible, and it's tearing me up inside.

"I'm broke, Viktor," she whispers. "This harvest *has* to be the best we've ever had, or I'm fucked. A-And I can't lose this place. It's the last memories I have of him."

For some reason, I feel responsible for Maggie and Lily. I can't let her lose this place either. Selfishly, I've grown to love the clean air and the clear, starry nights as much as I've grown to love her and her daughter. "Let me help."

Maggie sits back, eyebrows furrowed. Before I can stop myself, I smooth a thumb between them and cup the side of her face. For a moment, she leans into my palm, her eyelids fluttering shut.

"I still have access to my trust fund. Let me pay the debt for you. Let me take that burden for you." My voice is pleading, but I don't give a fuck. All I care about is making sure Maggie and Lily are safe.

When Maggie shakes her head, my stomach twists, sinking to the darkness of a bottomless sea.

"I'm not some damsel in distress who needs saving, Viktor." She pulls from my embrace and, begrudgingly, I let my arms fall away from the warmth of her body. Warmth I crave every waking minute of every day.

"Trust me." I smirk. "I know that."

Tears dried, her lips creep into a small smile. "I appreciate your offer, but I have a plan and, as long as everything goes accordingly, we'll be okay."

I don't like it, but I've learned during my time in the Wilcox house that Maggie is prideful and stubborn. No amount of bargaining or pleading is going to change her mind. Maybe there's a way I can help to make sure this harvest is as successful as she hopes. "You'll let me know if your plan *doesn't* go accordingly?"

"You'll be the first to know."

"Promise?"

"Promise." She holds her pinky up between us.

Chuckling, I link my pinky with hers and shake. The jerking motion causes her to lean forward until our mouths hover a hairsbreadth apart. "You know." As my voice drops to a gravelly octave, Maggie's lips part on a gasp. The pitiful sound shoots straight to my cock. My eyes flick to her mouth before returning to her eyes. "Lily and I have a surprise for you."

I expect the mention of her daughter to cause her to pull back, but Maggie is full of surprises. Her green gaze flashes with heat and falls to my mouth. "Oh?"

Screaming with the need to kiss her, I fight the bloodthirsty creature inside me. The one who only thinks about how sweet her blood would taste while I bury my cock deep inside her tight cunt.

She just bared her soul to me for the second time in the short period we've known each other. Her emotions are probably high from dealing with that slimebag this afternoon.

Thinking with my head, instead of my dick, I lean back and put some much-needed distance between us. It's getting harder and harder to resist the siren's call of her lips, yet I keep putting myself in these precarious positions.

I clear my throat, hoping to lighten the earlier growling timbre. "Yes. You've been under a lot of pressure lately with the upcoming harvest—and now the stress of the bank on your back. Lily and I came up with the perfect little break."

Disappointment flashes across her features, but she recovers into a tight smile. "Color me curious."

"My twin sister owns a luxury spa in the city. How would you feel about spending a day there? My treat, of course."

She fiddles with the hem of her shorts. "I don't know. There's still so much to do—"

My hand falls over hers, effectively stopping her fidgeting. "It's one day. And you deserve a break, country girl. Invite Antoinette... and anyone else."

"But Lily—"

I huff a laugh. "Will be fine here... with me. You won't let me pay your debt—" She opens her mouth to say something, but I hold a hand up to silence her. "Which I understand. So let me do this for you. Let me give you a day to recharge before the madness of harvest."

"You're relentless. You know that?"

I preen under her backhanded compliment, puffing out my chest. "You're not the only stubborn one around here."

She laughs, crossing her arms over her chest. "Fine. I'll see if Annie and Pen are free this weekend." Then she yawns, and I know it's time for our night to end.

"Good. I'll set everything up with Ness. Don't worry about anything," I say, standing from the swing. If I don't get out of here now, the last threads of my restraint will surely snap. "Goodnight, country girl."

"Goodnight, city boy."

The wheels in my brain turn as I zip down the path to the guest house. Barreling through the front door, I scramble to find my laptop before dropping into the chair closest to the fireplace. Maggie won't let me play the hero—rightfully so—but I have an idea of how I can ensure her harvest is the most profitable to date.

Pulling up an internet browser and a blank document, my fingers fly across the keys. Plotting and planning. I won't stand by and let Maggie lose the orchard.

CHAPTER 14

Maggie

By Saturday morning, I'm starting to realize just how much I need this spa day. A handful of workers called in sick the last few days, putting us behind schedule on filling the last grocery store order.

Jean-Luc assured me they would work overtime today to make up for it.

I pat the pocket of my yoga pants, checking that my cell phone is there. "And you're sure you'll be okay?"

Viktor slides the straps of my purse over my shoulder. Resting both of his big hands on my shoulders, he gives a reassuring squeeze. "Sweetheart, go get pampered. We'll be here when you get back. I have a whole fun day planned for Lily and me."

"Mini pizzas!" Lily chirps from his side, looking all too happy to get rid of me.

"Right, little one." He takes a hand off my shoulder to cup the back of her head, stroking over her curly ponytail. The gesture is so natural, making my heart skip a beat, like he's the missing piece of our family. "And what else?"

She smiles and bounces on her toes. "Ice cream! This is the best day ever!"

Warmth spreads throughout my chest, watching them interact. My little girl has Viktor wrapped around her finger, and I don't even blame him.

Not even a little bit.

A horn honks outside. "That's your ride, country girl. Have fun!" Viktor all but shoves me out the front door to the blacked-out town car waiting in the driveway. He went all out for the day, hiring a driver to take me to and from the city.

Once I'm settled into the back seat, I close my eyes and blow out a breath.

No worrying about the future today, Mags. Focus on enjoying the present. Enjoy being spoiled. Because it's been a hot minute since anyone has done something this nice for you.

After picking up Antoinette and Penelope, we arrive at Urban Oasis, the spa Viktor's sister owns. Housed in an old cathedral, it's nestled between two towering office buildings. No sign or markings of any kind hint at what awaits us inside.

"Are you sure this is the right place?" My eyes skim over the beautiful stained-glass window up to the gothic towers that climb toward the cloudless blue sky. Swinging my head back to our driver, I raise an eyebrow.

"This is the place," he confirms with a tip of his head and a smile. "Give me a ring when you're ready to head home." He tucks a business card between my fingers before climbing back into his car.

"I don't know about you two, but I'm ready for a massage and a pedicure." Annie grabs my hand and tugs me up the stairs to a set of double wooden doors.

"Did Cyrus do something to piss you off again?" I goad her as I push through the heavy doors. "Whoa." Immediately, I'm hit by a wall of warm, damp air.

Closing my eyes, I suck in a breath, and my body calms under a wave of eucalyptus and lavender. My ears perk up to the sounds of birds twittering above and a waterfall somewhere in the distance.

"This is—" Pen spins in a slow circle, her blonde ponytail swishing down her back when she tips her head to the domed glass ceiling high above us.

"Beautiful." Annie finishes Pen's thought and points at a babbling creek that cuts under the cobblestone path in front of us. I catch sight of bright orange-and-white Koi as they swim along the water.

The inside of the cathedral has been transformed into a serene paradise of towering tropical trees and vines. Winding paths surrounded by moss and exotic florals spread in different directions from where we stand.

Up above, the entire ceiling of this area is one giant work of art. Sunlight filters through the stained-glass masterpiece, sprinkling us in every color of the rainbow.

"Welcome to Urban Oasis." A soft voice draws my attention to a tall woman with rich brown skin and coils of dark hair. She's standing behind a reception counter that has flowering vines trailing all over it.

Taking a step closer, I'm drawn to her beauty. Her full lips split into a friendly smile, and I take note of the pointed ears that peek through her hair. Behind her back, a pair of translucent green wings shimmer in the sunshine. "I'm Melody. How can I help you today?"

Before I can respond, the door behind her opens to reveal another stunningly beautiful creature. *Is there something in the water around here?* Because I'll take some of what they're drinking. Maybe it'll get rid of the permanent bags under my eyes and the monster zit growing on my chin.

Settling a hand on Melody's shoulder, the woman speaks, her voice like a freaking angel singing. "I've got it, Mel. This is Viktor's guest and her companions."

How does she know who I—

The resemblance hits me then. The same pale, almost iridescent skin. White-blonde hair, except hers flows down to her waist in thick waves. The tall, lithe build and ethereal, almost otherworldly, facial features. *Vanessa.* "You're stunning," I murmur.

Glossy lips part on a blinding smile to reveal fangs nestled among straight white teeth. She rounds the desk to stand in front of me. "I was about to say the same about you. You must be Maggie."

Words escape me, so I nod.

"It's nice to finally meet the woman my brother is infatuated with."

My cheeks burn. I knew there was a mutual attraction between Viktor and me, but I guess I didn't realize just how deep it was for him.

Her fangs sink into her bottom lip in a lopsided grin. "I probably shouldn't have said that. Oops. I'm Vanessa, by the way." Her burgundy eyes lift over my head expectantly.

After a round of quick introductions, we follow Vanessa down the path to the left, passing by a waterfall. Tiny brightly colored birds splash in the falling drops of water, filling the humid air with their happy twitters. I smile. Viktor was right; this is exactly what I needed.

"Viktor booked you for a full day. Massages, facials, manicures, pedicures, and we'll finish with a fresh blowout and makeup application."

Jaw falling slack, my gaze flits to Annie and Pen, who stand behind me. Their eyes must be as big as mine when Vanessa rattles off the list of treatments like it's nothing.

Stopping in front of a single elevator, Vanessa presses the button. "We'll head up to the roof first. You can start with a dip in the serenity pool. The waters are enchanted to wash away any lingering stress or worries, so you'll get the full benefit of every treatment."

By the time the elevator dings and the doors slide open, I still haven't picked my jaw up off the floor. I'm definitely going to take advantage of every second before I have to head home.

"So... how *are* things with Viktor?" Annie waggles her dark eyebrows at me.

Tugging my fluffy white robe tighter around my chest, I bite my cheek to hold in the smile. But I fail—miserably—and my lips split into a goofy grin.

We're nearing the end of our spa visit. The last stop of the day is the salon. Annie sits in a massage chair across from me while one of the employees paints her toenails.

Behind me, another employee winds a section of my hair around a heated roller before pinning it to my scalp. "Fine."

A scoff to my left has my head turning. Pen sits at the manicure station, flipping through swatches of nail polish options. "Just *fine*? You've gotta give us more than that, Maggie."

"Okay, okay. It's been amazing! I don't know how I'll survive on my own after he leaves. And... and..." I blow out a breath, suddenly tongue-tied. "There's this obvious attraction between us, but I don't know if I can cross that line."

Annie clicks the button on her e-reader. Setting it in her lap, she gives me the full weight of her golden eyes. "Do you want to cross that line with him?"

I shrug. "I don't know. Isn't that wrong? He's an employee."

Pen chimes in, "You're both grown adults. I think Viktor can make his own choices. If he said yes, would you sleep with him?"

My cheeks burn as I think about his fangs dragging across my skin. Goosebumps rise on my arms, and I rub at my heated flesh, trying to get them to go away. "Have you seen him? Of course, I would!"

"So what's stopping you?" Annie asks.

Taking a drink of my champagne—compliments of the spa—I give myself a moment to gather my thoughts. The sweet bubbles burst on my tongue but do nothing to ease my dilemma. "Where do I start? He's so good with Lily. What if sleeping with him ends badly, and it fucks everything up?"

Annie's lips purse. "Valid point, but what if it's amazing? What if it *doesn't* end? Take Cyrus and me, for example... We hated each other." She cackles before sipping her champagne. "And look at us now."

"I don't know. His contract is up in another month, and I'm sure he'll go back to the city. He's supposed to start working for his father in their family business. The whole thing is a recipe for disaster and heartbreak." I sigh heavily as I rub my temples.

"You deserve something good and easy in your life for once, Mags. If you want to sleep with Viktor, then sleep with him. Otherwise, I guess invest in an arsenal of good toys." A wry smile spreads across her face, showcasing one of her fangs.

I choke on a mouthful of champagne. "Annie!"

"What? Gotta keep the pussy happy." She shrugs.

The pixie doing her pedicure giggles. "She's not wrong."

"I'm also scared." My heart clenches with the admission, and the hairstylist squeezes my shoulder in a show of comfort. "It feels like I'm cheating on Roman."

"Oh, Mags. Have you been with anyone since he passed?" Pen asks, blue eyes softening.

Grief clogging my throat, I shake my head.

"It's been over four years, so maybe now is the time to try. You deserve to find someone to make you happy again. It's time to live again, Mags." Pen gives me a small smile. "Roman would want you to *live*."

"She's right, Maggie," Annie says. "You've been surviving for the past few years, but wouldn't Roman want you to be happy?"

I shrug, closing my eyes. "Yes. But why do I feel so guilty? Like I'm erasing him."

Warm arms banding around me have my eyes springing open to find Annie on one side and Pen on the other, both hugging me.

"Oh, Maggie. Honey." Annie's voice is gentle when she pulls back. "It's okay to keep going in life. Moving on doesn't mean you're erasing what you had with Roman. You can keep his memory alive while being happy. Don't you think he'd want you to find someone to love you like you deserve... like he loved you?

"I-I guess." Sniffling, I wipe my nose and notice it's just the three of us. The staff must have realized this is an intimate conversation, leaving to give us some privacy.

"What if the roles were reversed?" Pen pipes up as the voice of reason. "Wouldn't you want Roman to find someone to help him heal? Someone to be there for him and Lily?"

"Yes," I admit. "But I'd haunt the bitch for life if she hurt him."

Joining in my laughter, we clink our glasses.

"I say, go for it, girl! Get yourself a piece of that hot vampire cake... even if it's temporary." Of course, Annie would be the one telling me to dive in headfirst, even after she fought her attraction to my brother-in-law tooth and nail.

"But it feels selfish," I squeak.

"Then maybe it's time to be selfish for once." Pen squeezes my arm. "Take that hot vampire for a test drive, even if it's only for one night."

Could I really sleep with Viktor and keep my heart out of the equation? I've never done that before. Sex has always been with someone I love, not just a physical release.

Whatever is happening between me and Viktor, it's getting harder to resist the lingering glances and soft touches. And something about how sweet and attentive he is with Lily gives him extra sexy points in my book.

Sleeping with him will either be the best thing, or it will ruin our perfect dynamic. Either way, my pussy is slowly hijacking this ride.

CHAPTER 15

Viktor

Grabbing my sunglasses and a baseball hat, I follow Lily into the garage. She carries her bug catching kit—essentially a small tote bag full of various sizes of plastic jars. If it's creepy and crawly and belongs outside, Lily Wilcox insists on catching it and bringing it *inside*.

The child doesn't have a squeamish bone in her body, and I've had to learn to be okay with every slimy worm and warty toad she throws my way.

"Four-wheeler ride?" Lily's smile nearly takes over her little face when she stops next to the vehicle in question.

"Umm." I eye the dirt-crusted red vehicle. It's... intimidating.

My gaze swings to the open garage door. "It's a nice, sunny day. How about a walk instead?"

I don't need a five-year-old judging me for my inadequacy when it comes to motorized vehicles. Years of living in the city have made me reliant on public transportation and walking. Honestly, I'm lucky I even have my driver's license. "We'll leave the four-wheeling to your mom. How's that sound, little one?"

"Okay!" She beams at me before taking off out of the garage as fast as her little legs will carry her.

We work our way through the rows of apple trees, looking for ladybugs. Apparently, Lily is on a mission to find every single one in the orchard today. "How many so far, Lily?" I ask as I squat down beside her.

Holding up the jar, her finger taps around the outside as she counts. "Ten, eleven... What comes next?" She squints up at me from beneath the brim of her hat.

"Twelve."

"Twelve, thirteen, fourteen, fifteen!" She lifts the jar higher for me to see, pride radiating from her little body.

"That's a lot of ladybugs! Should we—"

"*Mon petit bug!*" A gruff voice has my head darting up.

Jean-Luc cuts through the trees to get to us. We've interacted briefly, but he usually has a massive scowl on his furry face, so I steer clear.

My job doesn't concern him, so he seems to have given me a wide berth. Not that I'm complaining... Although, I could use his help with my plan.

Quest for bugs forgotten, Lily hops up and runs toward the minotaur, who scoops her into his huge arms.

And I mean *huge*.

I haven't come across many minotaurs in my time, since they tend to choose rural or more remote habitats for their homes, but I imagine Jean-Luc must be on the larger size for his species.

At six-foot-five, even I feel small next to him.

With Lily still tucked in his arms, he closes the distance between us, and my chin tips up to skim over his stern snout and wide horns. His red flannel and blue jeans look like they might split at the seams when he bends to place Lily back on her feet.

"*Bonjour,* Viktor." He extends a hand to me.

Even his hands are fucking *huge*. His grip is crushing, causing me to wince as we shake hands. Not letting the pain show on my face, I smile up at him. "Jean-Luc. Nice to see you again. Do you have a moment to chat?"

"*Oui*, but I need to keep an eye on the crew."

I nod. "Of course, lead the way."

As we follow Jean-Luc back the way he came, the orchard is abuzz with workers just a few rows over.

Winged creatures flit around the tops of the trees, picking fruit that's too high for anyone else to reach.

A troll carries a large bin full of apples to the bed of a waiting pickup truck. Swapping his bin for an empty one, he heads back to the trees.

This is the first time I've seen the harvest crew at work, and it has my chest swelling with hope. Hope that Maggie will be okay. Hope that she'll get to keep this place. Hope that Lily will get to experience the magic of the orchard for years to come.

And hope that maybe—just maybe—I'll get to be a part of that magic, too.

Jean-Luc braces his back against the side of the truck, crossing his arms over his chest. Imposing and stern, his dark eyes scan the workers before stopping on my face. "Alright, Viktor. *Ça va?* What can I do for you?"

Stepping closer, I lower my voice so the workers don't hear. Although, I'm not sure which ones might have sensitive hearing, like myself.

"Has Maggie told you about the state of the orchard?" I choose my words carefully, not sure how much Jean-Luc knows.

His eyebrows dip, and he blows out a breath. *"Oui."*

I wait a beat, hoping he'll expand. When he doesn't, I sigh and adjust my hat. "Well, I have a plan, but I need your help."

"Why would you help Maggie? You're just the nanny." His eyes slice from the trees back to me.

Just the nanny. Those words cut deep, but I brush it aside and forge on. "I care about her, and I'm pretty sure you do, too. Don't you want to do everything in your power to make sure this harvest is an absolute success?"

The hard set of his jaw softens at my question. *"Oui.* But Maggie is a prideful woman. How do you plan on helping without stepping on her toes?"

"That's where you come in, my new friend..." I spend the next ten minutes explaining the details of my grand plan to Jean-Luc. By the time I finish, the corners of his mouth twitch before spreading into a wide smile.

I knew I could get through his hard exterior.

"You really do care about her, don't you?" A heavy hand falls on my shoulder, squeezing.

Like it does every time I think about Maggie, my body tingles and my fangs ache. "More than you can imagine."

"Calvaire!" His voice softens, dropping to a whisper. Well, as much as a big minotaur can whisper. "She is your mate, *no*?"

I shrug, but a wide smile takes over my face. "I hope so."

"She has a dark history." The stony expression returns to his face.

"I know."

His eyes flit to Lily, who's somehow convinced a pixie to search for bugs with her. "I don't know you well, Viktor, but all I'll say is, be good to her. She deserves happiness and stability after what she's been through. If you can't be that for her, then leave her alone. I don't think she'd survive another heartbreak. *Tu comprends?*"

"Vampires are loyal to a fault." Just look at my mother, who refuses to leave Father, even though he's a colossal asshole. "My heart is set on Maggie, and I don't plan on straying from that path."

That big hand is back on my shoulder, squeezing a little harder than before. A warning. His eyes darken when they land on mine this time. "*Bon, mon ami*, because there are a lot of good places to bury a vampire out here. If ya catch my drift, Viktor."

I gulp a swallow and nod, thankful Maggie has someone like Jean-Luc in her corner.

"Viktor." Lily tugs on my hand, pulling my attention away from the brooding bull. "I'm hungry," she whines.

"Right. Okay. Grab your bugs, and let's head home for some lunch." I turn back to Jean-Luc. "Thank you for your help. I really appreciate it." And since I don't know when to shut my mouth, I push his buttons a little. "And maybe you could smile a little when you give those hayrides we talked about."

Before he can punch me—or worse, bury me under an apple tree—I grab Lily's hand and swing her onto my back, prepared to speed back to the house, but a deep chuckle meets my ears first.

"You know, I think you might be perfect for her, *vampire*."

CHAPTER 16

Maggie

My muscles are still Jell-O by the time the town car drops me off in front of my house. In fact, I don't think my body has ever been this stress free in my life. Certainly not in the past four years.

Somehow, the esthetician even managed to make the zit on my chin vanish.

Annie, Pen, and I spent all day getting pampered at Urban Oasis. Massages, facials, manicures, and pedicures—you name it, we did it.

"You deserve to be happy, Mags," I remind myself of Pen's earlier words. "It's time to start *living*." My heart flutters when I grip the handle of the front door, the cherry red paint vibrant in the fading daylight.

I'm greeted by a shrill giggle, then a growl, as I push into the house. The commotion filters down the hallway from the family room.

"Lava monster is gonna get you!" Viktor's voice is deeper than normal, like a ferocious rumble.

Following Lily's laughter, I head down the hall toward the back of the house. Peeking around the corner, I take a minute to observe their play. Pillows are strewn around the family room floor, along with the kitchen chairs, in a sort of obstacle course or mish-mashed pathway. Lily shrieks, hopping from a pillow onto the couch. "You can't get me up here, lava monster!"

On his knees in the middle of the chaos, Viktor holds out his hands, fingers curled like claws, and growls again. Quicker than I can blink, he jumps to his feet and grabs Lily by the sides, tossing her onto the soft cushions of the couch. "But the tickle monster can!"

At the first giggle to spill from my daughter's mouth, my heart melts.

With her laughter fading, she snuggles against him and lays her head on his broad shoulder. She's so small next to him. So fragile.

Viktor is good for her. He indulges in her playful and curious nature, feeds her need for knowledge, all while remaining a constant state of comfort.

In his short time here, he's become a comfort to both of us. I see that now.

"Looks like you two had fun," I say, finally making my presence known. Bracing my shoulder on the wall, I smile as Lily's eyes close.

Crimson eyes meet mine when Viktor's head snaps up, a soft smile playing on his lips. "We were just burning off the last bit of energy. I think she's ready for bed now. How was your day?"

Stepping closer, I take a seat in the oversized chair next to the couch. "I didn't realize how much I needed today. Thank you for arranging it. I already thanked Vanessa a ton, but you'll have to tell her again how much I appreciated her kindness. She's created a really amazing environment at Urban Oasis."

"She loves what she does."

"I think Annie might be a regular customer. She mentioned needing a massage package for when Cyrus pisses her off." I chuckle softly and reach out a hand to stroke Lily's back. She stirs, but presses herself deeper into Viktor's side. My ovaries might explode from the cuteness of my daughter snuggled up next to this sweet vampire. "I should get her to bed." I tip my head toward Lily.

Before I can protest, Viktor stands from the couch with Lily clutched in his arms, like she weighs nothing. She's definitely getting too big for me to carry, so I'm a little envious of his strength. He zooms to the stairs, stopping at the bottom to flash a smirk over his shoulder. "You coming, sweetheart?"

All I can do is nod and bite my tongue to hold back a needy mewl as I follow him up the stairs to Lily's room.

With a gentleness I've come to expect from him, Viktor lays Lily on her bed and tucks the blankets around her. I hadn't even noticed before that she's already in her favorite unicorn pajamas. "I figured she wouldn't want to go to bed until you got home, so I had her get ready before we started playing lava monster," Viktor whispers.

Before leaving her side, he brushes a kiss against her forehead and murmurs, "Goodnight, little one. I had fun with you today."

Sleepy green eyes blink open, and an equally sleepy smile spreads across her face. "Goodnight, Viktor. I love you."

And there they go... My ovaries officially burst at her sweet, sleepy words and the love shimmering in her eyes.

Viktor has woven himself deep into our lives, and as much as I want to let him in fully, I'm still scared shitless. I'm halfway in love with him, and admitting that out loud would give him the power to crush my already fragile heart.

Like Annie said, giving in to the sexual desire between us would be easy. No-strings-attached sex is one thing, but giving him my heart is totally different.

I don't know if I'm ready for that.

Stopping in the doorway next to me, he bends until his words warm my ear. "I'll clean up downstairs before I leave. Night, country girl."

My thighs clench, knees nearly buckling, and I clutch the doorframe behind me, but Viktor's already gone, blurring as he jets down the stairs.

I blow out a breath and kneel at the side of the bed. Brushing the stray hairs off Lily's face, I kiss her on the cheek and whisper, "I love you, Lily bug. More than anything in the world." Her responding snore lets me know she's already out cold, probably exhausted from a jam-packed day with Viktor.

With my nose against her hair, I inhale. She smells like sunshine and fresh air... and everything good in the world.

After one last kiss to her forehead, I switch on her unicorn night light before leaving the room and shutting the door behind me.

Standing in the middle of the hallway, the earlier conversation at the spa fills my mind. Roman would be pissed if he knew how stressed and lonely I am. I deserve happiness... and maybe being with Viktor can be the start of that happiness.

The full-length mirror leans against my bedroom wall, with my nightgown and a discarded towel draped over one corner. A pile of clothes lay on the floor near my bed. Clean or dirty? I'm not sure. "I really need to clean in here."

Even though I told him it's not part of his job, Viktor has been tidying and cleaning the rest of the house. I've made it a point to keep the door to my bedroom shut at all times, so he doesn't get any ideas about invading my private space.

I don't need the sexy-as-sin vampire finding the vibrators hidden in my nightstand.

Releasing a sigh, I wiggle a clean pair of panties up my thighs. The soft cotton settles against my hips.

As I raise my hand to the mirror, my fingers snag on the worn gray fabric of my nightgown, but my eyes are distracted by the sight of my naked body.

Annie and Pen said to go for it. To think with my vagina for once and give in to whatever chemistry is building between Viktor and me.

But would he even want me?

My fingers skim between my breasts. They aren't perky anymore. Not after nursing a baby for over a year. Like two deflated balloons, they sag closer to my belly button than they used to.

Dropping my hand, I let my gaze roam lower. My stomach isn't flat and it's laden with silver stretch marks below my belly button and along my hips. Not to mention, the horizontal C-section scar running between my hip bones, a constant reminder of the childbirth process and the fact I can't have any more babies.

I don't exactly hate my body, but I don't exactly love it either.

I'm grateful for the years it gave me with Roman and for gifting me a beautiful daughter.

But I didn't really "bounce back" after having Lily. And by the time life slowed down enough to focus on getting back in shape, tragedy struck, and I lost my husband—my partner, my whole damn world.

Tears sting my eyes, and I swipe them away. I can't go down that spiral right now. I won't.

Why would someone like Viktor want *me*? His beauty is god-like and otherworldly. Built like a marble statue, he's carved into the perfect specimen of the male body. All hard muscles and sharp angles.

His chiseled cheekbones and full lips have been the stars in all my dreams lately. Not to mention the heat flickering behind those ruby irises.

Even his hair is beautiful, for crying out loud. I finger a loose wave of my dirty-blonde locks. Sure, they look good tonight, after a professional blowout. But most days, I'm too tired or busy to style my curls properly, so they end up in a messy bun.

I'm a single mom with a rambunctious little girl and more emotional baggage than I can carry. How can I compete with his perfection?

Turning around, I peer over my shoulder to the one part of my body I've always loved. Roman always said I had the best ass. He could hardly keep his hands off it when we were younger.

I smile at the perky cheeks where they peek out from the bottom of my white underwear.

Not the sexiest, but they're comfortable.

And all my effort in the gym is paying off lately. Roman converted a portion of our large garage space into a home gym when we moved in. He was an avid weightlifter, a habit I picked up during our relationship.

Sure, I still have a layer of fluff over my muscles, but I'm strong. And I'm proud of the progress I've made, especially on my glutes.

I nod, straightening my spine and pulling the nightgown over my head. The fabric cascades over my body like a cool rain until my puckered nipples are on display through the thin fabric. "Viktor would be the lucky one."

If I did cross that line—because he's been throwing all kinds of signals my way—what would he do to me?

The memory of his lingering crimson gaze sets a shiver rushing through me, and I grab my thick knit cardigan from where it's draped on the end of my bed. Slipping it on, I pull the sides tight around my body, hugging myself.

Nostrils flared wide, I'm hit by a sudden wave of his unique scent. Rich sandalwood with a hint of sweetness, like caramelized sugar. My thighs clench when the heady notes invade my lungs.

He must have accidentally washed my sweater with his things.

I take another whiff, letting the ache build in my core until it's nearly unbearable.

Viktor and I have been balancing on a knife's edge for weeks now. Dancing around the obvious attraction between us. But who will break first?

"Fuck it," I mutter as I leave my room and slink down the stairs. It appears my willpower isn't as iron-clad as I thought.

The kitchen is dark, only illuminated by the glow of the single bulb above the stove. Grabbing the baby monitor from the counter, I shove it in the pocket of my cardigan.

My heart races as fast as my feet, scrambling to the back door, where I stuff them into the old rain boots I keep on the dirt-crusted mat.

I deserve to be happy.

Don't I?

Romantically speaking, I've been alone and miserable ever since Roman died.

He was my first love. My everything. Naively, I thought we'd grow old together, but our time was cut short by a devastating tragedy. What if Viktor is meant to be my next great love? What if our story is meant to fill the pages of the next chapter?

What if... I was meant to love and lose Roman so that I could find Viktor? My heart clenches at the thought.

I can't let my cowardice rob me of a chance at another happily ever after.

Hovering over the doorknob, my hand shakes. I blow out a harsh breath. *Suck it up, Mags.* Nerves coil like a python in the pit of my stomach, but I force my fingers around the knob and turn, pushing open the door and stepping into the cool autumn night.

Blood pounds in my ears with every step I take closer to the guest house. What if he rejects me?

How fucking awkward would that make things between us for the remainder of his contract?

I don't think I'd be able to face him.

My fingers tingle at my sides and my chest heaves with each breath when the faint glow of the guest house lights comes into view. "Don't think like that, Mags. You're a catch." Try as I might, the positive words simply roll off my back, but my feet trudge on until I'm standing at Viktor's front door.

Pretty sure I wasn't even this nervous for my first date with Roman all those years ago.

After one last calming breath, I bring my trembling fist to the door.

Knock. Knock.

Before I have a chance to change my mind and run back home with my tail between my legs, the door swings in, revealing a sight that has moisture dripping from my tongue... and my pussy.

"Holy shit."

Pale hair disheveled and brushing his shoulders, Viktor stands in the doorway dressed in nothing but a pair of low-slung pajama pants.

His scantily clad nature leaves all the snowy-white skin of his hard torso on display for me to devour.

And devour, I do.

I pull my bottom lip between my teeth, biting down to hold back a moan as I take in his chest muscles. The harsh dips of his abs lead my eyes straight to the bulge hidden behind the thin fabric of his pajamas.

When I finally make my way back up to his gorgeous face, his eyes widen. "Maggie. Is something wrong? Is Lily alright?" There's a franticness to his voice that has me melting. The fact that his first thought is concern for my daughter shows just how dedicated he is to his job.

A breeze ruffles my hair, and Viktor's nostrils flare wide, his eyes darkening as they peruse the length of my body.

Somehow, my nipples peak further, screaming *hey, look at me* through my thin nightgown.

"She's fine. I just—"

Now or never, Mags.

The adrenaline coursing through my body propels me forward. Wrapping my hand around the back of Viktor's neck, I pull his mouth to mine.

The first brush of my lips is tentative. Hesitant. Giving him a chance to back away, but he doesn't.

No, he does not.

Instead, he spins us, dragging me inside and caging me between the now shut door and his hard body, all while his lips stay sealed to mine.

The kiss turns frantic as Viktor consumes me, pressing my body harder against the wooden door and swallowing down every moan that sneaks past my lips.

My hands find their way to the cool skin of his chest, where his heart thumps rapidly under my touch.

He pushes the thick knit cardigan off my shoulders until it falls to the crooks of my elbows, leaving the thin straps of my nightgown exposed.

My lungs plead for oxygen, and I pull back, meeting his dark-red gaze. Cheeks heating, I brace my hands against his pecs. "I'm sorry. I shouldn't have done that. But there's this spark... this pull between us that I can't ignore anymore. I-I—"

Viktor leans his forehead against mine, voice quiet. "I know, Maggie. I feel it, too. It's been torture... wanting you, but not having you. You're driving me mad."

His lips call to mine, like a moth to a flame. I press another kiss to his swollen mouth before pulling back. "This is wrong." I kiss him again. "I'm your boss. And you're leaving soon."

Leaning back, he gives me some space. Well, as much space as he can while still keeping me caged between his body and the door. A single fang peeks out when one side of his mouth pulls into a smirk. *Damn, why does he have to be so utterly gorgeous?* "Technically, Cyrus paid my contract, so you're *not* my boss." The meaning behind his words is clear: he wants this as much as I do.

"Loophole." I chuckle before sobering. "But I'm damaged goods, Viktor. I have enough baggage to fill the trunk of your car... and mine... and then some. I-I—"

He cups my face in his large palm, the icy bite of his skin refreshing against my flaming cheek. "I know, sweetheart. What if we leave the feelings out of it? Just for tonight."

"Just tonight," I echo. "Are you sure?"

He nods, lips tipping up at the corners, but the smile doesn't reach his dazzling crimson eyes. Like he wants more than I can give him.

Accept what the man is offering, and for the love of god, don't overthink it, Mags.

Taking my own advice, I crash my mouth to his again, swallowing down his choked groan. Viktor's tongue laps at mine, stoking a fire between us that I've never experienced before.

Not even with Roman.

Unbridled passion spirals to life when he grips the backs of my thighs and hauls me up his body, pinning my weight between him and the door. A thick ridge in his pants catches me off guard when he grinds his hips between my thighs.

Each rock of his pelvis against mine sends sparks of pleasure straight to my clit.

He does it again, and I tear my lips from his to let out a broken moan.

My eyes skim down his muscled chest and abs, landing on where our bodies would be joined—if the thin barrier of my underwear and his pants weren't in the way.

The obscene bulge of his cock behind his pajama bottoms is *huge*.

Holy shit!

Doubt creeps into the back of my mind, washing away the euphoria, when he grinds against me again. His cock is big, like, bigger than I've ever had.

I've only ever been with one man. Roman. And he certainly wasn't this big, or a supernatural creature. What is Viktor even capable of?

Maybe this wasn't a good idea.

Suddenly, it's like I'm a blushing virgin. Which I'm not.

I've had sex. Lots of sex.

Great sex, in fact. But only with one man and not in a long time.

Viktor's tongue trails down the length of my neck. Closing his lips over my pulse point, he sucks, and I stiffen.

He must sense my hesitation because he pulls back until we're eye-to-eye, worry flashing across his face. "What's wrong? Did I do something wrong?"

The concern in his rumbling voice soothes my frayed nerves, but how do you tell your one-night stand, who happens to be your nanny, that you're thinking about your dead husband?

"Hey." He cups my cheek, and I lean into his cool palm. "We don't have to do anything you're not ready for. You're in control, Maggie. Always."

Swallowing, I push down my unease and nod. I'm not doing anything wrong. Roman would want me to be happy and feel pleasure again. "I'm okay. Just got a little distracted. Can we move to the bed?"

A change of scenery is certain to keep thoughts of Roman at bay.

Although I'm on the shorter side, I'm not the smallest woman, so I expect Viktor to set me back on my feet and lead me to the queen-sized bed in the corner, but he clutches me to his body. Swinging away from the door, he carries me with surprising ease. A squeak slips out of my mouth, and I wrap my arms and legs tighter around him.

"You're not going to drop me, are you?"

That damn smirk curls the corners of his lips again. "I can handle you, sweetheart. I promise."

Before I can respond, he tosses me onto the bed, my head landing on the pillows. I swear his eyes glow like two rubies as the mattress dips under his weight and he prowls up my body. I knew there was something wild lurking under his polished exterior, but this is the first time I've witnessed it. It's hot—*he's* hot.

Collaring my neck in one large hand, he tugs my head off the pillows and feasts on my lips. "You taste so fucking good, Maggie." His chest rumbles against mine when he growls into the kiss.

Soon, we're a tangle of limbs on the bed, making out like two horny teenagers.

Viktor consumes all my senses. Tongue dancing with mine. Low groans of pleasure filling my ears. His darkly sweet scent invades my nose. Rough fingers flirt with the hem of my nightgown, slowly pushing it upward to my ribs.

I wish I'd taken the time to put on something a little sexier. Not that I own any lingerie.

Roman always said I looked sexiest in one of his t-shirts, freshly fucked.

Stop thinking about your dead husband while you're under another man.

"Are you sure you're okay?" Viktor mumbles against my neck. *He really likes that spot.* "You're stiff as a board right now."

Giving me some space, he lies on his side next to me. Gentle fingers stroke the skin of my hip over my underwear.

Eyes on the ceiling, I blow out a breath, resisting the urge to cover my face with my hands. Instead, I ball them at my sides and speak in a quiet voice. "It's silly. I'm sorry."

"Don't." The command in his tone has my eyes widening and snapping to his. "Don't hide your emotions from me, Maggie. I can tell something is making you uncomfortable."

"R-Roman... he keeps sneaking into my head, but I shouldn't be thinking about him right now. I should be thinking about *you.*"

His hand moves higher until he grips the hem of my nightgown and tugs it back down, covering my body. Oh no, is this the end of our fun? Did I fuck it all up?

Tears prick the backs of my eyes, and I drop my head.

"Look at me, please," Viktor whispers.

Afraid the tears will fall if I look into his gorgeous eyes, I shake my head and keep my gaze on the bed between us.

Cool fingers hook under my chin and tip it up until all I see is his beautiful crimson eyes. Reflected in them, I find my own pain and sadness... like a mirror into my soul.

I latch onto them like a lifeline as a single tear slips free. Viktor brushes it away before tucking a stray strand of hair behind my ear. "Grief isn't linear, Maggie. It doesn't have an expiration date, nor is it the same from one person to the next. You're allowed to feel what you're feeling. Never apologize for that. When another wave pulls you under, we'll navigate the storm together. Okay?"

My lips tip into a meek smile, and I nod. "Together. I like the sound of that," I whisper.

"Me too. Do you want to stop?"

Do I? At that moment, my clit throbs and wetness coats my panties. My body is still keyed up and ready to go.

It's just like riding a bike. Get back on and start pedaling. "No. I need this. I need you to help me move on." Not to replace Roman. No one will ever replace him, but I can't stay stuck in the past any longer.

To drive home my consent, I muster every ounce of courage in my body and, with shaking hands, grip the bottom of my nightgown. The soft fabric glides up my body and over my head. I toss it away, until it's nothing but a puddle of gray cloth on the wooden floor.

CHAPTER 17

Viktor

I nearly swallow my tongue when Maggie rips off her night-gown and flings it to the floor. I'll be damned, she's just as stunning as I imagined.

Actually, scratch that; she's even more gorgeous than what I pictured in my head for the past few weeks every time I jerked myself to thoughts of her.

My fangs sink into my bottom lip as my jaw clenches, and I muster every last thread of restraint so I don't lunge on top of her and drive them into her flawless neck.

Pink tinges her cheeks, and trembling hands come up to cover her breasts, hiding her perfect body from my wandering eyes.

"Don't do that," I growl, my voice dipping lower than I ever knew possible. Reaching for her hands, I pin them to the mattress on either side of her head when I climb on top of her. My lower half settles between her spread thighs. The heat radiating from her pussy sends a shiver rippling down my spine. This is where I'm supposed to be. "Don't hide your beautiful body from me, Maggie."

"But you were just *staring* at me... I thought you didn't like what you saw."

The audacity. My chest rumbles like a caged animal is pacing inside me, low and menacing. Sitting back on my haunches, I glide my hands over her outer thighs until they rest on her wide hips. Tightening my grip, my fingers dig into her flesh. So soft. So smooth. "You call it staring. I call it admiring the peak female form. You're gorgeous, country girl."

My words only make her blush more, a furious trail of red winding down her neck and between her heaving breasts.

Hooking my fingers into the sides of her panties, I slowly peel them down her legs, giving her plenty of time to stop me. She's a little skittish, and the last thing I want is to take advantage of her.

"When was the last time this beautiful body was touched?" I ask. Divesting her of her panties, I chuck them over my shoulder and out of sight. "The last time you were worshiped like you deserve, Maggie? When was it?"

My eyes and fingers skim over the mottled skin on her lower abdomen. The scar that led to the precious child sleeping upstairs in the main house.

Leaning down, I place a soft kiss over the silver scar.

How does she not see how incredible she is?

Maggie's throat bobs, and she turns her head away from me. "It's been a while... Not since—" Her voice is barely a whisper, but vampires are blessed with astute hearing, so my ears pick up every heartbreaking word. No one has touched this beautiful woman since her late husband.

"Maggie." Running a finger along her jaw, I guide her chin toward me, until her sea-glass gaze meets my crimson one. Opposites in every way. She's the sunshine to my midnight. The warmth my icy touch has craved all my life. "We don't have to do this. And I should warn you that I have certain *tastes*. Certain proclivities as a vampire that you may not desire."

Her eyebrows furrow, mouth pinching into a grim line. "Like what?"

"I desire a more vigorous variety of sex. Rougher. Grittier. More primal. But the pleasure will be beyond anything you've ever experienced."

Chin clutched between my fingers, close enough to breathe the same air, I don't miss when her pupils double in size.

"Will you show me?"

It's on the tip of my tongue to deny her, this glorious creature, spread before me in offering. Deep in my heart, I know one night won't be enough.

One night will only open the Pandora's box of cravings already brewing in my veins.

She asked for no strings attached, but she already owns my heart. Every single beat is for her.

I can only resist my attraction to her for so long. If that makes me a terrible being, then so be it. Damn me to hell. I'll bask in whatever glory she'll give me. Morsels. Crumbs. I'll gobble them all up.

I give in to the bloodlust coursing through my veins, lost to its desire. "Yes," I growl, before slamming my mouth to hers.

Her throaty moans feed the darkness inside me, and my fingers wander to her chest, plucking and pinching her beaded nipples. "Has anyone ever touched you like this?" With a biting grip, I twist one nipple, then the other. Maggie's answering moans are the most pristine symphony to my ears.

"No," she whines, head thrashing against the pillow, hips lifting... searching. "But... don't stop. *Please*."

Just as I suspected, there's a darkness in Maggie that matches my own. A craving for something raw and primal. Is this why her body calls to mine? Like two long-lost lovers, the stars have finally aligned for us.

"Do you want to be my good girl tonight?"

"Yes." Her moans trail off into a gasp when I run my fingers through her pussy lips.

She's drenched. The insides of her thighs glisten with the evidence of her arousal.

"Do you like the sound of that?" I pump one digit into her perfect pussy. *Fuck, she's tight.* I can't take my eyes off the way her opening wraps around my finger, sucking it deeper inside her heat. "Viktor's good girl?"

Maggie's back arches off the mattress, thighs clenching around me. "God, yes. Please."

"You know what I'd like even more, sweetheart?"

Kissing a trail down her body—I'm careful not to nick her soft skin with my fangs—until her delicious cunt is right at eye level. Her arousal drips from my finger as I pump lazily in and out of her.

A pathetic whine fills the air when I remove my finger, and I chuckle. "So needy."

Maggie writhes above me, but I focus on her pretty cunt, spreading her lips with my thumbs and blowing on the wet, engorged flesh. She jerks, but melts back into the bed almost instantly, and a fresh trail of arousal leaks from her opening.

"Wh-what?" She's breathless, chest heaving when I add a second finger, pushing them into her as my thumb circles her clit.

"I want you to be my filthy whore."

My words hang in the air, silence settling between us. *Fuck*, I probably shouldn't have pushed her so soon. I get the feeling Maggie is relatively vanilla when it comes to sex, but I am not.

I don't want to hold back with her, especially if I only get tonight. Balls to the wall, as they say. I'm not about to hide my true desires from her.

Maggie's chest stalls. But her pussy doesn't lie. It spasms around my fingers, leaking the truth all over my hand: her desire to be degraded.

So I push further with a dark whisper. "Will you be my whore for tonight?"

On bated breath, I wait.

This is it.

The part where she says no.

The part where she takes back the promise of one night together.

Surely, my tastes are too depraved for her. I've miscalculated and scared her away before we've even begun.

The silence is almost too much to bear, stretching between us until the last thread of my sanity nearly snaps.

Surprising me, Maggie tilts her chin, defiance shining brightly in her pale-green eyes. "Yes." Her voice is confident and sure, no hint of the earlier hesitation.

Before I can catch myself, my eyes widen, disbelief washing over my features.

Maggie sits upright. Wrapping one hand around the back of my neck, she takes me down to the bed with her. My fingers slip free of her clenching cunt as I nestle my body against her, and my mouth hovers over hers. "Yes, I'll be your whore." Her lips curve against mine as they lift into a shy smile.

A rush of pre-cum dampens the front of my pajama bottoms at her words of consent. "Fuck me," I whisper.

Soft laughter puffs against my lips. "That's kind of the idea, Viktor."

I let loose a hearty chuckle that only has her grin growing.

"Mmm, you're not ready for me yet."

"Wha—"

I prowl back down her body to resume my ministrations. "You're wet, but I need you absolutely soaked before you take my cock." Without breaking eye contact, I lay the flat of my tongue against her opening and swipe up to her clit.

Her flavor bursts across my taste buds, and I nearly lose my load in my pants. She's perfect. Sweet and musky, with a hint of bitterness, like the perfect apple.

"Yes," she whispers as her back arches off the bed again. Her hands cup her breasts. Mmm, I can't wait to play with those while I fuck her. They're exquisite. Small and perky, lined with beautiful silver stretch marks that bear witness to the life her body has given.

Sucking her clit, I pump two fingers into her slick core, curling them until her eyes slam shut and she moans.

"Mmm. Just like that, Maggie. Show me how beautiful you are when you come on my fingers. Because next time, you'll be coming with my cock buried deep inside you. Stretching you wide and filling every inch of you."

At my proclamation, she strangles my fingers to the point that I can barely move them. She's close.

"D-don't stop. Please." Her hoarse cry is music to my fucking ears. I want her pleading on repeat for me all day and night.

My mouth goes back to her clit, licking and sucking at the engorged flesh until it happens. She *shatters*.

It's the most beautiful thing I've ever witnessed.

Maggie's fingers dig into the soft flesh of her breasts. Her back bows from the mattress, and her mouth opens on a silent scream.

Perfectly thick thighs tighten around my head like the filthiest pair of earmuffs.

But the best part? Her inner muscles contract around my fingers in a rhythmic pattern, pushing her thick cream out to coat them.

And, *holy fuck*, the monster inside me takes over at the sight of her arousal dripping down my hand. A ravenous energy possesses me, and I snarl. Baring my fangs, I feast on her until I push her into a second orgasm. Her thighs shake against my ears, her beautiful whimpers filling the air.

"Too much, Viktor." Palms against my shoulders, she pushes, but I drive my tongue into her alongside my fingers to lap up her essence. "Viktor, please."

At this point, I'm lost to the hunger. I've been celibate for decades, waiting for the right woman. For *this* woman. My hips drive into the mattress, rolling and bucking, trying to ease the tremendous ache in my cock, but it's no use. The only remedy for the pain is her juicy cunt.

She shoves my shoulders again with a breathy cry. More frantic this time, and the rational part of my brain takes over again. I pull back, sitting on my haunches and taking my fingers from her sweet heat.

"Sorry, I got a little carried away." I wince, but her eyes are still shut, a blissed-out expression on her face.

As soon as her flushed chest stops heaving, her lids drift open, and I'm transfixed by the way her pupils overtake the beautiful sea-glass green of her irises. "Holy fuck. I've never come like that before."

Pride swells my chest... and my cock. She really was made for me.

"Do you want to keep going?" I hold my fingers up between us, still covered in the sheen of her arousal. My tongue darts across my bottom lip, eager to clean them, but I have something else in mind. Something I hope she'll enjoy just as much as me.

Her head swings up and down. A few sweat dampened curls stick to her flushed cheeks. So beautiful.

"Be a good little whore and open your mouth."

Maggie whimpers, but her jaw drops open.

My rasped "good girl" has her pupils somehow blowing wider. Oh, she's definitely enjoying herself.

I plunge my fingers into her waiting mouth and rub them across her tongue so she really gets a taste of herself. "Good, isn't it?"

Closing her lips, she sucks and moans around my fingers.

"You know what would make it even better?"

Her eyes dart between mine. "Your cum?" she mumbles around her stuffed mouth.

My answering chuckle is ominous. "Are you hungry for my cock, whore?"

Maggie nods, making my fingers slide from her mouth. My hand trails down to collar the side of her neck. Hummingbird wings flutter against my palm, her heart racing under the warm skin.

Rising on my knees, I crowd her against the bed, forcing her head to tip back. "Oh, sweetheart." There's the slightest hint of pity in my tone. "Whores have to earn my cock in their throat and my cum in their belly."

The words pour out, shocking even myself with their possessive grit. This is what she does to me. Maggie brings out the darkness in me. I can only hope she doesn't back away when she sees the true monster.

"H-how?"

Shit. I'm running on instinct here. As much as I'd love to see my cock bulging in her throat and hear her gag around me, I've been dreaming of being inside her for weeks now. "Let's start with your pretty cunt. See if my cock will fit there. Shall we?"

"Yes. Please, Viktor."

Using my grip on her throat, I pull her lips to mine, needing another taste. "You think you can handle me?" I ask between bruising kisses.

Coasting down my body, her hands answer for her, tugging at the tie on my pajama bottoms. An uneasiness settles in my gut at what she's about to find when she reaches her delicate fingers into my pants and pulls my cock free. Based on the gasp that hits my lips, I don't think she's prepared.

Fingers not quite able to wrap around my thick shaft, she strokes me. Her palm skates over...

One.

Two.

Three.

Four.

And... five.

"Pierced? You're fucking pierced!?" A note of panic has her voice rising, and she pulls back.

"Is that a problem?" I arch an eyebrow as I sit back to give her a chance to admire me.

My cock juts out proudly from my groin, standing at attention for her. The five blood-red barbells gleam in the moonlight. A larger hoop, the same color, bisects the tip.

Maggie pinches her bottom lip between her teeth, eyes glued to my cock as I fist it and give a teasing stroke. A bead of pre-cum oozes from the tip, sliding down to coat my fingers. It's all for her. Every last drop.

"Ummm. No. I'm all for trying new things. Did those hurt?" With a single finger, she pokes at the barbell closest to my balls.

They draw up tight, and I groan, needing her hands on me. All over me.

I chuckle and take her hand in mine, guiding her to stroke me. "They didn't feel good. That's for sure." What I leave out is that I wanted the pain. Welcomed it as I stayed celibate, waiting for the perfect woman. Waiting for *her*.

Admitting that now would make me sound downright insane, and surely have her running from my bed, so I swallow it down, locking it away for another day.

"How do they feel?"

More pre-cum drips from my cock at her question. Truth is, I haven't been with anyone—monster or otherwise—since getting pierced, but all my research points to them being pleasurable for both parties involved. Imagining pushing inside her tight cunt one rung at a time has me threatening to lose my mind. "Why don't we find out? Together."

"Yes, please." Maggie uses her feet to push my pants farther down my legs, all while stroking my cock at a tortuously slow pace. *Tease.*

Slipping my pants off completely, I brace one forearm next to her head.

Suddenly, the rational part of my brain interrupts. "Shit."

"What?" Maggie's eyebrows scrunch together when I sit back, and her hand falls away from my cock.

"I don't have any condoms. I wasn't exactly planning on having any sex while I was here." Rubbing a hand over the back of my neck, my cheeks flame as I wince and peer at Maggie.

"Oh. Umm, I'm clean and covered, if that's what you're worried about."

"You sure?" I lean over her again, braced on one hand.

"I'm a big girl, Viktor. I'm sure." Smirking, she wraps her arms around my neck and tugs my forehead to hers.

My other hand goes back to my cock, lining the tip up to her entrance. "You have no idea what you do to me."

I shouldn't be saying things like this. It's too close to the "feelings" territory we've vowed to avoid, but I can't help it. I don't want just one night. I want every night for the rest of time.

The little minx slips one hand down to my cock. Her grip tightens, and her legs come up on either side of my hips. "I'm pretty sure I have some idea." She smiles, laughter evident in her voice. "Just fuck me already."

So impatient.

"As you wish, sweetheart." There are too many things to focus on as I press my hips forward, her heat engulfing the tip of my cock. Her eyebrows dip, eyes locked on mine. A soft sigh falls from her parted lips. Her hands go to my back, sharp nails digging into my skin.

My cock is surrounded by her warmth, and it's better than anything I've ever felt.

"More," she whines, thighs squeezing me.

A dirty idea sparks in my head. "I want you to count for me, whore."

"W-What?"

"You heard me... Count each piercing as it slides into your wet little pussy." Without warning, I punch forward, giving her the first rung.

"One!"

Her eyes shut, cheeks flushed red, and I give her the second.

"Two!"

She's panting now, chest heaving as it brushes against mine. "More?"

Maggie nods, pinning that damn lip between her teeth again. I want that to be my fangs, sinking into her sweet flesh and drinking her down. "More. I can take more."

"Good girl," I croon, rolling my hips forward so the third piercing slips into her stretched pussy with a squelch.

"Three," she gasps.

Leaning down, I hold my weight on both elbows until she's pressed into the mattress, and bring my mouth to her ear. "You're doing so well, little whore. Your cunt is taking me beautifully. Ready for the last two?"

She whimpers. "Yes."

The single word snaps the final thread of my control, and I plow forward until my balls slap against her ass.

"Four. F-Five," Maggie chants. Her inner walls spasm around my cock, already starting to milk me.

I pull back to meet her eyes, combing my fingers through her hair before cupping her cheek. Her skin is so warm, glowing bright pink from her earlier orgasms. "Holy fuck, I'm in. All the way in, sweetheart. You took it all like such a good girl."

Her kiss-swollen lips curl into a seductive smile. "Now what, city boy? Are you gonna fuck me like a whore?"

Holy mother of— Does sweet little Maggie Wilcox have a bratty side? Oh, I can't *wait* to explore that more. I press my lips to hers, giving her pussy one last moment to adjust to my size. "You're something else, sweetheart."

Then I do as she asked. Sitting up straight, I take a second to admire where our bodies join. The sensitive skin around her opening is red and soaked with arousal. Her cunt is stretched wide to take my shaft, which is glistening, too. Maggie shivers as I run a finger over where we're connected. "Damn, sweetheart. Such a masterpiece."

Once I've committed this moment to memory—for future use—I slide my hands to her hips, where my fingers dig into her supple flesh. She squeaks when I lift her lower half off the bed as I rise higher onto my knees. The first drag of my piercings out of her pussy has both of us groaning. So fucking tight.

There's no way I'm going to last long if every thrust is this euphoric. The first inklings of my orgasm have already taken root in my balls.

I push that thought aside and let loose. The inner monster claws at his cage, but I don't let him out yet. My hips piston, driving my cock in and out of Maggie at a frantic pace. Her pleasure-filled cries grow louder with each thrust, and it's a good thing we're so far away from the main house or we'd surely wake Lily.

My eyes snap to the nightstand, where Maggie managed to set the baby monitor before we gave in to our sexual desires. Lily is still fast asleep in her bed.

"Stay with me, Viktor." Maggie's words have my head snapping back to the goddess in my grip. Her breasts bounce with each punishing snap of my hips, hands braced against the headboard as every thrust inches her up the bed. Pale eyes are glued to me, almost glowing in the moonlight.

With a growl, I drop her hips, dropping my hands to the mattress by her shoulders. I continue to drive forward, fucking her deeper into the cushion of the bed. At this angle, I can curl my hips at the top of each thrust in hopes of stimulating her clit and hitting the elusive G-spot.

I must be doing something right, because Maggie moans and thrashes under me like a banshee. Her hands go to my back again, and I revel in the first slice of her nails through my skin. "Yes, sweetheart. Let it out. Give it to me."

Electricity races down my spine, and my balls draw up tight to my body. *Not yet.* I need Maggie to come first.

"Come on, whore. Come on my cock. Mark me as yours." For good measure, I sneak a hand between our bodies and strum her clit like a man possessed.

For the third time tonight, Maggie explodes in my arms, wailing as she clamps around my shaft.

And as much as I want to come inside her warmth, the overwhelming need to mark her skin as mine wins out. Sitting up again, I pull from her still spasming cunt, instantly missing the heat of her body. My hand flies up and down my cock in a death grip until the orgasm finally takes flight. The first spurt of milky-white cum lands on her perfect breasts. The next on her soft belly. And the last few coat the red flesh of her used pussy.

She's magnificent, lying spent in my bed. Wearing my cum.

"You took me so well, Maggie."

She moans, eyes fluttering shut, hands limp at her sides.

"You were perfect." I continue to praise her while I swipe my fingers through the mess on her pussy. Gathering as much cum as I can, I push my fingers into her. She whines, but her hips rock like a gentle ocean wave.

Can I make her come one more time before she leaves?

Give her a night she'll never forget.

Hooking my fingers against her G-spot, I press my other thumb over her clit. When she doesn't protest, I add a little pressure. "One more, sweetheart. I know you have it in you."

Eyebrows drawn together, eyes closing, her hands fist in the sheets like she's concentrating, trying to give me what I asked for. "One more." The words are so soft, I doubt they'd be audible without my exceptional hearing.

Permission granted, I work my fingers faster, harder. But not too hard. I don't want to hurt her.

I may like to degrade and call her a whore, but I never want to inflict physical pain on Maggie. In fact, nausea roils in my gut at the thought. I'd rather die.

Maggie's hips rock faster, riding my fingers and drawing my focus back to her. "That's it. Good whores get to come over and over and over."

"Yesss," she hisses. This time, when she comes, it's like a wave washes over her body as her head tips back on an airy sigh. Her back arches, and her thighs clench around my hands, keeping them in place until the wave is taken out by the tide and her body settles back onto the bed.

As much as I want to lie down next to her and pull her body to me, my cum still lingers on her skin, sticky and cold now that some time has passed.

Making a quick trip to the bathroom, I wet a washcloth with warm water. Remembering the scratches on my back, I twist until I can see them in the mirror, but my skin is already healed. Damn my vampire genetics. The one time I wish I didn't heal at lightning speed. I want her marks on my skin.

With a sigh, I leave the bathroom and swing by the fridge to grab two bottles of water. My head is already dizzy, so I can only imagine how Maggie feels after four orgasms.

When I return to the bed, her chest rises and falls in a gentle motion. Huh. She must have fallen asleep. Anticipation rushes through me at the thought of Maggie sleeping in my bed, and the prospect of having her one more time. But alas, I can't keep her here. What if Lily wakes up? What if she has a bad dream and needs her mom?

It would be stupid and selfish of me to keep Maggie in my bed. Hopes dashed, I swipe the cloth over her skin, wiping away any evidence of our time together.

"Thank you." Maggie's soft voice startles me. Her lids spring open, and I'm met with two glittering gemstones. "That was pretty freaking amazing." She smiles wide, my favorite gap between her teeth on full display, and my heart pinches. *Stay*, I want to say, but I know she can't give me more. She can't give me her heart.

"Yeah," is all I can manage as I finish cleaning her up.

Silently, we drink our water and get dressed. "One night" is over, only to remain as a memory I revisit often.

Walking her to the door, I resist the urge to pull Maggie back to the bed and keep her there for another round. I can't, though. If I'm already this far gone after being in her pussy once, it'll only be worse the more times I take her.

"I guess I'll see you in the morning, then?" She chews on her bottom lip and fiddles with the bottom of her cardigan. Both are sure signs that she's nervous.

"Bright and early." *Idiot*. Tell her to stay. Tell her you've waited decades for her.

Rising onto her toes, she places a kiss on my cheek. "Night, Viktor."

Then she's gone. Out the door like nothing happened.

I can't take my eyes off her as she retreats to the main house. She fades into the darkness until she reappears on the back deck, illuminated by the soft glow of the outdoor lights. Hand resting on the door handle, she hesitates. *Interesting*. My heart hammers when she turns to glance over her shoulder before going inside. I swear there's a hint of regret in her pale eyes, but even my vision isn't precise enough to catch it at this distance.

The light flicks off a second later, but I can't tear my eyes away, my enhanced vision still able to decipher the outline of the closed door.

My cheek burns from her lips when I finally turn away, bracing my back on the wall and letting out a groan. I knew it. I fucking *knew* it.

One night with Maggie isn't enough, and I don't know if I'm strong enough to resist her.

And honestly, I'm done trying.

Chapter 18

Maggie

The other night with Viktor was fucking amazing. Hands down, the best sex I've ever had. "Sorry, Roman," I mutter to the ceiling after closing the cabinet door.

The kitchen is quiet. Only the soft chirping of the few remaining songbirds coming in through the open window. Harvest season has descended upon the orchard. Lily started kindergarten. And Viktor started tutoring at the community center a few nights a week. Which means, somehow, we've barreled straight into mid-September, and we only have a month left with Viktor.

And after our passionate night together, I hope the next month will be filled with the same heated kisses and orgasmic touches.

Except... it's been a week, and he hasn't touched me. Maybe he really did only want one night.

Granted, we've all been adjusting to a new routine now that Lily is in school.

My eyes lift from the window, turning toward the family room to find Lily engrossed in her tablet. Her finger slides across the screen, probably playing one of the letter tracing games Viktor loaded onto it.

Since she's occupied, I let my brain wander. Back to that night.

The night I was Viktor's whore... and his good girl.

For a little while, I could turn off my brain and let the pleasure consume me. Let *him* consume me. No worries about my looming debt or making sure Lily is okay. I was simply a toy for Viktor to use.

And use, he did.

Wetness drips from my pussy, and I clench my thighs against the ache forming in my clit. I've never been degraded in my life, but the mix of praise amongst his dirty words had my skin buzzing.

Fuck, it's still buzzing even days later.

I want more.

Sighing, I fill a large pot with water and set it on the stove to boil. Viktor's lack of initiation surely means he's done with me, right?

One night. No feelings.

That's all he wanted, and I stupidly gave it to him, thinking that's all I wanted, too.

Boy, was I wrong. My nipples pebble every time he enters the room, and the man has the ability to soak my poor panties with just one heated glance of his beautiful red eyes.

Lost in thought, I grip the handle of the pantry door and push it open. A hand snaps out, gripping my wrist and tugging me into the closet-sized room.

Before I can scream, another hand slaps across my mouth, muffling my squeaked protests.

"Shhh, sweetheart. It's just me." I melt at the deep rumble of my vampire's rich voice.

My vampire?

Not yours, Mags. No feelings, remember?

"What are you doing? I thought you had a tutoring session tonight," I hiss when Viktor removes his hand.

My back is plastered to the closed pantry door. Thick arms come up to cage me against the hard wood.

"Not until later." Viktor dips his head, nestling his nose against where my pulse is beating at a frantic pace in my neck. His chest brushes against mine as he fills his lungs on a choked groan. "You smell so fucking good."

This spot, where my neck and shoulder meet, seems to be a favorite of his. He showered the skin with attention during our heated night together. Does this mean he wants to bite me? Feed on me?

The thought alone has a needy exhale spilling from my lips and my already drenched panties soaking through with arousal.

"Fuck, you're wet for me, aren't you? I can smell your arousal. What were you thinking about in the kitchen, naughty girl?"

His hot tongue follows his filthy words, and my skin scorches under the attention.

Gripping his trim waist in shaking hands, I tug his groin to my core. He's hard. His thick, pierced cock strains against the front of his slacks.

My mouth watered at the sight of him the other night. Long and thick. So thick, in fact, I could barely wrap my hand around him.

Dark-blue veins ran up his shaft, visible through his pale skin.

Yes, even his beautiful cock is pale, like the rest of him.

But my favorite part is the ladder of piercings running up the underside. Five metallic crimson bars perfectly spaced along his cock. And a massive ring bisecting the tip.

I shiver, remembering the way each ridge stretched my pussy as he slid inside.

"You must be thinking about something really good. You're soaking the front of my pants, and your scent is so thick, it's practically choking me," he murmurs against the burning skin of my neck.

And my cheeks heat to match. I'm probably as red as the freshly picked tomatoes on my kitchen counter. "Why haven't you touched me again?" Internally, I cringe at the pathetic whine in my voice, but I'm too worked up. Too horny. It was never like this with Roman.

Not that the sex was bad or anything. But I wasn't desperate, vibrating with the need to be fucked.

"We said one night—"

My fingers dig into the soft material of his shirt, the muscle underneath hard as granite. "I-I know, but I need you again."

Viktor's nostrils flare against my neck, like he's taking one more hit, before he pulls back. "I can't stop thinking about you. The sweet taste of your lips. The way your body trembled with anticipation. And the tight hug of your cunt every time I drove deep inside you. I need you again, too, Maggie."

"Viktor." I brace my hands on his chest, his heart beating just as fast as mine. "What are we doing?"

"I don't know, sweetheart, but one night wasn't enough. I need more of your moans. You're so beautiful when you come. Let me see you come again." Crimson eyes plead with mine, tugging on my heartstrings until I don't know if I'll be able to say no to him. "What if we keep our feelings separate?"

I swallow, trying and failing to resist the pull of his body as he cages me against the pantry door, fingers toying with the ends of my hair. Right now, I want him more than anything. "Like friends with benefits?"

Lips splitting wide, those sexy fangs are on full display when he smiles down at me. I still remember the pinpricks of pain as he scraped them against my neck the other night. I'd be a fucking fool to deny myself another experience like that.

The pleasure. The hint of pain. The perfect mixture to send me careening toward the best orgasm of my life.

With a wink, Viktor ends my little daydream and answers my question. "Yes. Exactly like that."

"You won't catch feelings?"

His gaze drops, focusing on a curl of my hair while he wraps it around his long, elegant finger. "I won't catch feelings."

Silence fills the small pantry until it's nearly suffocating. We're both lying to ourselves if we think feelings won't be involved in this arrangement.

But at this moment, I want to be selfish. Reckless.

For the first time since Roman died, I want to think only of myself and my needs.

I don't want to be Maggie, the single mom or business owner.

I want to be Maggie, the woman who lets a vampire ravish her on a nightly basis once the rest of the world has gone to sleep.

I want to take every drop of pleasure Viktor is willing to give me, and I won't apologize for that.

Gripping the back of Viktor's neck, I pull his mouth to mine in a heated kiss. "Then you better make good on your words and take another taste." Bracing my hands on his shoulders, I push until he drops to his knees in front of me, eyes glowing in the dim light of the pantry.

Cool hands coast up my legs under the hem of my sundress. "Fuck, country girl, what are you doing to me?"

Instead of answering, the air stalls in my lungs when his fingers curl around the sides of my panties. Viktor slides them over my hips and down my legs, stuffing them in his pocket. "For later," he says, voice laced with a promise as he winks.

Then his hands are back on my skin, like an icy river cutting across my heated flesh. My back arches, and I shiver as he pushes the skirt of my dress up until my soaked core is exposed to him. "Do me a favor, sweetheart?"

"Anything," I breathe.

Pushing the soft fabric into my hands, his eyes never leave my pussy. "Hold this for me so I can eat." His chest rumbles with a growl, his tone commanding.

Oh my— Fuck. I adore the gentle Viktor, who's so good with Lily. But I crave this hungry side of him. The monstrous side he hides from the rest of the world.

The growl deepens when he leans forward and buries his nose in my pussy. He sucks in a breath. "Fuck, I can't resist you." His words are hushed, almost too quiet for me to hear.

And maybe I wasn't supposed to hear them because we said no feelings. But Viktor's lust for me boosts my confidence, and I widen my stance, giving him better access to what he wants.

The heat of his mouth moves to my inner thigh as he hooks my leg over his shoulder, opening me wider for him.

I suck in a breath when something sharp pricks my inner thigh. Not breaking the skin, but testing the limits. *His fangs.*

"Viktor," I moan.

He groans. "Do you have any idea how much I want to taste you, Maggie? You smell so sweet. So perfect. Fresh apples. Sunshine."

"Do it."

He shakes his head, rubbing his nose against my inner thigh, sucking in a breath. "Not yet. I want to take my time when I finally drink you down. I don't want to be interrupted or rushed."

Oh. Right. I almost forgot about Lily in the other room.

"No. Right now is about you. Making you feel pleasure." His long fingers drift back to my pussy lips, and he spreads them wide for his view. Crimson eyes burn into my exposed skin, sending a trickle of arousal leaking from my core.

I whimper. "Please."

"Are you going to be quiet?"

The first lap of his skilled tongue has my legs shaking.

"Yes, Viktor," I squeak before biting my tongue against the moan crawling up my throat.

"Good girl." Then he's on me, tongue swirling against my needy clit, fingers teasing my entrance.

Clamping a hand over my mouth, I close my eyes and focus on the pleasure building at the base of my spine; the petals of my orgasm unfurling like a spring bloom. Each swipe of his tongue pushes me higher.

My fingers dig into my cheeks, and my lips curl around my teeth, trying to keep the moans of ecstasy from spilling free when he presses two fingers into my core.

I'm so wet; he's met by almost no resistance when he pulls out and pushes three fingers back inside me. "Fuck, Maggie, you think you can take one more?" His eyes meet mine, one dark eyebrow raised.

I nod vigorously, rolling my hips to meet the curl of his hand.

"Are you going to stay quiet?"

Nodding again, the coppery tang of blood fills my mouth when I bite down on the inside of my cheek.

My consent spurs him on, adding a fourth finger into the mix, and I'm so *full*. So fucking full that my toes curl and my pussy flutters.

"Good girl. Now come for me, sweetheart." Viktor curls those long, elegant fingers inside me over and over again, swiping my G-spot every time and driving me up to the stars.

When he suctions his lips around my clit and flicks it with his tongue, my eyes slam shut, and I detonate. Flashes of color dance across the backs of my eyelids and my legs shake. The fingers in the skirt of my dress curl tighter around the soft fabric. And the hand over my mouth clamps down harder.

"Open your eyes, Maggie." This time, Viktor's voice comes from right in front of me. *When did he stand up?*

My eyes spring open, met by crimson orbs dancing with humor. One fang pinches his bottom lip, like he's holding back a self-satisfied smirk. "You good? I think I lost you for a second."

Lowering my hand from my mouth, my cheeks burn. "I-I'm good. Thank you."

Leaning in, his lips brush mine as he growls, "Good, because next time, I want you screaming my name as loud as you can, country girl."

As he pulls back, the smirk finally breaks free, lighting up his whole face. Reaching onto the shelf next to him, Viktor grabs a jar of pasta sauce and thrusts it into my hand.

I gulp, fingers wrapping around the glass jar. *Next time.* I can't fucking wait.

"Momma! I need help!" Lily's voice comes from the other side of the door. *Shit! How long have we been in here?*

"Duty calls," I say lamely, clutching the pasta sauce to my chest and opening the pantry door.

Peering over my shoulder, my gaze catches on a pair of devilish red eyes peering through the cracked door. An equally devilish smirk stays on his lips, fangs on full display. *Later*, he mouths before slipping into the laundry room.

When I turn around, I find Lily on her stool, reaching for the cookie jar. "Do you need help, bug?"

"I'm hungry, Momma. Can I have a cookie?" She lays her best pout on me, but I'm no fool.

"Dinner first, then you can have a cookie. I'm making your favorite."

"Spaghetti?" Her little mouth breaks into a wide smile, showcasing the gap from the tooth she lost a few days ago.

Heading to the stove, I find the water boiling, so I dump in the box of pasta before getting to work on the sauce. "It'll be ready soon. Why don't you go clean up your toys?"

Leaving me to my racing thoughts, Lily scampers out of the kitchen and into the family room. My eyes linger on her while I finish cooking.

Viktor and I said one night, but it's like neither of us is able to put the lid back on the can of worms we opened. There's an ache deep inside me that only his touch satiates. Could I really move on and be happy with Viktor?

After what he just did to me in the pantry, this doesn't feel like just sex anymore. Not with the way my heart skips a beat when he comes through the front door every morning, or how much Lily laughs and smiles when he's around.

He's not only good for me, but he's also good for her.

"It's only temporary," I mumble, turning to the sink to drain the pasta. His contract ends in a month. Plus, his father expects him to stay in the city and join the family business. *You'll probably never see him again. Enjoy it while you can, Mags.*

CHAPTER 19

Viktor

"You know, you don't have to cook on the nights you tutor," Maggie says when she steps out of her office and closes the door behind her.

Setting the tray of roasted veggies on the stove, I flip the dish towel over my shoulder and turn toward her. Today, she's wearing a long, flowy dress. And it's taking every bit of my restraint not to tear it off her. Ever since I feasted on her pussy in the pantry the other night, I've become ravenous for another taste.

Alas, life has gotten in the way.

I started tutoring and volunteering at the community center in town now that Lily is in school. It's taken up most of my free time, but... Idle minds and all that. I needed something to keep mine off the beautiful creature currently standing before me.

Above the neckline of her dress, her chest flushes pink. The light-blue floral material brings out the last hints of the summer tan on her skin, hugging her small tits to perfection. "I like cooking for you and Lily. Remember? Food is my love language."

She rubs her stomach with a smile. "Mmm. You don't have to remind me. I had the leftover lasagna for lunch today. You really outdid yourself with that one, city boy."

She brushes behind me, and I jump at the sharp pain in my left butt cheek. *Did she pinch me?* Like nothing happened, Maggie continues on her way to the sink and washes her hands. But she flashes me a cheeky little wink over her shoulder.

I like this playful side of her.

"Brat," I say, sliding up behind her and returning the favor. My fingers sink into the supple flesh of her perky ass, and she squeaks when I squeeze.

"Viktor! What if Lily sees?" Her head snaps to the kitchen table, where an explosion of craft supplies surrounds her daughter.

Plastering my body to hers, I rock my rapidly hardening cock into the valley of her ass. With my nose nestled against my favorite spot on her slender neck, I breathe in her sweet apple scent. "She won't." I grind my hips forward, and Maggie moans. "I just want a kiss goodbye, country girl."

"You're leaving? But it's Friday." There's a hint of disappointment in her voice.

Turning off the water, I spin her to face me. I take the towel from my shoulder and dry her hands before tossing it into the sink behind her. "Yes. There's a woman at the community center who needs help learning English, so I volunteered to assist her. Tonight is one of the few nights she has off."

Maggie smiles up at me and smooths her hands over my vest before adjusting my tie. "You have such a big heart, Viktor."

Her words have the organ in question speeding up and warmth spreading across my face. "I just like to help."

"I know." Pressing onto her tiptoes, she seals her lips against mine for a kiss that's nearly as sweet as her. My tongue swipes at her lips, and she opens willingly for me.

The familiar ache in my fangs pounds to life, and I pull back before I accidentally bite down on her bottom lip. It's for the better, I realize, when a commotion to my left has my head snapping up.

"Uh-oh." Lily's voice follows closely behind.

At the table, a large pile of purple glitter spills from its jar and onto the paper in front of Lily. Tiny shimmering bits are scattered across the table and on her fingertips. If I had to guess, it's also in her lap and on the floor.

Eyes the size of dinner plates and mouth agape, she meets Maggie's gaze, then mine. "It was an accident."

When my eyes flit back to Maggie, her hand is clasped over her mouth. Cheeks reddening, moisture coats her lash line. Her shoulders shake with— Is she... *laughing*?

"What's so funny?" I ask, head swinging between the two of them.

Maggie presses a hand to my chest, and I step back. She's still laughing as she grabs the trash can from the cabinet under the sink and heads to the table. "Didn't you notice how there wasn't any glitter in the house before you bought her some?"

I shrug, using some of the paper to scoop the glitter into the trash. "Glitter is fun. Kids love glitter."

"Yes." Maggie points a finger at me as she stifles another laugh. "But it gets everywhere, and it's impossible to get rid of. I bet we'll be finding purple glitter for the next decade."

"I didn't mean to. I promise." Lily sticks out her bottom lip in a pout.

"We know, Lily bug. But how about we save the glitter for supervised art time." Maggie's gaze falls to her hand, and she winces. Purple sparkles coat her palm. "Why don't you say goodbye to Viktor and go wash up in the bathroom?"

She hops down from her chair. "Okay. Bye, Viktor!"

Little arms wrap around my waist, and I pat the back of her head. "Bye, little one."

Looking back at her mother, Lily whisper-shouts. "Tell him about our surprise for tomorrow." Then she's running down the hall to the bathroom.

Maggie laughs.

"Surprise?" My eyebrows rise.

With the glitter crisis mostly cleaned up, Maggie stacks the crayons and markers in their container and closes the lid. "Are you going to the city this weekend?"

"No," I answer, closing the coloring book and setting it in the bin of craft supplies. With each passing day, the city feels less and less like home. Even the prospect of one of Phil's famous cinnamon rolls at brunch with Ness isn't enough to entice me anymore.

"Good. Meet us here at ten tomorrow morning." She gathers the bin in her arms and steps into my space. Her eyes turn heated, lids dropping to rake over my chest and down to my crotch. My cock twitches under her blatant eye-fucking. Yeah, I *definitely* like this side of Maggie. "And as much as this vest and pocket watch combo makes my panties wet, you're gonna want to wear some jeans, city boy." She winks before smacking a kiss on my cheek. "Have a good tutoring session."

Maggie giggles, and when I try to hook an arm around her waist, she sidesteps me on her way into the family room. "Tease."

"Night, Viktor."

Slipping my watch from my pocket—the very one that makes my country girl *wet*—I find it's time for me to leave for the short drive to Maple Ridge Hollow. Me and my big heart. *Fuck*. No more stolen kisses, heated glances, or chaste touches... until tomorrow.

"**A**nyone home?" I call out when I slip through the sliding glass door into Maggie's house. I woke up early today, body riddled with excitement.

I spent the morning working on my plan to help Maggie with her debt. As much as I want to tell her about it, it's too soon. Everything has to be perfect first.

Unfortunately, I was interrupted by a call from my father. His reminder about the upcoming gala looms over my head. "Bring a date... an appropriate date," he commanded in that authoritative tone he's used all my life. An appropriate date, AKA a vampire female fit to his impossible standards.

I doubt one exists unless she's of his choosing. Rolling my eyes, I banish all thoughts of my father from my mind and focus on what's in store for today.

Breakfast plates, coloring books, and an array of crayons are scattered across the kitchen table. The sight has my lips curling into a dopey smile.

My instincts kick in, and I reach for the plastic plate in Lily's usual spot, a half-eaten pancake coated in an obscene amount of syrup sticking to the pink surface. Out of nowhere, Maggie slips between me and the table.

Not sure how she got the drop on me. My vampire abilities must be clouded by my daydreams of spending every morning at this table with my girls.

My girls.

"Nope." She smacks my hand away. "No cleaning this morning. It's my turn."

Lily is nowhere to be found, so I take the opportunity to quench my thirst for this radiant woman. Leaning into her space, she gasps when her ass collides with the table.

My hands skim up the rough denim of her jeans. Like always, they're so tight they must be painted on, showing off her amazing ass and thick thighs. Maggie's paired the dark denim with a sleeveless red flannel that's tied at the small of her waist. "Morning, country girl," I purr, lips hovering over hers.

Her pupils dilate, and her gaze stays locked on my mouth when she mumbles, "Morning, city boy."

"I'm gonna kiss you now."

She nods, but I need those gorgeous green eyes on me when I take her sweet lips. Sliding my hand up the side of her neck, I use my thumb to tip her chin up until our gazes collide. Her breaths come faster, puffing little bursts of hot air against my lips when I close the distance between us.

At the first taste, I groan, and my fingers tighten around her throat. Her pulse thunders under the skin, urging me on. My free hand finds its home on the small of her back, pressing her closer to me as I ravage her mouth.

"I've missed your lips, Maggie. I need a whole lot more of this." We said no feelings, but the lines are becoming increasingly blurred with each and every day. And I'm past the point of caring.

She's awoken a hunger within me that I've never experienced before. My fangs ache when I'm around her. All my life, Father always made his opinion clear; Ness and I would settle down with vampire mates when the time came, but that's not how I see the trajectory of my life.

I just want to love someone who will love me back. Wholly. Unconditionally. Someone I can be myself around and not feel judged. Someone who laughs at my stupid jokes. Someone who makes my heart flutter. And it's become painfully obvious that *someone* is Maggie Wilcox.

"Momma!"

Lily's voice is like a bucket of ice water, and I rip my lips away from Maggie's in a blur. My ears perk up to the pitter-patter of little feet above us.

"Momma! Where's my butterfly net?!"

Maggie sighs, wiping the corner of my mouth with her thumb.

I take a step back and give her some space. In my pants, my erection presses painfully against the front of my jeans. *Yes*, I wore jeans like Maggie instructed.

Her eyes drift down to my crotch as I adjust myself.

"See something you like?" I can't help the crooked smirk that stretches across my face when her cheeks flush a delightful pink.

If there wasn't a child upstairs, I'd have my country girl bent over the table. Taking my cock like a good girl and screaming my name like a good whore.

But... *priorities*.

"You know I do. And I'll be seeing a lot more of it... later." She winks before leaving me—and my raging boner—to help Lily.

And even though she told me not to, I spend the next few minutes tidying up the kitchen table and washing the dishes. On the counter, there's a large wicker picnic basket with a patchwork quilt draped over the top.

As much as I want to peek inside, I resist the urge to ruin whatever surprise they have planned.

"Okay, crisis averted," Maggie says when she re-enters the kitchen a few minutes later. Lily bounces behind her with a wide grin on her face and a giant butterfly net in her hands... happy as a clam. "We thought we'd show you one of our secret spots since the weather is still warm. Ready?"

"Lead the way." Like a gentleman, I hook my arm through the handle of the picnic basket and sweep my free hand toward the garage door.

Parking the four-wheeler next to Maggie's, I switch it off and remove my helmet. For my first time driving the beastly machine, I'd say I didn't do too bad. No broken bones or bruises, and I didn't even hit anything.

I tug on my hat as my eyes eat up the secret oasis spread before me. Hidden away near the back of the orchard, the trees give way to a small pond. The water is a brilliant turquoise, sparkling under the late-morning sunshine.

Vibrant green lily pads float in a gentle motion along the top of the water. Cattails protrude from the surface, creating the perfect habitat for croaking frogs and buzzing dragonflies.

Surrounded by the birds singing in the trees, it's... *magical*.

Adjusting my hat, I let it shield my sensitive skin from the warmth of the sun. "This is beautiful."

After taking off Lily's helmet, Maggie grabs the blanket from the back of their four-wheeler and spreads it out near the base of a giant oak tree. The branches and bark are withered and worn by age, like it's lived a thousand lives. "This was Roman's favorite place." She rests a hand against the trunk of the tree.

"We used to bring Lily here as a baby." When her gaze meets mine, her eyes swim with tears.

My long legs eat up the distance between us, and I wrap her in my arms. "I'm so sorry, Maggie."

She tips her head up and wraps her arms around my waist, returning the embrace. Deep in her eyes, an emotion that matches the one I've been hiding for weeks now shimmers back at me... *Love.* "I'm okay. I promise. But I wanted to share this place with you, well, because you're special to us. To Lily... and me."

My hand cups her cheek, and she nuzzles into my palm before placing a soft kiss on my palm. "I feel the same way, Maggie. I—"

"Look! A frog! Momma, can I catch it?" The queen of inconvenient timing strikes again. Lily splashes near the edge of the pond, and a frog hops along the sand near her feet.

"Thwarted again, city boy." Maggie pats my chest. "Can you finish setting up the picnic while I help Lily catch her frog prince?"

"Sure thing, country girl." I wink just so I can bear witness to her flushing cheeks again.

Smiling and shaking her head, Maggie bends to where the picnic basket rests on the ground. She grabs a glass jar from inside before jogging to her daughter.

While I work to spread out the food on one corner of the blanket, the girls' laughter keeps me company. I can't help but smile, knowing Maggie wanted to share something with me that once belonged to her and Roman. It makes me think, just maybe, her heart is healing enough to let me in.

I don't want to replace Roman. A first love is something sacred, and it's not my intention to erase his memory. I simply hope to add more happy memories to the next chapter of Maggie's story while honoring Roman's memory.

When I stand, my eyes catch on something carved on the side of the tree, in the same spot Maggie touched earlier.

R + M
4ever

Roman and Maggie? It's the only logical explanation. My throat thickens when I lay my hand over the carving, the weathered bark rough against my hand. Closing my eyes, I lean my forehead against the tree and breathe deep. "Thank you for loving her, Roman." A squeal, followed by a burst of giggles, has my eyes snapping open and head swinging toward the pond.

Barefoot, with her jeans rolled to her knees, Maggie splashes in the shallow water with her daughter.

"I caught one!" Lily squeals, hands cupped around what I can only assume is a wriggling frog.

Sea-glass eyes lift from the water to meet mine, and I can't help but smile at the joy radiating from Maggie's brilliant gaze.

Yeah, this is where I'm meant to be from now on. Tapping my hand over the carving once more, I whisper, "I'll take it from here. I'll protect them both for the rest of my life."

CHAPTER 20

Maggie

"She's out cold. After all that fresh air today, I'm sure we won't hear a peep until morning," I say when I get to the bottom of the stairs. The sight before me has my pussy fluttering and my mouth watering.

There's a literal god on my couch. One arm resting on the back, Viktor's tall frame takes up almost half the couch. His thick thighs strain in his dark jeans, legs spread in that sexy way men do.

His shirt sleeves are rolled up to expose the tantalizing veins running under his pale skin. The top few buttons of his shirt are undone, and his hair is a bit messy from wearing a hat all day, making him even more appetizing to my suddenly starving pussy.

On the floor near his feet, there are two baskets of laundry. Folded to perfection, I'm sure. Because everything this vampire does is nothing short of perfection.

Once I'm within reach, Viktor wraps his big hands around my waist and guides me to straddle his lap. This has become our routine over the past week. After Lily goes to bed and on nights he doesn't volunteer, we make out on the couch like teenagers until, somehow, he ends up with his mouth between my thighs and I'm screaming his name.

It's a good thing my daughter would sleep through a zombie apocalypse. The last thing I need is her wandering downstairs while Viktor's making me come. Talk about an awkward conversation I'm most definitely not ready for.

We haven't taken things further since that first time. It's like he's focused solely on my pleasure, which I appreciate. But I want *more*. I want to touch him again. I want to taste him. I want him inside me again.

Today, I shared a piece of my past with him, and I'm hoping it only strengthened this bond growing between us. Because whoever decided we were keeping our feelings out of this situation was a damn liar. My heart is invested now, even if I haven't admitted it to anyone out loud. So I'm pushing us off the cliff tonight and taking the next step.

"I had fun today," he says, his soothing voice bringing me back to the present. "I may have let all the frogs go while you were putting Lily to bed." One hand goes from my hip to the back of his neck, and his cheeks turn an endearing shade of pink.

I giggle. "Thank you. She'd keep every creepy crawly or slimy amphibian if I let her. And thank you for folding the laundry." I tip my chin to the baskets on the floor.

Viktor's flush deepens. *Cute.* "I don't mind. Plus, I'm faster, so it only makes sense."

"You know..." Skimming my hands up his broad chest and around his neck, I thread my fingers into the silken strands of his hair. I tip his chin up until our eyes lock. "All the little things you've been doing around here." I place a kiss on his lips, pulling back before things get too heated. "The laundry." Another kiss. "Cooking." And another. "It hasn't gone unnoticed."

My lips land on his jaw, and he groans. His fingers tighten on my hips, and he bucks his crotch up to meet my core.

"I appreciate everything you've done for us since you got here." Continuing down his throat, my lips make a heated trail while my fingers work to unbutton his shirt.

"Don't stop, Maggie." His broken moan of pleasure fuels me to keep going.

Sucking the spot where his neck and shoulder meet, I peel his shirt open. As I sit back, I admire his chest and abs. *He's so beautiful.*

I run my fingers down the ladder of muscle while slipping to my knees between his spread legs. The plush rug is like a cloud against the warm skin of my legs. Working farther south, my lips and tongue slide against the ridges of his abs. From beneath my lashes, I peer up to find his big body shuddering when I unbuckle his belt and lower the zipper on his pants.

"That feels so good, sweetheart." Viktor weaves his fingers through my curls when I continue to lick and suck my way down until I reach the top of his pants.

Leaving bruises behind, possessiveness flares in my chest as I mark him as mine.

"Maggie." My name is a prayer on his lips. "You don't have to."

Resting back on my heels, I let my best sultry smile spread across my lips. "Sometimes you don't know when to shut up, Viktor. I want this. I want to be on my knees for you. I want my hand wrapped around your thick cock. And I want to feel each piercing scrape against my teeth as I taste you."

"Holy shit." His eyes burn with a raging inferno as he stares down at me, my hands resting on his thighs.

I may be the one on my knees right now, but it's clear I'm the one with all the power as I reach into his pants and work Viktor's pierced cock free.

It's bigger than I remember, the piercings cool against my fingers as I give him a testing stroke. His thigh muscles tense, his hips buck, and a bead of pre-cum oozes from the tip. It drips down to coat the red hoop bisecting the head of his cock.

Not wasting a second, I lean down and catch the runaway drop before it goes to waste. Salty and warm, his flavor bursts against my tongue, awakening a craving for more.

More of him.

All of him.

Starting at the base, my tongue runs up the ladder piercing the underside of his cock. His groans continue, urging me on and telling me he likes what I'm doing. That he likes my mouth on him.

Courage builds in my chest, heart thumping like a herd of wild mustangs, and I swirl my tongue around the head of his cock before slipping him between my lips.

I give a light suck, and Viktor mumbles a curse when the first piercing in the ladder clicks against my teeth.

"That's it, Maggie. Suck me like a good girl."

His words spur me on, and I work my mouth up and down his shaft until the first three piercings are slick with my saliva.

Viktor's fingers thread into my hair, gripping near the scalp. He stops me, growling, "Sweetheart, I need your eyes on me while you suck me dry like a good little whore."

I moan around his length, but my eyes flick up at his dirty mouth.

This stunning vampire is the picture of pleasure when I peer up at him through my lashes. Head tipped back, the corded muscles of his neck constrict when he grits his teeth. With one long, lithe arm spread across the back of the couch, his knuckles are white where he has the cushions in a death grip. His broad chest heaves as I lick and suck him, but he lets me have control, and I take another piercing into my mouth. Four in total now. Only one left.

"That's it, Maggie. Take every inch."

On the floor, I squirm, wedging one heel against my clit and grinding down. The rough denim presses just right against the sensitive spot, and lightning zips up my spine with every rock of my hips. Fuck, that feels good.

The salty flavor of his pre-cum only has me doubling down. I need him to come. To fill my mouth with all of him. Adding my hands to the mix, one strokes the bottom of his shaft, the part I can't quite fit in my mouth. With the other, I tug at his balls, rolling and kneading until Viktor's chest vibrates with another rumbling growl and his hips thrust up to meet my mouth.

The ring in the tip of his cock hits the back of my throat, and I gag, spit dribbling down the sides of his length.

It's messing and raw—and so fucking hot. Like nothing I've ever experienced before.

"Sweetheart, *fuck*, keep that up, and I'm gonna come."

Pulling back, his dick slips from my mouth with a pop, but my hands continue to twist and stroke his glistening shaft. I smirk, fluttering my tear-stained lashes. "That's kind of the idea, city boy."

His lips pull into a grin that rivals mine, fangs on full display. "You have a little bit of brat in you, don't you?"

As my fingers tighten around his balls, he groans. "Is that a problem?"

"No." The word is choked, almost a cough. "I like my whore to have a little fire in her." Like the fire he speaks of, his eyes flare, the red brighter than I've ever seen. "Now, be a good *whore* and swallow my cum. Every drop, Maggie. Show me you can handle it."

The fingers in my hair flex, leading my mouth back to his cock. Taking as much as I can into my mouth, I swallow around his length before pulling back.

"That's it, country girl. You're doing so good."

His mix of degrading words and praise has me working harder, faster. One final suck and one final squeeze, the first spurts of hot cum fill my mouth. Choking a bit, I swallow down as much as I can, but some sneaks out the sides of my mouth and dribbles down my chin.

Viktor moans, and it's the sexiest sound I think I've ever had the pleasure of witnessing. Once his fingers relax in my hair, and I've swallowed as much as I can, I pull off his softening cock.

Faster than I can blink, he has me hauled into his lap again and his mouth is on mine. His tongue plows into my mouth, swiping against mine. *I'm so turned on right now, fuck.* I grind down on his lap and sigh into the kiss.

"I need to taste you, Maggie," Viktor mumbles against my lips, not bothering to break our kiss.

"Do it. Please," I whine and roll my hips against his lower abs. My panties are so wet, I wouldn't be surprised if my arousal has soaked through my jeans.

Laying me down on the couch, Viktor makes quick work of removing his clothes and mine. As much as I want to cover my body and hide the imperfections from him, the unfettered desire in his eyes has me thinking otherwise. Instead, I arch my back and spread my legs to accommodate the wide berth of his shoulders as he settles his face over my pussy. My inner walls pulse with anticipation.

Licking my inner thigh, Viktor trails his tongue closer and closer to where I ache. Where I need to be filled. "Tease," I moan, wiggling my hips and cupping my breasts.

"Takes one to know one, Maggie." He winks before diving headfirst into my pussy, lapping at the sensitive flesh.

I squeal and pinch my thighs around his head.

One hand clamps around each thigh, holding them hostage and spreading me open. "I thought you wanted me to taste you," he goads, words muffled by my flesh.

Huffing a breath, I grip some of his platinum hair and tug his mouth from me. Meeting his smoldering gaze, I clarify. "I meant bite me, Viktor. Feed from me. D-Don't you think it's time?"

The heat cools in his gaze, replaced by sincerity. "You're sure?"

Swallowing, I nod. "Yeah. I'm sure."

Viktor's mouth drops open on what can only be described as a snarl. His fangs lengthen, doubling in size. Moving back to the junction of my thigh, he swipes his tongue along the flesh. Fingers brush my pussy lips before thrusting inside. They curl against that perfect spot right as Viktor rears forward and sinks his fangs into me.

Burning pain rushes through my veins, and my mouth falls open on a silent scream. This is not what I imagined—but before I can shove Viktor off me, the pain turns to a burst of euphoria.

Holy shit! On impulse, my back arches off the couch, and my pussy clamps down on his fingers. The instant orgasm radiates from where Viktor's fangs are sunk into my skin to the tips of my fingers and toes.

It's more powerful than any orgasm I've ever experienced. And it's fucking amazing!

The first pull of his lips against my skin has aftershocks of a smaller release shooting through my body.

After one more swallow, Viktor retracts his fangs from my skin. He swipes his tongue over the spot before placing a kiss there.

From head to toe, my body buzzes with pleasure when he prowls over me, settling his hips into the cradle of mine. He's hard again, because... of course he is.

"You okay?" The longer fangs peek out from under his top lip, creating divots in his bottom lip. Sharp nails brush some stray hairs off my face. And, for the first time, I notice his eyes are lit up in the dim light of the living room.

"I'm more than okay. Are you? Your eyes are... glowing. And your fangs are bigger. And—" I pull the hand from my hair and run a finger over the long, black claws that have replaced his nails. "You have claws."

Springing up, Viktor's head snaps to the mirror mounted on the wall above the couch. "Holy—" The rest of his words fall away as he pulls at the skin under his eyes and prods at his fangs. "This has never happened before." He swings his head back to me.

"What does it mean?"

Chapter 21

Viktor

"What does it mean?" Maggie's soft voice is nearly drowned out by the pounding in my ears.

The creature staring back at me in the mirror only confirms what I already knew. *She's my mate.*

According to everything I was told as a child, vampires only transform into their true form after feeding on their mate.

But we said no feelings.

I can't very well tell her the truth right now. Not when we've barely gotten started.

No.

I'll keep it to myself for now and give her time to adjust to the idea of us being more.

"I'm not sure. It's been so long since I fed on a human." I shrug, sitting down on the couch. "But you're okay? I didn't hurt you?" Pulling her onto my lap, I position Maggie so she's straddling me and run a thumb over the two puncture marks on her inner thigh.

"You didn't hurt me," she confirms, head tipped down and eyes locked on my finger. "Why isn't it bleeding?"

"My saliva stops the blood flow and heals the wound when I'm done feeding."

She smiles. "That's a pretty neat party trick."

You have no idea.

"Are you ready for more?" I ask, gripping her hips and grinding her down onto my hard cock.

She answers my question with one of her own. "Will you make me come like that again? W-While biting me?" Eyes flicking down, her cheeks darken.

My country girl is still a little shy.

I can't help but chuckle when her gaze meets mine again, and there's a sparkle of hope shining back at me. My fingers sweep up the soft skin of her cheekbone, tucking a strand of golden hair behind her ear, before they coast down to grip her chin. "Is that what you want, my beautiful whore?"

Her head bobbles in my grip, and she wiggles her hips with enthusiasm. "Yes. I've never come that hard in my life."

"A vampire's bite is one of the greatest aphrodisiacs in the world. If you're not careful, you might get addicted." *I hope you'll get addicted.*

"Sounds pretty good to me," she purrs before sitting back and gripping my cock. The red tip drips with pre-cum, and I can't wait to fill her cunt with my seed.

Last time, I pulled out to mark her flawless skin, but now, I need to claim her womb, too. She'll be mine in every way.

"Do you remember our first time?" I ask, stroking her cheek.

"How could I forget?" Her teeth sink into her bottom lip.

I run my tongue over the tip of my new, larger fangs and taste the last remnants of her blood. Coppery, with a hint of sweetness. "I promised you something dark and depraved. Is that still what you want?"

"Yes." Her consent is a whisper. A prayer. *A promise.*

And along with her blood still on my tongue, it unleashes the monster within me.

"Hands behind your back, sweetheart." My voice dips to a feral growl, my restraint slipping.

First one, then the other, Maggie obeys like a good girl and places her hands on the small of her back, wrists crossed.

Wrapping my fingers around her wrists, I restrain her. "That's my good whore."

Her head tips to the side and she whimpers as her eyes fall shut.

Using my free hand, I gather the soft flesh of her breast and feed it into my mouth. Sucking a bruising mark on her tit before I pull back, my fangs scrape against her skin, and she shudders. Moving to her nipple, I pinch the sensitive peak between my teeth and give a gentle tug.

"Fuck," my country girl hisses. Hips rocking faster, she slides her dripping pussy along my cock, not yet breaching her. "Do that again."

"Ask nicely."

She groans, voice laced with irritation. "Tease."

"Brat."

"Please," she pants, rising onto her knees to try to get my cock inside her. But I'm not ready for that yet.

"Good girl." Switching to the other breast, I suckle her flesh before giving her nipple a sharp tug.

Her back arches, and she cries out. "I'm gonna come."

She's right where I want her. And at her admission, I take my hand from her breast, using it to line my cock up with her entrance. With the grip on her wrists, I slam her down on my shaft at the same time my fangs sink into her breast.

Maggie's spine bows. "Viktor!" Head tipped to the ceiling, she screams my name at the same time her inner walls strangle my cock.

Somehow, I resist the overwhelming urge to coat Maggie's womb with every drop of cum I have to offer.

Her body collapses against my chest, and I tuck her head into the side of my neck. Soft blonde curls tickle my nose when I bury it in her hair and breathe in her familiar scent, only it's tinged with a hint of sweat this time, somehow making her smell even better. "That was only number two, country girl. You've got at least one more in you. I know it."

She whimpers, but nods against my throat.

I let go of her wrists. "Put your hands on my shoulders and hang on tight. Dig those pretty nails into my skin and make me bleed, sweetheart."

Obeying, Maggie sits up, eyes glazed and a little unfocused. But she does as instructed, wrapping her fingers around the thick muscles on my shoulders.

I groan at the slight prick of her nails. The pain zips to my balls, and my cock leaks inside her. "Good girl. Are you ready for me to fuck you like my whore?"

A shiver rolls down her spine, but she moans and digs her nails farther into my skin.

Letting the monster take over, my vision flickers red at the edges when I hook my hands under the backs of her knees, effectively making her legs useless. Then, I unleash all the pent-up sexual frustration from the past week, and I pound into her sweet pussy, impaling her on my pierced cock over and over again. "Your cunt is so fucking tight."

Breasts bouncing, blood trickles from my earlier bite, and the crimson liquid calls to me like a siren to a wayward sailor. Leaning down, I lap at the wound, savoring the coppery tang as it coats my tongue.

My fangs ache.

My cock weeps.

And Maggie lets me use her body like the perfect whore.

Moans spill from her mouth in a broken staccato. It's the most beautiful symphony I've ever heard.

Consumed by pleasure and the need to make her come, I sink my fangs into her skin again and let her sweet nectar fill my mouth with every swallow.

We shatter in unison, her cunt seizing and triggering my release. It's spectacular. Everything I've ever dreamed of, and it only solidifies what I already suspected—Maggie Wilcox is the love of my life and my mate... and I'm never letting her go.

"Well, that was—"

"Fucking spectacular," I rasp breathlessly.

Maggie giggles. Peering up at me, her eyes sparkle, a direct reflection of all the emotions rushing through my veins. But when her eyes drop to my chest, the corners of her mouth turn down and a deep furrow forms between her eyebrows. "I got blood all over you." She swipes a finger through the crimson staining my skin and lifts it between us.

I grip her slender wrist, and my nostrils flare, filling with her addictively sweet aroma. "Trust me, Maggie, I don't mind a little blood." Entranced, my eyes lock on a small red drop as it rolls down the side of her finger. When my tongue darts out, I moan.

Salty and sweet, her essence fills my tastebuds. The exquisite flavor gets better each time I taste her.

A small gasp hits my ears when I suck Maggie's finger into my mouth, tongue lapping at her skin and not missing a single drop of blood.

My eyes flick to hers, finding heat in them. Her chest rises and falls in quick succession. She pulls her finger from my mouth with a pop, swipes it through the mess on her chest this time, before raising it to my lips once more.

How did I find such a perfect woman? A perfect *mate*.

Proving my point, Maggie's fingers twine into my hair. Her grip tightens, and she leads my mouth back to the oozing wound on her breast.

Fuck. I was so caught up in everything—in us—earlier that I forgot to seal the bite.

I swipe my tongue across the sticky, blood-smeared skin, cleaning up my mess and healing her at the same time. A moan rumbles out of my chest as I swallow down the last mouthful of her. Tipping my chin up, I meet her gaze and admit the thought flowing through my head. "I'm already addicted to you."

Somehow, the red flush to Maggie's skin deepens further, glistening with a fine layer of sweat. Unruly golden curls tumble over her shoulders and back. She gives me a shy smile, but there's a mischievous spark in her eyes.

She's beautiful.

"I'm gonna go clean up," Maggie says, breaking the moment between us. She winces when she slides off my lap and cum trickles down her leg. "I'll be right back. Don't go anywhere."

While I wait for her, I do a quick cleanup of my own in the kitchen. Picking our clothes up off the living room floor, I fold them into a neat stack on the side table before finding a blanket and laying back on the couch.

When Maggie comes back into the room, in all her naked glory, my cock twitches. *You were literally just inside her. Cool it.*

None the wiser to my internal battle with my dick, Maggie wiggles her body between the back of the couch and mine. Lifting the blanket, I make room for her.

Her head rests on my chest, and my arm bands around her shoulder, fingers burying themselves in the back of her curls.

The quiet stretches between us, but it's not awkward or uncomfortable.

"This is more now, isn't it?" Maggie breaks the silence.

I hum, stroking her back. "What do you mean?"

She props onto her elbow so we're face-to-face. "Us. What we're doing. We said no feelings, but it sure feels a hell of a lot like there are feelings involved."

"Country girl," I rasp. "My feelings have always been involved. I've wanted you since the first moment I laid eyes on you." I smirk when she sits up, her perfect tits on full display. Seems like not long ago, she would have hidden her body from me, but not now.

Eyes dropping to her beaded nipples, I lick my lips.

Maggie hooks a finger under my chin, directing my gaze away from her chest and up to her eyes. *No fun.* "So you lied to me?"

"If I could only have you for one night, then I damn sure wasn't missing that opportunity. You're a fucking catch, Maggie Wilcox." I shrug, not ashamed of my selfishness. I'm speaking the truth. "Are you mad?"

"I should be, but... no, I'm not. Viktor, you healed a part of me that was broken. You showed me that I'm capable of experiencing pleasure again, capable of being a sexual creature again. But—" Her eyes flash with doubt before dropping to my chest, and her shoulders curl.

Cupping her face, I guide her eyes back to mine. "What is it?"

Voice small, she asks, "What happens now?"

"Whatever you want, Maggie. You're always in control here."

Lying down again, she snuggles back under my arm with her head on my chest. I hope she doesn't notice how fast my heart is beating. "Can we go slow?"

"As slow as you want, sweetheart. Always."

"I'm not ready to tell Lily yet, either. She's had a lot of adjustments recently, so I want to make sure this is permanent before we tell her."

Do her words hurt a little? *Sure.* But I'm determined to prove just how serious and permanent this is. "Of course, Maggie. I want what's best for Lily, too." Like magnets, my fingers make their way back into her curls. The claws seem to have retracted now that my appetite for blood is satiated.

The claws... the eyes... Will that happen every time I feed on her? Only time will tell.

"I do need a date for my father's annual charity event. Would you like to accompany me?"

"Hmm. Will there be food?" She yawns before snuggling deeper into my side.

I chuckle. "Yes. And drinks. And dancing. We could stay the night in my apartment in the city."

"I'd love to go." Her head pops up, eyebrows knitting together. "But I don't have anything fancy to wear!"

Sweeping a finger over her freckled cheek, I smile. "Don't worry, country girl. Just call me your fairy godmother, because I'll take care of everything."

There's a pep in my step as I walk back to the guest house. Opting to not use my enhanced speed, I tuck my hands in my pockets and whistle. The gravel crunches under my shoes and the soft breeze ruffles my hair.

Energized by excitement, my body hums. Excitement about the charity gala this weekend. Excitement about Maggie meeting Mother and Ness.

Fuck Father.

I don't give a flying fuck what he thinks anymore.

Most importantly, excitement about the future and finally being out from under his suffocating grip.

When I get inside, I slip off my shoes and collapse into the chair next to the fireplace. I still didn't tell Maggie she's my mate, but she said she wants to go slow. So I didn't want to ambush her with a lifetime commitment or anything.

Huffing a sigh, I pull my phone from my pants pocket and dial the one person who I always talk through tough situations with.

"Hello, dear brother. To what do I owe the late-night phone call?" Her tranquil voice is like a balm on my stuttering heart.

"Ness, I need your help." I rub the bridge of my nose before tipping my head back and staring at the ceiling.

She hums. "Ah, so you've finally realized who the smart twin is." I can hear the smugness in her tone.

I growl. "I'm serious, Vanessa."

"Hi, Serious. I'm Vanessa, it's nice to meet you." She giggles, then snorts. Glad I'm amusing her.

"Ugh, *Ness*. Maybe I should have called someone else."

She laughs. "You're too easy, Viki. What can I help you with?"

"It finally happened, Ness. I fed on her."

"Please, keep the details to yourself."

I roll my eyes. "Ugh, Ness. Real mature—"

"Never claimed to be," she sing-songs.

"*Focus*. I fed on Maggie, and it happened... the claws, the longer fangs, the glowing eyes. All of it."

She's quiet for a beat, and I almost ramble more, but she finally says, "So she's a compatible mate." Vampires can have several mates over their lifetime, but based on my body's reaction earlier, Maggie is one of mine. The only one.

"Yes."

"Did you tell her?"

Running a hand over my hair, I shake my head. "No. We're taking things slow. But I'm bringing her to the charity gala. That's why I need your help, Ness. Can you send some dresses from the city?"

She squeals, and I rip the phone from my head before she shatters my damn eardrum. "Yesss! I'll take care of everything, Viki. Dresses, shoes, bags, jewelry. Oh, this is so exciting! It'll be like the times we used to wear Mom's dresses and shoes when we were little."

"Yeah, until Father found us and made sure to burn it into my brain that real men don't play dress up."

Vanessa's sigh echoes down the line. "Speaking of Dad. How do you think he'll react to you bringing Maggie to the gala? She's human, Viktor. You know he's going to lose his shit."

Somehow, I swallow down the unhinged, possessive growl that threatens to break free from my chest. "I'll protect her. I won't let her out of my sight all night." *I hope.* "He won't have a chance to ambush her or be his dickish self."

"I'll help run interference, but you should probably warn her ahead of time."

I pick at the worn arm of the chair, hating that my father is such a colossal asshole. "I will." Suddenly, the rush of adrenaline I had after leaving Maggie crashes, and I stifle a yawn. "Thanks for your help, Ness. I'll see you Saturday. Love you."

"I can't wait to see Maggie again! She's a gem, Viki. Hold on to her tight."

A smile curves my lips, and I relax against the soft cushion of the chair. "I plan to."

CHAPTER 22

Viktor

My fingers brush over the silken fabric of my bowtie, adjusting it for the millionth time in the last few minutes. Nervous energy hums in my veins as I wait for my country girl to come downstairs.

Tonight is my father's charity gala.

Equal parts dread and anticipation filled my body for the past week... a week that passed in a blur as my relationship with Maggie grew stronger with each passing day.

We're still careful to keep things platonic in front of Lily, but I no longer retreat to the guest house after dinner. Instead, I help with everything from her bath routine to bedtime.

And once Lily is sound asleep upstairs, Maggie and I curl up on the couch, recounting the ups and downs of the day. At some point, my cock usually ends up down her throat or pounding her pussy until she's begging for my fangs in her sweet flesh.

I haven't had to rely on synthetic blood powder since the first night she asked me to feed on her.

Everything is perfect. I'm finally living my dream, and it's pure, domestic bliss.

Except, my father's ultimatum still looms over me. I have to tell him that I'm not cowering to his orders this time. And I have to tell him *tonight*, so my future with Maggie can finally flourish.

"Is this the part where I threaten to kill you if you break her heart?" Cyrus rumbles, coming to stand near the bottom of the stairs with me. He and his mate, Antoinette, are here to watch Lily while Maggie and I attend the gala and stay the night in my apartment in the city.

"Afraid that ship has already sailed. Jean-Luc beat you to it." I tuck my hands into the pockets of my tux pants and rock onto my toes.

His chuckle takes me off guard. Cyrus is a few inches shorter than me, but he's twice as broad and stacked with thick, bulky muscles. Intimidating, to say the least. But he smiles and extends a hand to me.

When I grip his hand, he tightens his hold and pulls me close, until our chests nearly brush. His voice drops to a low, threatening tone, and his eyes bore into mine. "Just know, I'd help him bury the body in a heartbeat."

I gulp, but he releases my hand. Stepping back, he slaps me on the back. *Hard*. And I splutter a cough. "I-I have no intention of hurting her. I—"

"You love her. Don't you?" His hard features soften, eyes landing on his mate, where she sits on the couch, reading a book to her niece.

In contrast, my face hardens, jaw pulsing in an expression I hope doesn't give away how deeply I love Maggie. "We're taking things slow."

Icy-blue eyes swing back to me. "Good. She's been through a lot. She deserves someone who will give her the world."

I nod. "Something we agree on."

"Momma looks like a princess." Lily's awe-filled voice has my head snapping to the top of the stairs.

She's... "Stunning," I murmur, trying to remember how to breathe as she descends one step at a time.

Her curvy body is poured into a slinky navy dress—one of the options Ness picked out for her.

Its neckline dips in the center of her chest, exposing a tantalizing sliver of cleavage.

The fabric clings to the dip of her waist and the flare of her hips, making my mouth water.

With each step down the stairs, I get a flash of her sleek, sun-kissed leg through the slit in the dress. On her feet are a pair of shimmering gold heels. They sparkle like the sun that's currently dipping below the horizon, casting her in its final rays.

"Do I look okay?" Maggie asks once she's in front of me. There's a slight tremor to her voice, like she's unsure. Like she doesn't realize she's the most beautiful woman to ever exist. To ever pull me into her orbit.

Reaching up, I tuck a stray coil of hair behind her ear, careful not to disrupt the rest of her curls, where they've been artfully pinned into an extravagant updo.

More glittering gold adorns her ears from her dangling earrings, like a spray of shooting stars. "You are perfect, Maggie. In every way. You'll be a goddess among mere mortals tonight."

Crimson darkens the flesh of her cheeks, and her chin and eyes drop to the floor.

"None of that, country girl." Cupping the side of her neck, I use my thumb to tip her chin up. "You are absolutely radiant and should never be ashamed."

This time, her eyes stay locked on mine, and her lips tip into a playful smirk. "You don't look so bad yourself, city boy. Give me a spin." She twirls her finger in the air. "I need the full effect."

Humoring her—because, of course, I want my mate to be just as infatuated with me as I am with her—I puff out my chest, adjust my tux jacket and spin in a slow circle. Really letting Maggie eye-fuck me as much as she desires.

Once I'm facing her again, her eyes flare with lust, and she has her bottom lip trapped between her teeth. Our bodies brush when she steps into my space and slides her hands up my chest.

I shiver when she runs her nose up the side of my neck, and her lips tickle my ear.

"I can't wait to peel this off you later, city boy." Her throaty whisper has me biting back a groan, my hands squeezing her hips.

Before I can steal a taste of her lips, there's a tug at the fabric under my hands. "Momma! Are you a princess?"

Maggie pats my chest, breaking our flirtatious moment. She squats down so she's eye level with her daughter. "For tonight, I think I am." Her green eyes flick to mine, shining with adoration before her gaze returns to Lily. "We'll be back in the morning. Be good for Cy and Annie. Okay?"

Lily nods, then wraps her arms around Maggie's neck in a big hug. "I will. I love you."

"I love you, too, bug."

The towering buildings of the city grow larger on the horizon as we approach downtown. Anxious energy has my hands running up the sides of the steering wheel before gripping it tight. The leather creaks beneath my fingers.

I haven't seen my father since I walked out of our last family lunch, and our last phone call didn't exactly go well.

Even the soft music filling the car does nothing for my nauseous stomach. Peering over at Maggie, I clear my throat, and her head tips my way. "Stay with me or Vanessa tonight. Father is *prickly*, and I don't want him cornering you alone."

Maggie's hand lands on my thigh, and she squeezes. Her touch is exactly what I needed, a soothing balm for the tension in my muscles. "I know. You told me. I promise I'll be a good girl." Her saucy wink has me chuckling before directing my attention back to the road.

I briefed her earlier this week about how Father may try to corner her and scare her off. He's said hurtful things to his own children in the past, so I can only imagine what he would say to Maggie, a stranger.

Of course, Maggie called him more colorful names than I've ever heard and turned up her nose. *I'm a big girl, Viktor. I can handle myself.* Her words echo in my head.

She's proven time and time again to be able to take care of herself, but she's never met an adversary quite as cunning and ruthless as Kasmir Bielski.

"You're nervous," Maggie states, fingers stroking my thigh.

I manage to unwind my white-knuckled grip on the steering wheel and, instead, thread my fingers through hers. "Yeah."

"Why? If you're anything like me, your brain has come up with all sorts of impossible scenarios about tonight. So tell me, what's the worst that could happen?"

I sigh. "He could insult you to the point you run away crying, and I'd be forced to kill him."

A chorus of angels surrounds me as Maggie laughs. I can't help but smile at the beautiful sound.

"One." She holds up her free hand with her index-finger extended. "I won't waste my tears on a man who can't support his children. And two." Another finger extends. "I own about ten acres and a few shovels. It wouldn't be too hard to make him disappear."

"You're diabolical, Maggie Wilcox."

She squeezes my hand and gives me another wink. "Only for you, city boy. How about I distract you? Ask me anything."

"Do you want more kids?" The question pops out before I can stop it, and I wince.

Maggie's silent for a beat. When I glance over at her, the city streetlights cast her down-turned mouth in a soft glow. She clears her throat, speaking in a quiet voice. "I actually can't have any more. My pregnancy with Lily was... rough, to say the least. And the delivery was pretty traumatic, so I decided to have my tubes removed."

This time, I squeeze her hand, pulling it farther into my lap. "Oh."

"Does that bother you? That I can't give you a baby."

Thankfully, we've made it to the gala, so I pull into the parking garage and kill the engine. Giving Maggie my full attention, I cup her cheek. "Never, sweetheart. I'll take you—and Lily—any way that you'll have me."

She leans in, sealing her mouth to mine in a sweet kiss. "Thank you, Viktor. You truly are a blessing in our lives. Now... I believe you promised food and dancing. You ready to deliver?"

CHAPTER 23

Maggie

Viktor's hand is clasped tightly in mine when we enter the ballroom. True to his word, he hasn't left my side. I have to remind myself not to gawk at the extravagant decor or the artwork lining the walls. "So all this art is up for auction?" I ask as he leads me toward the dance floor.

"Yes. All the proceeds go to a charity started by my mother. It's a non-profit that helps house monster children who have been abandoned by their parents."

My thoughts land on Annie. When she told me the story of her upbringing, my heart broke, and I gained a whole new level of admiration for the dragon shifter. Her mother abandoned her when she was still a teen, so she was forced to navigate the world alone and live in hiding until she came to New York.

Viktor's arm tightens around my waist, pulling me against his body and closing any space between us. He moves us around the dance floor with ease, his steps perfectly in time with the soft classical music.

One song bleeds into the next, and I'm lost to the gentle sway of our bodies and the steady beat of Viktor's heart beneath my hand. "You've been quiet tonight. Are you not having fun?"

The evening has been a blur of scrumptious food, copious amounts of expensive champagne, and Viktor showing off his dance moves, which are impressive, to say the least.

Like Lily said, I do feel a little bit like a princess.

I smile up at him, stroking my fingers through the ends of his low ponytail. "I'm just taking it all in. If your father puts on this big event for charity every year, he can't be all bad, right?"

Lips pursing, Viktor hums. "Mother is the reason for this event and any philanthropic acts my father does." His eyes are fixed over my head, searching for something... or avoiding someone. "Their relationship has always confused me. How someone so kind and gentle could love someone so emotionless."

"Maybe he's different around her?" I shrug as the music ends, and Viktor leads me toward the bar.

He introduced me to his mother, Evelina, when we arrived, but she was swept away by some potential investors for the charity. She seemed sweet and kind from our brief interaction. The only glimpse I've gotten of his father is when he and Evelina delivered their speech during dinner.

Before we reach the bar, a slender arm wraps around my waist and steals my attention from Viktor.

"Maggie! You look simply radiant!" Vanessa braces her hands on my shoulders, smiling down at me.

My cheeks heat under her compliment. "Thank you. Someone with impeccable taste picked out my dress."

She giggles, twining her arm through mine like we're old friends. It really does feel like I've known her for years. There's the same easy comfort that I get with her brother.

Is it a twin thing? Or simply their auras?

Both light and free, promising no judgement.

"Viki, can you grab some more champagne? Maggie and I are headed to the restrooms."

"Oh," I squeak. I don't really have to pee, but I did drink a lot of champagne.

Viktor's gaze meets mine, darkening as his sister tugs me in the opposite direction.

I'll be fine, I mouth. He acts like his father talking to me would be the worst thing in the world. Surely, Mr. Bielski can't be that bad, right?

"Love looks good on you, Maggie," Vanessa says, pushing through the double doors that lead out of the banquet room and to a quiet hallway.

Love? Is that what this is? My heart quickens at the thought, nearly skipping a beat. It should be scary, letting someone into my heart again after losing Roman. But with Viktor, I feel calm and safe for the first time in a long time. Like maybe the future is brighter than I'd ever imagined. And maybe tonight is the perfect opportunity to tell him. "It feels good, too," I respond, admitting my feelings out loud.

"He might be my brother, so I'm a little biased," she says, holding the bathroom door open for me. "But there aren't many men, monster or not, out there like Viktor."

My chest swells, and I smile. "I'm starting to realize he's quite a catch. And having fresh baked goods in the house all the time is a real perk." I wink.

Vanessa's giggle fills the air, and we part ways inside the bathroom, which is just as fancy as the rest of this place. There's even a luxurious couch in the lounge area by the doors.

Once I take care of business, I wash my hands and reapply my lip gloss while I wait for Vanessa.

One minute turns into two. *Did I miss her? What if she's waiting outside for me?*

Stepping out of the bathroom, my head swivels from left to right in search of the tall, willowy vampire, but she's nowhere to be found.

"So you're the woman my son is infatuated with," a gruff voice rumbles from behind me.

Whipping around, a broad figure emerges from the shadows, and I find myself alone in a secluded hallway with Viktor's father. Who is currently glaring down his nose at me.

I've never been the type to shrink away when someone is rude to me, but this giant vampire is truly intimidating. He's the same height as Viktor, but nearly twice as broad. The seams of his tuxedo strain under the thick muscle lining his body. His piercing dark-red eyes skim my body, one lip pulling into a sneer. "Just know you're a passing fancy, my dear. Viktor belongs in the city with his own kind, not playing house with some country bumpkin."

My mouth drops open, but I'm too dumbstruck to form words.

He takes a step closer, until he's in my space. "Don't get attached. Come his birthday, he'll be where he belongs, and there's not a thing you can do about it. So save yourself the heartbreak, little girl, and walk away now. It'll only hurt worse for you and your daughter the longer you string this along."

That's it. I can't hold my tongue anymore. Leaning close, I let the venom filling my veins drip into my voice. "Listen, Mr. Bielski. I don't know why you hate me, considering we've just met, but Viktor is a grown adult capable of making his own choices. And beyond that, he's your son, for fuck's sake! Your child. Not some pawn you can move around on your chessboard or some robot you can control. Can't you see how miserable he'd be if you forced him into the life you've chosen for him? He's *good* at what he does and, more importantly, he loves it. And... and I love *him*! So, no, I won't walk away, and I sure as shit won't stand by while you take that joy away from him!"

My chest heaves and, honestly, I can't believe all those words flew out of my mouth as this intimidating vampire glares down at me. Dark eyes sear into mine with a rage that's brighter than a thousand suns. His jaw tightens, the muscle jumping under his pale skin. *Oh, shit*. Maybe I should have just walked away.

"Maggie." Viktor's voice comes from behind his father. "What's going on? What did he say to you?" Pushing past his father, my vampire comes to stand in front of me. His head whips over his shoulder, red eyes narrowed on the older vampire. "What did you say to her?"

"Nothing you didn't already know, Viktor. She's not your future. She's not important."

A growl vibrates Viktor's whole body. "Yes, she is. Maggie and her daughter *are* my future. They're the *most* important things in my life. Verbally berating the woman I love is beneath you, Father. You can belittle me all you want, but not her. Never her."

Stepping up behind Viktor, I wrap an arm around his waist in a silent show of solidarity.

"You're so stuck in the past, Father. So stuck on the idea that men are expected to work certain jobs. And that we're expected to breed with our own kind. Open your eyes, old man. Time's have changed. I don't care if you cut me off and disown me; I will not be coming to work for you, and I will not be leaving Maggie."

"Kasmir Bielski!" Every head in the deserted hallway turns to Viktor's mother. "I've had enough of this! He is our *son*, the only one you have." Stepping up to the big vampire, she jabs a finger into his chest. "Viktor is right, my love. It's his life, and it's time you butt out!"

"Evie—"

"No! Not this time, Kas. Let them be." Turning toward me and Viktor, she says, "Maggie, it was lovely to meet you. I'm extremely sorry for my husband's behavior. Viktor, I love you, I'm proud of you, and I will call you tomorrow." With that, she grips the front of her husband's tuxedo jacket and hauls him away.

Viktor faces me, a small smirk on his lips. "I didn't think she had it in her," he says before cupping my face between his hands. "Are you okay?" he whispers, leaning his forehead against mine.

"Yeah. You love me?" I somehow manage to croak, because this whole confrontation is surreal. My fingers tingle from the adrenaline still rushing through my veins when I curl them around Viktor's wrists.

He chuckles, the deep sound soothing my frazzled nerves. "Yeah, country girl. I've loved you since the moment I first saw you. Since you first opened that cherry-red door and compared me to Mary Poppins."

I can't help but giggle at the memory.

"And where the fuck is Ness?"

Heels click on the tile behind us. "I'm so sorry, Viki. A client caught me outside of the bathroom, and I got sidetracked. Maggie, I'm so sorry. I had eyes on you, then I blinked, and Dad was there. Are you okay?"

I nod, swallowing down the emotion from Viktor proclaiming his love for me. "Yeah, nothing I couldn't handle." My head swings back to Viktor's, our eyes locking.

"I heard what you said, you know? You love me, too." His hand slides up the back of my neck, anchoring me to him.

"Well, things are under control, so I'm just gonna..."

But Vanessa's words fade away when Viktor's lips land on mine, and he walks me backward until my back hits the wall. "Say it again."

Smiling against his lips, I whisper, "I love you, city boy."

I'm not sure how we got back to Viktor's apartment. Something about him needing to be inside me, cursing the New York traffic, then he was speeding through the streets of the city with me in his arms. I'm not really sure; everything after the confrontation with his parents is sort of a blur.

I don't think his lips have left mine for more than a few breaths ever since I said I love him.

My vampire is desperate.

Desperate for *me*.

"Fuck, Maggie, do you know how hot it was when you stood up to my father?" Viktor grips my hips and backs me into his bedroom while kissing down my neck.

Frantically, my hands push off his tux jacket, then get to work on his bow tie and shirt. "Mmm... need you naked now, Viktor."

Lips pressed against my throat, Viktor chuckles. It's deep and rich, sending a tremor of need down my spine. "Slow down, sweetheart," he murmurs against my heated skin while steering me toward his bed. "We have all night, and I plan to take my time with you."

I bite my tongue to stop the needy whine from escaping my mouth. It takes everything in me to not scream, *just fuck me already*. The whole night has been foreplay of the most delicious kind. Even now, as Viktor gives my shoulders a gentle shove and my butt lands on the bed.

Eyes blazing, he kneels in front of me and takes my foot in his hand. Long fingers unbuckle the thin strap of my heeled sandal and lift the shoe off my foot. All the while, Viktor's gaze never drops from mine, and my skin burns with my ever-growing horniness. "Viktor, please."

Removing the second sandal, he sets the pair side-by-side next to his nightstand. With a click of his tongue, he stands. "You're not going to rush me with your impatience, Maggie. Now that I have you in my space, I want to savor every moment until your poor little pussy is begging to be pounded by my cock."

God, the mouth on this vampire. I may spontaneously combust from his words alone.

He takes advantage of my silence and switches our positions, moving me like a rag doll until I'm standing between his spread thighs and he's lounging on the edge of the bed. Beams of moonlight bathe us in a soft glow, accentuating the smooth ridges of Viktor's abs when he reclines on his elbows. Those crimson eyes skate up and down my body, and I roll my shoulders back, sticking my chest out.

"Strip for me, country girl." His tongue flicks out, wetting his lips before his fangs sink into the bottom one.

"But—" I peer over my shoulder at the wall of glass behind me. The room is cast in a dim light from the bedside lamps, but anyone outside could probably see in. "The window. What if someone sees?"

Viktor's fangs gleam when his lips curl into a lascivious smirk. "Let them. I want the whole world to know you're mine, Maggie. And I'm yours."

His mutual claiming boosts my confidence, and I maintain eye contact as I reach behind me to unzip my dress. One at a time, I slip the straps from my shoulders, catching the fabric with an arm over my breasts.

I've never stripped for anyone, and I don't think of myself as sexy. Sure, I'm cute. Pretty, I guess. But... *sexy*? Definitely not.

Viktor's hoarse groan washes away any thoughts of self-doubt. Sliding his hand into the front of his black tux pants, he pulls out his cock.

It's thick and hard, and my mouth waters.

The red barbells catch the moonlight as his hand works up and down his shaft. Slow. Teasing.

At least he's not only edging me, but himself, too.

Under his penetrative stare, I drop my arm, breasts spilling free as the fabric slinks to my hips.

"Fuuuuck, sweetheart. Do you have any idea how stunning you are? My perfect whore."

I tremble and moan. Whore. *His* whore.

Pushing the dress over my hips, it falls to the ground, a puddle of navy satin around my feet. I never thought I'd be into degradation, but Viktor somehow mixes in the perfect amount of praise, and it has me burning up inside.

As I step out of the dress and scoot it to the side with my foot, he continues to work his cock.

Voice laced with honeyed seduction and dark promises, he asks, "Where are your panties, country girl?"

With my eyes entranced by his fist stroking up and down his hard shaft, I answer, "I didn't want panty lines." Finally pulling my gaze from his length, I lift a shoulder in nonchalance.

As he licks his lips, his eyes darken, flashing with what I'd call appreciation and *hunger* as they drag across my naked form.

"Turn around," Viktor commands, finger swirling lazily in the air.

So I do. Spinning, I face the window, the midnight glow of the city illuminating my reflection in the glass.

"Hands on the glass."

The slap of my palms against the cool window echoes around the small bedroom. I shiver with anticipation, lust overtaking my senses.

My eyes catch on a couple passing on the street below us. *What if they can see me?* The idea alone has my back arching.

Who knew I had an exhibitionist streak?

A menacing growl fills the air behind me. "Bend over and show me how wet your needy little cunt is, whore."

Oh my God.

Chapter 24

Viktor

"Goddamn, that's a pretty sight." Arousal glistens on the insides of Maggie's thighs when she hinges at the hips and presents her sweet cunt to me. She's perfect in every way.

Obedient, yet bratty.

Timid, yet confident.

A bead of clear fluid rolls from her sopping pussy lips, and my body vibrates with a deep rumble of approval. "Touch your pretty cunt for me, Maggie."

She whimpers, but one hand leaves the glass. Snaking between her legs, two fingers plunge into her pussy.

"Good girl," I growl, voice so low, I barely recognize it.

Tonight, we put all our cards on the table, finally proclaiming the mutual love we feel for each other. And I want to cement myself under her skin and inside her heart, which I plan to do by claiming every part of her right now.

"Don't stop until I tell you." Opening the nightstand drawer, I grab the small bottle inside before standing.

"Are you going to fuck me, or what?" As her fingers slowly pump in and out of her heat, Maggie shakes her hips and peers over her shoulder. Green eyes shimmer with mischief. Brat.

Shucking off my pants, I toss them to the side and approach Maggie. "So impatient, little whore."

When I step up behind her and grind my pierced cock between her ass cheeks, she moans.

My knees collide with the soft carpet as I drop down behind her, putting both of her glorious holes right at eye level. Cupping a dimpled cheek in each hand, I spread them apart, and my eyes feast on the sight before me.

Two fingers curled into her cunt, her thumb flicking her swollen clit.

Suddenly, I'm ravenous, salivating for my mate, so I lean in and devour her.

Above me, Maggie moans, rocking her hips against my face.

My tongue slips inside her—alongside her fingers—before venturing to taste her clit. With each swipe, she gets wetter and wetter, until her essence coats the lower half of my face. It's messy. It's raw.

It's fucking glorious.

Pushing Maggie's hand away, my fingers replace hers, and my lips suction around her clit. A symphony of moans spills from her throat, and her core convulses around my fingers. *That's one.*

But I need more. The monster inside me howls, driving up the bloodlust in my veins.

Before the last part of my sanity snaps, I pull away and grunt, "Need to feed, sweetheart."

"Yes." She whimpers her consent, pushing her ass into my face.

I strike. Hard and fast, my fangs sink into the supple flesh of one cheek.

Warm, sweet liquid fills my mouth, sliding down my throat with each gulped swallow.

As I feed, my fingers curl against Maggie's G-spot until she's screaming through another orgasm. *That's two.*

Sitting back on my heels, I swipe my tongue over my bottom lip. The combination of the metallic taste of blood and Maggie's tangy arousal is exquisite. It's a flavor I could get drunk on.

"You okay, sweetheart?" Black claws tip my fingers now that her blood has entered my system. My tongue drags across the lengthened point of my fang.

One hand still on the glass, Maggie holds the other over her shoulder in a shaky thumbs-up. "So good. Need your cock." Her words are a little slurred, making me chuckle.

"And you'll have it, sweet whore. We're far from done." As I stand, my eyes stay locked on her ass. The puncture marks on her cheek ooze a steady trail of blood. Each crimson drip feeds the monster inside me, and he rattles the bars of his cage.

I plaster my chest to her back, reaching between us and feeding my throbbing cock into her opening.

Head hanging between her arms, Maggie sighs, like my cock filling her is the answer to all of life's problems.

My claws curl against the cool glass as I brace my hand on the window next to hers. The other hand snakes between her heaving breasts to collar her delicate throat, lifting her head until her gaze meets mine in the reflection on the window. Glowing red against soothing green.

Not breaking eye contact, I lean in until my lips brush her ear. "I want to fuck you like a whore, but love you like you're my serenity."

Turning her head, Maggie's eyes meet mine, and I nearly drown in the emotion crashing through the sage orbs. "I love you, Viktor."

Her words make my heart sing, and our lips collide. Hand on her throat, I devour her mouth while my hips smack against her ass with each thrust, pushing us both toward our peaks.

"Bite me again. Please, Viktor," she pleads against my lips.

"Who am I to deny my perfect whore what she wants?" My fangs extend, scraping down the side of her throat to where her pulse gallops under the skin.

Maggie's scream of pleasure fills my ears as I sink the sharp teeth into her flesh. *That's three.*

One more, and I'll allow myself to fill her with my cum.

Pulling my cock from her pulsing cunt, I bend down and grab the bottle I stashed by my feet.

I need to claim every part of her tonight.

My pelvis and Maggie's ass are smeared with red. Blood trickles from the puncture wounds on her left cheek, the crimson drops rolling down the valley between her supple ass cheeks. Fingers dragging through the warm liquid, I smear it around her tight back entrance.

"Anyone ever fuck you here, country girl?" I apply a little pressure to the tight pucker, and Maggie shivers.

"Yes. But it's been a while..."

Roman. "Did you like when your husband fucked you in the ass, Maggie?"

Opening the bottle of lube, I pour some on my bloodied fingers before slipping one inside, careful not to hurt her with my claws.

"Oh, God. Yes!" Maggie moans.

Adding a second, I can't take my eyes off the way her tight ass stretches to accommodate the girth of my fingers. "I want all of you tonight, Maggie. No more holding back."

She rocks her hips to meet the slow thrusts of my fingers. "You have me, Viktor. I'm yours."

When I manage to drag my gaze away from the absolute masterpiece of blood splattering her ass, our eyes collide in the window again, and hers flash with heat.

"*Mine,*" I growl, low and predatory.

"Yours."

Once Maggie's muscles relax around my fingers, I slip them free and lube up my cock. I tremble as my hand glides over each rung in the ladder. Lining the pierced head up with her ass, I push inside.

She's so warm and tight, the breath stalls in my lungs.

Pushing forward again, her ass swallows the second and third piercings. "Fuck, sweetheart. You're taking every inch of me so well."

A little more lube before one more gentle thrust, and my pelvis is flush with her heated skin. She gasps once my cock is buried deep inside her.

Sweat beads on her back, slicking us together when I lean over her again. One arm bands under her breasts to hold her tight to me.

The fingers on my right hand thread through hers, palm still on the glass. "Move, Viktor. Please."

So I do. My thrusts are slow and shallow, not wanting to tear her up. Skin slaps skin. Moans and grunts surround us.

Tightening her fingers in mine, she drags our hands from the window to her pussy. She's soaked, ribbons of arousal dripping down her legs. "You love this, don't you, my pretty whore? Getting fucked in the ass by a vampire."

"Oh my god, Viktor."

My fingers curl into her cunt, hers going to her clit. Her ass grips my cock with each retreat of my hips. Tingles start at the base of my spine, the first signs of my orgasm.

I've staved it off long enough. It's time. Coasting my arm from her waist up to her throat, my fingers tighten around the soft flesh.

Blood from the open bite wound on her neck seeps through my fingers, bathing both our skin in crimson. My eyes eat her up. She's so beautiful, covered in life's sweet nectar.

I guide her mouth to mine and whisper, "Fall with me, Maggie. And I promise I'll be there to catch you. Always."

With her lips on mine, I let the wave of pleasure take me under, filling her with my cum. For the fourth time tonight, Maggie orgasms, eyes rolling to the back of her head as her mouth falls open on a silent cry. She's real and beautiful... and all mine.

As my climax fades, my knees buckle. Ripping my hand from her core, it slaps against the cool window, creating a smear of blood and cum on the otherwise spotless glass. A masterpiece I won't be wiping away any time soon.

Maggie's legs shake against mine, and she whimpers when my cock slips free. Limp and sated... for now, at least. "Come on, country girl. Let's clean you off so I can get you dirty all over again."

Joyful laughter fills my ears, and my heart, when I swing her into my arms and head for the bathroom. She gives me a lust-drunk smile and snuggles into my chest. "Yes, please, city boy."

CHAPTER 25

Maggie

My bladder burns with the need to pee, the pressure almost unbearable. Eyes fluttering open, pillars of light stream through the window next to Viktor's bed.

Viktor's bed. Smiling, I snuggle deeper into the sheets as my brain recounts every way he used my body last night. First, in front of the window, where anyone could see. Then again, in the shower.

Like he said, he washed the cum and blood from my body, only to dirty me up again.

And I loved every second of it.

Afterward, he made me drink an entire bottle of water and eat a snack. Something about needing to keep my energy up for round three.

Finally, we collapsed in his bed, and I had the best sleep of my life, cocooned in his strong arms. The steady rise and fall of his chest against my back, like the most soothing lullaby.

The arm draped over my waist tightens, pulling me into a cool body. Viktor nuzzles his face into the crook of my neck. "Mmm... Too early." Grit and gravel coat his voice, making my clit light up in anticipation. But... then the pressure in my bladder takes over again, demanding attention.

Turning my head, I press a kiss to his soft pale hair, whispering, "My bladder is about to explode. I'll be right back."

Sleepy crimson eyes meet mine as he lifts his head. "Promise." His lower lip presses out, like the cutest pouting puppy.

A lock of hair falls over his strong brow, giving him a boyish appearance this morning. Automatically, my fingers smooth it back before I press a kiss to his lips. "Now who's the needy one?"

My bladder screams again, threatening to burst. *Must pee now!*

Pulling away from the Adonis next to me, I slide out from under the sheets. Viktor tugs my pillow into his arms and promptly falls back asleep.

After all the emotions and fucking into the early hours of the morning, he must be exhausted.

Surprisingly, I feel refreshed and better than I have in years.

Viktor's white dress shirt is draped over the back of the chair by his dresser. Snagging it, I slip my arms into the sleeves and fasten one of the buttons to hold it closed. Like a warm hug, his scent surrounds me, and I pull the collar to my nose, sucking in a greedy breath.

After emptying my poor bladder, I go to the sink to wash my hands. In the mirror, I barely recognize the woman reflected back to me. Curls in a disheveled halo around my head after going to bed with wet hair last night. Rosy cheeks accentuate the spray of freckles on the bridge of my nose.

Bunching my hair on the top of my head, I spot the twin puncture marks on my neck.

Heat thrums in my veins and my pussy clenches. The marks solidify Viktor's words from last night. That I'm *his*. And he's *mine*.

Being claimed by him feels so right. After years of grieving, I'm finally ready to open my life to this kind and caring vampire.

Pulling myself from my thoughts, I spot a small glass jar of hair ties on the counter. I steal one—Viktor won't mind—and throw my curls into a bun.

Since I'm taking advantage of Viktor's hospitality, I also snag a swig of his mouthwash. No one likes morning breath. Spitting the minty liquid in the sink, my gaze flicks back to the mirror. The skin under her eyes is finally free from the dark circles that had become permanent residents on my face.

The woman in the mirror is happy.

Unbelievably so, for the first time in over four years.

"You deserve it, Mags. You deserve *him*." With a smile, I turn and exit the bathroom.

Back in the bedroom, I find Viktor still asleep. One leg hooks over the covers so his perfect pale butt is on display. I bite my bottom lip, eyes wandering from his broad shoulders and down the hollow of his back to the juicy cheeks of his ass. There's something about a man with a nice, round, *biteable* ass. Bringing my fist to my mouth, I groan.

I might have to try that later.

Viktor may not be the only one who enjoys biting in this relationship.

Letting my vampire rest, I find my way to the kitchen for some morning caffeine.

A fancy coffee machine waits on the counter for me. In the cupboard above, there are single serve pods in various flavors.

"Can't go wrong with a breakfast blend." I slip a mug under the machine, pop the green coffee pod in, and hit *Brew*.

Before I close the cabinet door, my eyes catch on a black plastic tub on the bottom shelf. *Crimson Destroyer* is emblazoned in blood-red block letters above a shirtless gym bro. His skin is pale, and veins protrude along the boulders of muscle lining his upper body. Snarled lips showcase sharp fangs dripping with blood. And his eyes have a predatory gleam that's downright frightening. *Gnarly.* This must be the synthetic blood supplement Viktor uses.

Unscrewing the lid, I sniff. A pungent, acidic odor hits my nostrils, and I pull back before I cough all over the powder inside the container.

This is what he's been drinking?

Shrugging, I dump a scoop into the steaming coffee, mixing thoroughly before getting to work on my own.

By the time I come back into the bedroom, Viktor is sitting with his back propped against the tufted headboard. He scratches his chest and yawns.

"Good morning, Sleeping Beauty. I wasn't sure how you take your coffee, but I found the blood powder in your cupboard. What's up with the dude on the label?" Holding back my laughter, I take a seat on the edge of the bed and extend the mug to him.

His chuckle is thick with sleep when he takes the mug. "The model is some famous body builder, but it's the only brand I've found that tastes close enough to the real thing." The thick muscles of his throat constrict when he drinks. "It's perfect, country girl. Thank you." Another sip and he sets the mug on the nightstand.

Over the rim of my coffee, I peer at him, curiosity rippling under my skin. "What...um. What does it taste like? The fake blood?"

Smirking, twin fangs glint in the morning sun. "Do you want to try?"

Before I can answer, his hand blurs, and he takes the mug from my hands, setting it next to his. Big hands wrap around my waist, and he pulls me into his lap, my naked core settling against his hard shaft.

I'm still reeling from how fast he managed to get me in a compromising position as he grabs the mug of blood coffee again and lifts it to my lips.

"W-Will it hurt me?"

"No, but I don't think you'll like it. It's... an acquired taste." He winks.

Hesitantly, I wrap my mouth around the rim of the mug and take a miniscule sip. The bright notes of coffee hit my tongue first, followed by an acidic coppery tang. It's not terrible, but… "Definitely an acquired taste," I croak before running my tongue around my mouth, but the unsavory flavor lingers.

Viktor chuckles, setting the mug to the side again. His fingers band around the sides of my throat in a possessive hold as he brings my lips to his. The kiss is slow and sweet until his tongue snakes against mine. He must get a taste of the lingering blood on my tongue because he groans.

"*You* taste so much better, country girl. Sweet. Succulent. *Perfect.*"

The fingers of his free hand dig into my ass, and he guides me to grind against his hard length. It lays flat against his stomach, so my clit bumps against the piercings on the underside with each rock of my hips.

Sparks fly behind my closed eyelids, and my fingers weave into his hair, soft like fine strands of silk.

"I love you, Maggie. My mate."

My eyes spring open, and my lips part from his with a *pop*. "Mate? What does that mean?"

Cyrus and Antoinette are mates, but she's a dragon shifter, not a vampire. Are mate bonds the same for all monsters?

Suddenly, my back hits the mattress and heated ruby eyes bore down on me, Viktor's large frame looming over mine. "Do you remember the first time I fed on you?"

I nod, heart beating a little faster as I clutch his biceps. "You grew claws, and your eyes glowed. The same thing happened last night."

Even now, there's a luminosity to his beautiful irises that's not normally there, like my blood is still coursing through his system.

"I knew that first night, but I was a coward. Afraid you'd run if you knew the truth. But my body's reaction to your blood... It means you're my mate. It means—if you accept—our souls would be bonded together forever."

All the air leaves my lungs when his hand finds my throat again, and he tips my chin to his. "When I look at you, my whole life makes sense, Maggie."

"B-But you're immortal. And I'm... not." My stomach twists. "How would that work?"

Viktor sighs, closing his eyes and resting his forehead against mine. "I'm still working on that part. Do you trust me?"

Again, I nod. "Yes. I love you, Viktor. You brought me back to life." The words tumble from my lips without any hesitation.

He rocks his cock against my core, and I moan, back arching. My nipples harden. Each rub against the inside of my shirt sends sparks of pleasure down my spine.

With a single touch, a single glance, Viktor is able to set my blood on fire.

His hand leaves my throat just long enough to unbutton the shirt, exposing my breasts to his hungry eyes. Then his long fingers are back on my pulse, like he needs to feel the steady thrum of my heart while he eases his cock inside my pussy.

Every roll of his hips solidifies the bond between us, clicking each puzzle piece into place. My future doesn't seem so uncertain anymore, not with Viktor there as my lighthouse. The storm of grief I've been waging for the past four years doesn't seem so overwhelming with his presence guiding me.

Together, we reach our peak, and it's soul-shattering. All-consuming.

When I leave the bedroom—after cleaning up again—Viktor flits from the stove to the fridge and back again. Today, he's dressed in a crisp white button-down, the sleeves rolled at the forearms, and a pair of eggplant-purple slacks. I bite my lip and admire the way he moves with ease while cooking. This is his happy place.

"I hope you're hungry." His wrist flicks, the omelet in the frying pan flipping with ease.

Right on cue, my stomach growls. "Guess I'm not used to all this sex. If you plan on fucking my brains out every chance you get, you'll have to start feeding me more."

One dark eyebrow arches, and a fang sinks into his bottom lip. "Is that a challenge, sweetheart?"

Laughing, I plop onto one of the stools at the counter. "I'll never say no to sex and food." I wink, picking up the fresh mug of coffee he made for me and taking a sip.

A sleek laptop is open, and my eyes snag on an aerial picture of... *my orchard?*

Gulping down my coffee, the hot liquid chafes my throat. "W-What's this?"

Viktor slides the omelet onto a plate and sprinkles it with some extra cheese before joining me at the island. He sets the plate in front of me, along with a fork. "Eat. This is my attempt to save *Sweet Orchard Dreams*."

My brow dips. "What?"

"You wouldn't accept my money." He holds a hand up when my lips part in protest. "Rightfully so. I understand that now, Maggie. I overstepped and tried to swoop in and take away your power. I'm sorry I was inconsiderate."

"Thank you. So what's this?" I ask, swallowing roughly.

Fingers blurring over the keys and mouse pad, Viktor pulls up a few more documents. "I still wanted to contribute somehow. Call it white knight syndrome, but I had to make sure your harvest was a success this year. So I came up with the idea of a harvest festival to draw in more customers and drive up profit by offering additional avenues for them to spend money."

Every word that comes out of his mouth has tears coating my lash line and butterflies erupting in my stomach. "You did all this for me?" I take my eyes off the screen to meet his.

"I'd do anything for you, Maggie. You have so many memories with Roman there. I can't let you lose that."

Those butterflies plummet, and my gut twists. "Viktor." Drawing his hand into mine, I squeeze. "I'm so sorry. I've been so focused on keeping Roman's legacy alive. That's not fair to you."

Snowy-white locks brush his shoulders as he shakes his head. "No, Maggie. That's not how I see it. I'm not trying to replace or erase him. You still love him. You probably always will. But your love for him doesn't make me feel any less loved by you. He was your first. And I hope to be your last."

Bringing his hand to my mouth, I press a kiss to his knuckles. Tears trail down my cheeks, but Viktor is there to brush them away. "Have I mentioned how much I love you?"

"You may have mentioned it a time or two last night, but I'll never get tired of hearing it. I waited my whole life for you, sweetheart."

Cheeks heating, my eyes flick to the laptop screen. "Tell me more about this festival of yours."

I take in the Ferris wheel and food trucks. There's a beer and wine tent. Viktor rattles off the details of the festival, which is planned for opening weekend—next weekend.

"This is actually perfect. I can run some social media ads to bring in more people. Maybe hang some fliers locally."

"That sounds like a great idea."

"And." I tug on his hand until he's forced to bend over the counter. Pressing my lips to his, I speak against his lush mouth. "I will be paying you back every cent that you spent. This isn't you rescuing me, Viktor. I don't want you for your money."

"You don't have—"

My hand lands over his mouth. "Shush. I will pay you back."

He nods, but the way his eyes shine tells me I'll have to fight to get him to take every cent.

Satisfied, I remove my hand from his mouth as he pushes the omelet in front of me again. Humoring him, I pick up the fork and tuck into the food, which is delicious.

Of course it is. Everything Viktor makes is out of this world.

Eyeing me over the rim of his mug, he says, "No more sneaking around. Okay? I want us to be official."

My heart leaps. "Does this mean you're staying?"

The question has a cheeky grin brightening his handsome face. "I dare you to try to get rid of me, country girl." In fact, his smirk is downright devilish, and my panties would be drenched... if I was wearing any.

But his expression sobers, and he sets his mug on the counter, wrapping both hands around it and leaning on his elbows. "Last night, I pretty much told my father to fuck off. I doubt he'll be speaking to me for a while—if ever again."

I run my fingers up his forearm. "Oh, Viktor. I'm sorry it's come to this." He straightens, rounding the island to gather me in his arms. One hand cups my cheek as he smiles. "Nonsense. I got you and Lily out of the situation. Seems like a pretty great deal to me."

"I think we're the lucky ones." What I don't say is that the orchard finally feels whole again with him there. "Let's go home and tell *our* girl." At this point, it's obvious he loves Lily just as much as he loves me.

Drooping to half-mast, his gaze scans my body in a lazy caress. "Sweetheart, as much as I love you in nothing but my shirt, I think you need clothes first." When his eyes meet mine again, they're filled with a familiar heat, and he winks.

Those damn winks. From the moment we met, they've been my weakness.

A thought dawns on me at the mention of clothes. "Your car is still at the gala."

Giving my ass a firm pat, he spins away from me and grabs his keys and pocket watch from a little tray on the island. "Stay here and finish eating. Look over the festival plans, and make sure there's nothing you want to add or change. I'll be back soon."

CHAPTER 26

Viktor

She's mine. She's mine. She's mine. Each pounding beat of my heart plays the words back to me. If only I can figure out a solution to this pesky immortality issue.

Vampires usually mate with other vampires, or find a new mate if they outlive a mortal one. But I don't want anyone else.

I only want Maggie.

She's it for me, and I doubt she'll want to outlive her daughter, so I'll have to make a sacrifice. I'm all too happy to give up my immortal life to spend just one lifetime with my girls.

There has to be a solution.

Rather than use my enhanced speed, I head in the direction of last night's gala at a normal pace. I need the extra time to think.

Rounding the corner a few blocks later, the pink flying saucer logo of Cream Me Up beckons me like a mirage in the desert. Some mysterious force tugs my feet to the entrance. The little bells at the top of the door chime as I stumble through the doorway.

"Viktor!" Maria waves from behind the diner's counter. Her iridescent wings flutter behind her back as I approach, a sunny smile lighting up her face.

Maria is a pixie and Phil's wife. Speaking of the big, green fella, he shoulders through the double doors of the kitchen as I settle on one of the pink barstools. "Vik, my man! How's it going?"

Phil's arm wraps around Maria's waist, and he smiles down at her. Cream Me Up has become a pinnacle of the New York monster community, with this loving couple at the center.

Pixies are known for their powerful magic, so if anyone can help me out of my predicament, it's Maria. "What do you know about immortality and mate bonds?"

While I explain the situation to Maria and Phil, my fingers twitch and shake, so I pull my pocket watch from my slacks. Twirling the chain around one finger, I flip open the lid and click it shut again.

Maria's luminous amethyst eyes flit to the watch in my fidgeting hands, and her lips flirt into a smile. "I have an idea." She extends a delicate palm across the countertop, fingers beckoning me to place the watch in her grasp.

So I do.

"Thank you again for watching Lily." Maggie wraps her arms around Cyrus in a loose hug.

"Not a problem, Mags. She's a good kid." He yawns. "But man, she has a lot of energy."

Giggling, Maggie pulls out of the hug, only to draw Antoinette into her arms.

Unsure of my place in this conversation, I hover near the front door and tuck my hands in my pockets. My fingers brush the cool metal of the newly enchanted pocket watch.

It's been a constant weight on my mind since we left the city, but I want to wait until we're alone—for the perfect moment—to broach the subject of mating.

Suddenly, Cyrus is beside me, his shoulder bumping mine. "So did you tell her?"

"Tell me what?" Maggie's gaze ping-pongs between me and her brother-in-law, delicate eyebrows drawing together.

I clear my throat and wrap an arm around Maggie's waist. When I pull her close, her warm body melts into my side. Eyes on Cyrus, I say, "Not that it's any of your business. But... yes." Then my attention is focused back on my mate. "I told this amazing creature that I love her. I love her and Lily. And I'm officially staying."

The breath is stolen from my lungs when Maggie's lips split into a blinding smile, showcasing the gap between her front teeth. Amazing. Perfect. Mesmerizing. Beautiful. I doubt I'll ever run out of adjectives to describe her.

"So now we can stop tiptoeing around the 'will they, won't they' sexual tension? I thought Antoinette and I were bad—" His words cut off on an *oomph* when a small elbow collides with his stomach.

"Be nice, Wilcox," his mate chides. "It wasn't too long ago that we were in their shoes. I, for one, am happy you found each other." Her eyes flutter up to the brute of a human beside her. Something akin to the emotions swirling through me reflect in her golden irises. "Everyone deserves to find love. You taught me that, Cyrus."

Cyrus raises a hand to cup the side of Antoinette's face. "I know, princess. I was just teasing." He looks back at me and Maggie. "Sorry if I was an ass yesterday before you left, Viktor. You seem like an alright guy, and if you make Maggie and Lily happy, then that's all that matters."

I guess I'll take that. He extends a hand to me. As I grip it, he adds, "But I meant what I said about if you hurt her."

"I'll hold you to that, since I'd rather die than hurt either of my girls."

After another round of quick goodbyes, the couple leaves for the drive back to the city.

"So what did he threaten you with if you hurt me?" Maggie locks the deadbolt and spins to face me.

Stepping closer, I crowd her until her back hits the door, head tipping back to meet my gaze. "Cyrus? Oh, just that he'd help Jean-Luc bury my body if I broke your heart."

Her hands slide up my chest, playing with the buttons on my shirt. Giving in to temptation, I lean down, eliminating the distance between our mouths. In the next breath, I'm reminded why I love this strong, stubborn woman. "I'm pretty handy with a shovel, too."

My chuckle puffs against her lips. "Duly noted, country girl. But I have no intention of breaking your heart. You're stuck with me for good now."

"Good." Her fingers tighten in my shirt until her lips seal to mine once more.

That same fire ignites in my veins like every time we kiss. It's addictive and all-consuming.

With need of their own, my hands find purchase on her wide hips, sliding up to her waist and reveling in the soft skin exposed at the waistband of her leggings. Before things turn too heated, Maggie cuts the kiss short. Too short for my liking.

With panting breaths, her flushed chest heaves. "We still need to tell Lily that we're together. That you're staying."

Before I can object, she threads her fingers through mine and leads me down the hall. "Where is she anyway? It's suspiciously quiet." I turn to search the family room, only to find it empty.

"Maybe she slipped up the stairs when no one was looking?"

How can a five-year-old disappear so quickly?

A soft hum hits my ears, and I pull Maggie toward the kitchen. Near the fridge, a mop of dark-blonde hair catches my eyes. "Found her."

"What are you doing, bug?"

Coming to stand behind her, my eyes drift to the permanent marker in her hand. *Uh-oh.*

"I'm adding Viktor." Her little tongue pokes out of her mouth as her hand moves along the wall. Framed by a few scuff marks, a stick figure drawing of three people adorns the light-green paint.

Maggie kneels next to her daughter, placing a hand on her back. "Adding him to what?"

Smiling, she swings her pretty green eyes toward me. The same breathtaking color as her mother's. "To the family."

Maggie's soft gasp fills the air, tears glistening in her eyes.

Squatting to Lily's level, I cup her cheek. "You're okay with me staying?"

She nods. "I heard you talking to Uncle Cy. You love me and Momma. And I love you. So you stay with us now." The simple logic of a child, but she's not wrong. I would do anything for her and her mother.

Taking the marker from Lily's hand, Maggie puts the cap on and shoves it into her pocket. "Do you understand what that means, Lily? Viktor staying?"

Lily's brow furrows. "That we're a family?"

Maggie nods. "Yes, but it means Viktor and I are together."

Something clicks in Lily's head, and her eyebrows shoot up. "Oh! Like Brittany in my class! Leo is her boyfriend."

I bite my tongue to stifle a laugh. I can only imagine what the concept of a boyfriend is for a kindergartener.

A laugh slips out of Maggie's mouth before she clears her throat. "Sort of like that, but Viktor will live with us, and not in the guest house anymore. He'll sleep in bed with me. He'll be here when you wake up and when you go to sleep at night. Is that okay with you?"

"Yes! Viktor can do bedtime stories!"

"I can definitely read all the bedtime stories you want from now on." At my declaration, tiny arms hook around my neck, catching me off guard. I fall on my ass and Lily lands in my lap, no vampire grace in sight.

"I love you, Viktor."

Opening my arm, I beckon Maggie into the hug, too. She wraps her arms around us, and the last puzzle piece clicks into place. *This* is my home now, with these two perfect creatures. Tightening my arms around them, I say, "I love you, too, little one. Both of you."

"And Miss Lily, we will be having a conversation about where you found this permanent marker," Maggie says.

Lily giggles. "I saw you hide them in the big drawer... in your office." Her head pops up, eyes swinging between Maggie and me. "Am I in trouble?"

CHAPTER 27

Maggie

Bright afternoon sun glints off the metal beams of the Ferris wheel, the buckets rocking with the gentle turn of the big wheel. Lily tugs my hand, eyes wide and head swinging from side to side, taking everything in.

The festival is staged near the entrance to the orchard. A large Ferris wheel and a few smaller rides take up one area. Near the main drive, food trucks line the gravel, serving customer after customer.

Over by the barn, a big yellow tent has been erected. Inside, visitors can try different beer, wine, and hard cider.

And, of course, people can pick their own apples or enjoy a hayride with Jean-Luc. *Hopefully, he remembers to smile.*

Hoards of people mill about taking part in different activities. We only opened an hour ago, and already, there are more people here than I get in an entire season.

Viktor wouldn't let me help with the setup over the past week, something about still wanting everything to be a surprise, even though he showed me his master plan. My vampire is a romantic to his core, and this is his grand gesture.

"Look, Momma!" My daughter points a little finger at a bright blue food booth. "Cotton candy! Can I have some?"

Not only does the harvest festival coincide with our opening weekend, but it's also Lily's sixth birthday. So, to her, this is all a giant party in her honor.

Deciding to let her indulge, I follow her to the attendant, and she picks out a light-pink cloud of candy fluff. I'm sure I'll regret it later, when she's bouncing off the walls and refusing to go to bed. Viktor can fight the sugared-up birthday girl at bedtime tonight.

Speaking of... "Where is Viktor?"

Cool arms slip around my waist, pulling me into an equally cool but hard chest. Sharp teeth nip at my earlobe before a rough voice whispers, "Having fun, country girl?"

Spinning in his embrace, I find Viktor, with Vanessa trailing close behind. She volunteered herself and some of her spa employees to work in the beer and wine tent for the day.

I hook my fingers under his suspenders and drag his lips to mine in a quick peck. "Everything is perfect, Viktor. Thank you for this."

With a tilt of his head, he smiles. "Anything for you, Maggie."

He takes a step back, slipping his hand into mine as we stroll past the food trucks.

Dark, pressed jeans hug his lean thighs, accentuating the bulge between his legs. My gaze heats, scanning his perfectly fit pale-green button-down. When I reach his face, fangs peek out from behind his smirking lips, and crimson eyes flick to my mouth. Gripping his suspenders again, I tug his mouth to mine.

This time, the kiss is slow and drugging, but I find the will to pull away before things turn indecent. We are in public, after all.

Ever since the night of the gala, it's been like this. Insatiable need courses through me every time I lay eyes on my vampire.

After telling Lily about Viktor and me, he's slotted into our lives effortlessly. From helping to get Lily ready for school in the morning, to sleeping in my bed every night. It's what I dreamed my life would be like.

Even the constant ache over missing Roman isn't unbearable anymore, because I have a partner who helps me through when a wave of grief hits.

Up ahead, Jean-Luc stands next to his idling tractor, arms crossed over his barrel chest. Impatience ripples off him as people settle on the hay bales in the trailer. God, I hope he remembers to at least pretend to like these people so they give us a glowing review and, just maybe, come back next year.

"Who's that?" Eyes darkening, Vanessa's gaze locks on the minotaur, and her tongue skims the tip of one fang. "That's one bull I'd like to ride."

"Ness!" I scold. "He's my employee!"

Her eyes roll, but the smirk on her lips stays firmly in place. "So? *I* don't work for you. Come on, Lily girl. I think we need to go on a hayride!"

"Can I, Momma?" Lily clasps her hands under her chin, lips pouting.

"Go on. It is your birthday. Go big, or go home."

Ness cheers. "And it's your birthday?"

Lily nods, taking Vanessa's hand. "Feels like my birthday, too," she murmurs, eyes never leaving Jean-Luc.

Curly blonde ponytail bouncing, Lily is all too happy to tag along, none the wiser to Vanessa ogling my foreman.

Viktor chuckles, wrapping his arms around me again. "Could you imagine? Those two together?" He shakes his head before nuzzling his favorite spot, where my neck and shoulder meet. My pulse spikes, but before we can get too engrossed in our PDA, I spot Cyrus and Annie exiting the beer tent.

She rolls her golden eyes at something he says and smacks his chest, but the corner of her mouth quirks into a small smile. His boisterous chuckle fills the air as they walk toward us.

Plastic cup in hand, Cyrus waves his arm around the festival. "This is amazing, Mags!"

"Thanks, but I can't take all the credit." I peer over my shoulder at Viktor.

"I couldn't let you lose this place, sweetheart. Not after everything you've been through."

"Lose this place? What's he talking about, Maggie?" Cyrus's brow buckles.

Shit! I never told him about the debt and being behind on payments.

Guess it's time to clear the air. I blow out a breath before meeting his crystalline-blue eyes, so similar to Roman's, it's like a punch to the gut. "I may have gotten a little low on funds over the past year and been on the verge of foreclosure."

Now, his dark-blonde eyebrows climb up his forehead. "Why didn't you tell me? I would have loaned you the money."

"That's exactly why I didn't tell you." Breaking out of Viktor's embrace, I step up to my brother-in-law and clasp his hand in mine. "It's been four years, Cy. I can't keep relying on you to save me. It's time for me to stand on my own... without Roman. This was my burden to bear."

He squeezes my hand. "You're not a burden, Mags. Never. I understand that it hurts your pride, but tell me in the future. Okay? Even if it's just to be there as your support system. You're not alone. You're still my family." Then his big arms are around me, enveloping me in a warm hug.

Tears blur my vision as I sink into his body. "I know." When I pull back, swiping away the tears, I manage a smile. "And I do owe you a thank you for hiring a nanny." Glancing over my shoulder, I throw Viktor a saucy wink. "Who knew things would play out so well?"

Cyrus chuckles and knocks his shoulder with mine. "It's good to see you happy again, Mags. It's what he would want."

Before I can say anything else, a menacing growl splits the air like a lightning bolt. "You've got some nerve showing up here!" His body blurs past mine so fast that my eyes can barely keep up. When they finally do, Viktor stands toe-to-toe with his father, of all people.

Okay, I was not expecting to ever see Kasmir Bielski again.

"Excuse me," I say, leaving Cyrus and Annie to enjoy the festival while I break up the Bielski family feud.

All three vampires tower over me, but I roll my shoulders back and get ready to support Viktor.

Evie elbows her husband, and he clears his throat, dark eyes swinging to *me*. "Ms. Wilcox. I believe I owe you an apology. The way I treated you at the gala was completely unacceptable. My wife has put some things into perspective for me." He pats her hand where it rests on his forearm. "You make my son happy, and that's all that matters. I hope you can forgive me."

Dumbfounded, I simply nod.

Next thing I know, a business card is thrust into my hand. "If you ever need a backer, I would love to help fund this place. It seems you've brought the whole community together."

Clearly finished with me, he turns to Viktor. "I'm sorry, Son. I know I've been a shit father. And I shouldn't have put my beliefs and my dreams on your shoulders... or your sister's. It wasn't fair to either of you. Thanks to your mother, I see that now." His eyes flit to his wife, who smiles and leans closer to him.

"Keep going, Kas. Just like we practiced," she encourages him.

His face softens, and his thick throat bobs with a swallow. "I-I'm taking some time away from work to repair my relationship with Vanessa... and your mother. I know I don't deserve it, but I hope you'll forgive me, too."

Next to me, Viktor's jaw tenses, the muscle jumping under his skin. I thread my fingers through his in a silent show of support. His eyes never stray from the older Bielski male, dripping with fury. "I need some time, Father. But maybe someday," he all but growls, chest heaving.

Kas nods. "That's all I can ask."

Suddenly, Viktor's lips curve into a mischievous grin. "You can start by enjoying the festival. Spend lots of money."

"Viktor!" I smack his chest as they walk away.

One dark eyebrow lifts. "What? They can afford it. Think of it as the first step to an apology."

I roll my eyes. "Fine. Are you okay after all that?" I wave a hand at his retreating parents.

Hand in mine, he shrugs and guides me toward the Ferris wheel. "His opinion doesn't matter when it comes to you and Lily. As long as I have the two of you, nothing else matters."

CHAPTER 28

Maggie

My eyes must be playing tricks on me. I shuffle through the papers again, mentally tallying the totals. "It can't be."

"There you are." Viktor leans against the doorframe of my office, arms crossed over his chest. "Lily was out cold as soon as her head hit the pillow."

I'm not surprised. She spent all day dragging Ness, Cy, and Annie around the festival. Pretty great sixth birthday, if you ask me.

My eyes linger on his long legs as they eat up the space between us. Once he's in front of me, he cups the sides of my neck and places a chaste kiss on my lips. "I thought for sure you would be soaking in a nice hot bath after such a long day." His thumbs knead the aching muscles at the base of my neck, and I moan, eyes fluttering closed.

"I wanted to check the numbers first." My voice is breathy as he continues to work out the knots in my sore shoulders and his lips caress mine languidly.

Eyelids drooping, I give in to the relief for just a moment. My hand drops to my side, the papers rustling against my skin. *No, wait!*

My eyes spring wide, and my heart threatens to beat out of my chest when I bring the papers between us. "We did it, Viktor! We made double what I needed!"

Squeezing me tight, he steps away from my desk and spins us in a circle. "That's amazing! I'm so proud of you, country girl!"

When he settles me back on my feet, his eyes shine with so much love that it sends me floating above the clouds. "And this is only the electronic payment numbers. Jean-Luc and I will have to count the cash after the weekend is over. Did you see how many people came today?"

"All because of you, sweetheart."

I shake my head. "No—"

"Yes, Maggie. I saw it with my own eyes. People flocked to you today. Telling you how much they loved the orchard. How much they loved the apples. I even heard a few people say they'd be back next year with their friends. This is only the beginning."

My belly swoops. Only the beginning... in more ways than one. Ideas for the future of the orchard flooded my brain all day as I interacted with customers. Some wished the festival was more than just this weekend. Others asked if we did weddings or had other seasonal events.

Now that Viktor's out of the guest house, it could be used as a bed & breakfast.

And with Kas as an investor...

Slow down, Mags. There's plenty of time for all of it.

"Your gears are turning, aren't they?" Smiling, Viktor's fingers tap my temple.

Rivulets of unfettered energy rush through my veins. I doubt I'll get any sleep tonight. "I'm excited for what the future holds—for the first time in a long time, things don't seem so bleak."

"And you deserve every single amazing thing that's coming your way."

I blink rapidly, trying to stave off the happy tears as they fill my eyes.

"How about one more surprise?"

I pull his hand to my racing heart as he boosts me onto the desk. "I don't know if my heart can take any more excitement today."

A flirty wink, then he says, "You'll like this surprise. I promise." One hand tucks into the pocket of his slacks before drawing out in a closed fist.

Using the bulk of his body, he parts my thighs and crowds into my space. "Remember when I asked you to be my mate?"

I nod, locking onto his crimson eyes.

"And I asked you to trust me to find a solution to our little immortality dilemma?"

"Yes." My eyes dip to his fist when he uncurls his fingers, revealing his pocket watch.

Except now, the chain is longer, like a necklace. And the watch is smaller, the size of a locket. "What? I don't understand."

"The morning after the gala, when I went to get my car, I stopped to see a friend. She's a pixie with powerful magic. She enchanted my watch." He holds it up between us, and the aged gold glints in the low light of my office. "If it's filled with your blood and I wear it, then you will become immortal." He pops the lid open to reveal the watch face, the hands still ticking, but the space behind is translucent and empty. "Combined with a mating bite, this would bind our souls more permanently."

In the silence, the only sound is my harsh swallow and the ticking of the watch. "W-What about Lily?" My eyes meet his.

"She would continue to age as normal."

"I don't think I could watch her grow old and die." The thought alone has bile crawling up my throat.

"There's a second option." His free hand slides to my hip, bringing our bodies flush. "If the pendant is filled with my blood and you wear it, my clock would begin ticking, and I would age with you."

I suck in a breath. "You'd give up your immortality... for me?"

"Maggie, I'd give up *everything* for you. You and Lily are my whole world. I'd cease to exist without you in my life." He brings the pendant to his chest, thumping it before saying, "This heart beats for you. These lungs breathe for you. One mortal lifetime with you is worth more than all the immortal lifetimes I've spent wandering the earth without you. I love you, Maggie."

Finally breaking free, tears spill down my cheeks at his confession. He'd rather live one lowly human lifetime with me than live forever?

My fingers find purchase on the back of his neck, crashing our mouths together. I sob into the kiss, because I never thought I'd find another love like the one I shared with Roman. I never thought I'd be able to open my heart to anyone after him.

But Viktor changed everything. "I love you, Viktor. My beautiful, kind vampire."

He smiles against my lips. "So option two?"

I nod, too busy devouring his lips to come up for air. He indulges me for a few minutes, feasting on my mouth. Nipping and sucking. Rocking his hips against my core, which grows wetter and wetter by the second. "Are we doing this now?"

He chuckles, lips against my throat. "No time like the present."

Pushing his shoulders, he leans back, giving me some space to think. "Okay, how do we do this?"

"I don't know, country girl. It's my first time." Laughter dances in his ruby irises, and I smack his chest. "Sorry, you walked right into that one. Normally, when vampires mate, their fangs release a special toxin that will cause the mating bite to become permanent. So I guess we do that, then fill the pendant with my blood." He shrugs, like it's the most logical thing in the world.

I raise an eyebrow. "You guess? I'm not a vampire. What if it doesn't work?" Nerves flutter in the pit of my stomach.

His warm chuckle melts over me, easing the worry a bit when he loops the necklace over my head and settles the watch between my breasts, like it was meant to be there all along. It feels *right*.

"Then we try something else. We try whatever it takes until our mate bond is solidified." As if proving his point, nimble fingers work the buttons free on the front of my dress, peeling the blue fabric off my shoulders until I'm left in nothing but a basic nude bra. Viktor's eyes follow his finger as it traces the curve of my heaving breast. "Mmmm... Right here looks like the perfect place to mark you as *mine*. What do you think, little whore?"

Like a switch flips inside him, the monster comes barreling to the surface.

I moan when his other hand snakes behind my back and unhooks my bra, peeling it from my body. Under his ravenous gaze, my skin burns and my nipples ache, peaking into tight buds that scream for his attention.

As if he can read my mind, he bends to take one nipple into his mouth, sucking until my back arches and my head falls back on a moan. "Yeah, that's the spot," he mumbles against my flesh.

"Yes," I agree, rocking my hips against the front of his jeans. Somehow, in the chaos of our kisses and conversation, my dress is bunched around my waist, leaving my top and bottom halves exposed.

He grinds down, the rough denim rubbing against my clit through my thin underwear. Sparks ignite behind my closed lids, and I grip the back of his neck. "Viktor, please. I want to be yours." I already am in every way except one. "Fuck me," I beg.

"That's a good whore," he coos, followed by the snick of his zipper lowering.

Long fingers hook into the sides of my panties, tugging un-til—*rrrip*—the fabric gives way. Then the pierced tip of his cock is nudging against my entrance. I spread my legs wider, accommodating his body as he leans over me, his eyes locked on where his length slides into my pussy. "Fuuuuck, Maggie. You always feel so damn good."

I groan as each rung on the underside of his shaft massages me, stretching me so perfectly.

With a grunt, he bottoms out. Dropping his forehead to mine, his expression softens. "You're sure about this? You're sure you want me?"

I hate the doubt that flashes across his gorgeous eyes. Cupping his face, I hold his gaze. "Yes, Viktor. I want *you*. Not for your money. Not for your name. Not as my nanny, but as my partner." My lips turn up in a smile. "I mean, I won't say no if you keep doing the laundry and the cooking and the dishes—"

I squeak when pain radiates through the side of my ass as his hand connects with it.

"Brat," he growls.

Sobering, I press a kiss to his forehead, each eyelid, his nose, and finally his lush lips. "I love you, Viktor. And that's never going to change, so mark me as yours."

My words must break the last thread of whatever's holding him back because he unleashes, hips pistoning to drive his cock in and out of me at a furious pace.

Breasts bouncing, I moan as he pummels my pussy in only the way he can. His piercings drag with each retreat, adding a delicious friction that has the first signs of an orgasm blooming in my core. "Yes, Viktor. Don't stop."

I need his skin on mine... ice against fire. So I claw at the buttons on his shirt, until they pop open and his sculpted chest is on display. Slowing his thrusts, Viktor shrugs out of his suspenders and shirt, then crowds me until I'm forced to lie back on the desk. The wood sticks to my sweat-slicked skin.

He braces his hands near my shoulders, and I wrap my legs around his narrow waist.

Arching my neck, I bare it to him, foreign instinct telling me he needs to feed. Carding my fingers into his hair, I guide his mouth to my hammering pulse. My free hand slides between our bodies in search of my clit. "Feed, Viktor," I moan, working my fingers over my clit. It's slippery with our combined arousal.

My eyes slam shut in preparation for the pinch of pain I know is coming.

As his hips pick up their pace again, his body lays over mine like an icy shield. "I love you, Maggie." The gentle declaration is a direct contrast to the brutal way he fucks into me.

Then, he strikes, sinking his fangs deep into my neck. My pulse skyrockets and my blood burns.

Until... I'm floating on the fluffiest of clouds as euphoria takes hold of my body. A kaleidoscope of brilliant colors dance across my closed lids, and pulses of pleasure radiate from my core where it clamps around Viktor's cock.

His guttural moans vibrate against my throat, and his thrusts stutter before he holds deep. The first splash of his cum against my womb pulls a groan from my lips.

He gulps down my blood before pulling back. Crimson drips from his elongated fangs. His eyes—*Fuck*. They glow a brilliant red.

Combined with his disheveled snowy locks, it should be frightening. He's an apex predator, and I'm trapped beneath him.

But Viktor would never hurt me. He only wants to bring me pleasure and love. Something he's proven over and over. Proving my point, he dips down, and his hot tongue drags along the wound on my neck. The movement causes my inner walls to flutter as I moan. "Did it work?"

His lips caress the skin, like butterfly wings, before he pulls back to meet my eyes. "We'll know in a few days if the bite mark turns into a scar instead of healing. Ready for your part?"

My brow furrows as Viktor sits me up, cock still buried deep inside me.

He brings his wrist to my lips. "Bite, country girl."

That same nagging instinct rears its head again, and I obey. My teeth sink into his wrist, breaking the skin. Tangy, rich liquid fills my mouth. For some reason, I have the urge to swallow a mouthful before I release him.

The warm blood slides down my throat and settles in my stomach.

When I release his wrist, Viktor has a knowing smile on his face. "We have to hurry before it heals."

Grabbing the watch pendant from between my breasts, I bring it between us and flip open the lid.

My body acts on its own, somehow knowing exactly what needs to be done, even though I have no fucking idea what I'm doing. Through a small hole in the top, Viktor's blood fills the interior of the watch, drop by drop.

Soon, the face is tinted red. It shimmers when it catches the light. The hands keep ticking like normal. "Do you think it worked?" Dragging my eyes from the watch face, I find Viktor's.

His eyebrows are pinched in the middle, his jaw tight. "I don't... I don't know."

Then he groans and drops to his knees. *Oh, shit!*

Face pinched in a pained expression, he clutches his chest.

"Viktor!" Ignoring my state of undress, I scramble off the desk, crawling in front of him. When I place my hand over his heart, it's beating way faster than it should. My gut twists. *Did we do something wrong? What's happening?*

Another pained groan, and his eyes roll to the back of his head as he collapses.

"Viktor!" Tears blur my vision as I do the only thing I can think to do... start compressions on his chest. But the beating of his heart is noticeably absent.

Oh my god! This can't be happening again. Am I cursed to find love, only to have it ripped from my grasp every time?

Sobbing, I lay my head on his chest, my body growing numb. *Thump.*

I press my ear closer to his chest.

Thump. Thump.

His heart.... It's beating again.

Viktor's eyes fly wide, and he sucks in a breath. His chest heaves as he gasps for lungful after lungful of air.

Tears pour down my cheeks, their salty flavor coating my trembling lips. "Viktor. Holy shit! Are you okay?"

Relief washes over me as I scoot closer and gently prop his head on my lap.

He rubs at the skin over his heart. When he sits up, one hand goes to my chest, right over my galloping heart. The fingers of his other hand wrap around my wrist, laying my palm on his chest. Under the skin, his heart beats perfectly in time with mine. "They're in sync. Bonded. I-I think it worked, Maggie." Sleepy eyes flit to mine before closing on a long blink.

"You're mortal?"

Releasing my hand, his fingers wrap around the pendant that hangs between my breasts. "I think so, but let's not find out, yeah?" He chuckles.

Helping him to his feet, he wobbles when I lead him to our bedroom and straight to the bathtub. "I thought you were dead," I say, leaning him against the counter and turning on the tap.

Hot water fills the tub as I help Viktor undress. "I'm not going anywhere for a very long time. You're stuck with me, country girl." His thumb swipes back and forth over the puncture marks on my neck.

"Sounds pretty damn good to me, city boy."

Viktor presses a kiss to my forehead, then my lips. Now that the shock of almost losing him has worn off, the mating bond thrums under my skin as Viktor's love pours through our connection.

It'll take some getting used to, but I like the feeling of him always being with me.

I tug him by the hand into the tub, where we clean the blood from our skin and start planning for the future of *Sweet Orchard Dreams*.

EPILOGUE

Maggie

Christmas Eve: The Swiss Alps

The cabin door clicks shut. A soft giggle followed by a deep chuckle has my lips curving into a smile. Turning off my e-reader, I set it on the coffee table next to my mug of hot cocoa. "How were the slopes today?"

Viktor wanted to celebrate his birthday—and our first Christmas as a family—with a big trip. So here we are, in a ritzy cabin in the Swiss Alps. Since I'm not the most coordinated person in the world, I gave up on skiing after day one.

After falling on my ass more times than I can count, I settled on staying cozied up by the fireplace with a good book while Lily and Viktor hit the slopes. We've been sightseeing in the evenings and enjoying all the local cuisine, too.

It's been a magical vacation... the first of many, if Viktor has anything to say about it. Which I'm sure he does.

Lily kicks off her boots and shrugs off her winter coat, leaving them in a pile on the floor before running to me. "Viktor fell down... twice." She's beaming at his blunder, the missing teeth in her grin tugging at my heartstrings.

With a heavy sigh, my vampire collapses onto the couch on my other side. "I believe the second time, you fell on me and took me down with you, little one." His lips morph into a smile when he reaches across me and tickles Lily's side.

"What happened to your supernatural grace, city boy? Did you forget it at home?" After syncing our lifespans, Viktor didn't seem to lose any of his extra abilities, like his speed or enhanced senses, but it's still fun to give him a hard time.

"Brat," he mutters, pulling me in for a hug. His lips press against the top of my head, and I melt into his cool body. He's even chillier after being out on the slopes all afternoon, but the roaring fire in front of us staves off my shiver. "Little one, should we give Mom her present?"

Lily squeals, then hops to her feet and sprints toward the bedrooms.

My eyebrows knit together as I turn to face Viktor. The picture of calm, his features give nothing away. "I thought this trip *was* the present?"

"You know I love to spoil my girls. I couldn't help myself." He shrugs, playing innocent.

Before I can pry more information out of him, Lily flies back to the couch and hands something to Viktor. His fist swallows whatever it is before I can catch a glance. "What are you two up to?" I ask, pulling Lily into my lap. She wraps her arms around my neck and snuggles close.

But Viktor is on the move, slipping from the couch to kneel in front of me. *On one knee.*

Is he going to—

"Maggie." His ruby gaze glitters as he searches my face, finally landing on my eyes, tears burning the backs of them as he brings his fist between us, opening it to reveal a small red velvet box. "I've loved you since the first moment I saw you. And every minute I spend with you, I fall deeper and deeper into the depths of your love. You always say that I brought you back to life but, country girl, you did the very same for me."

He peels open the lid of the box, and nestled inside is the most beautiful ring I've ever seen. Side-by-side on a white gold band, a sparkling ruby sits with a crystal-clear diamond. "Is that my wedding ring from Roman?"

"I hope you don't mind. It only felt right."

All I can do is nod as tears cloud my vision. "It's beautiful, Viktor."

"You and Lily mean the world to me, Maggie. And I'll spend the rest of my life spoiling you both rotten and showing you how much I love you. Will you marry me?" His dark eyebrows crouch low over pleading eyes as he stares up at me.

How could I say no to this amazing vampire who clicked into my life perfectly when I didn't even know I needed someone like him?

"Yes! Of course!" Holding out my trembling left hand, Viktor steadies it in his and slides the ring onto my finger.

It's then I notice a smaller diamond nestled between the two larger stones, near the band of the ring. "That's for me!" Lily exclaims, wiggling in my lap and pointing at the smallest stone.

He thought of everything. Connecting the past chapters of my life with the new chapters yet to be written. "It's perfect, Viktor. Thank you." The first tear slips free, rolling down my cheek when he leans in for a kiss.

"Not as perfect as you, sweetheart."

The rest of the evening passes peacefully as the snowflakes dance through the darkening sky outside. Cuddled by the fire, we eat and play some of the board games provided by the resort. Eventually, Lily's eyes grow heavy, and Viktor offers to put her to bed.

Viktor

"Goodnight, Lily. I love you." Bending, I press my lips to her forehead before tucking the blankets tighter around her.

"Viktor?" The question in her sleepy voice has me settling on the edge of her bed.

"Yes, little one."

"If you're marrying Momma, does that mean you're my dad now?" Her dark-blonde eyebrows crease in the middle as her eyes meet mine.

On the inside, my stomach knots, but I keep my tone even. "It doesn't have to change anything, unless you want it to." I stroke the flyaway hair back from her face. "But I'd be honored to be your dad. I'm honored just to know you, Lily."

Her lips twist as she hums. She hugs her stuffed unicorn close to her chest. "I think I'd like for you to be my dad."

My heart nearly erupts, it's beating so fast. I can't keep the smile from spreading across my face. "Okay."

"Can I try it out?"

Curling my lips over my teeth, I fight back a laugh. "Yes, of course."

"Goodnight, Dad. I love you." She beams as she says the words, and I return her smile.

After one more kiss goodnight—and another round of "I love you"—Lily burrows under the blankets, and I doubt we'll hear a peep from her until morning.

Closing her bedroom door, I cross the hall to the room where Maggie and I are staying. Dark wood furniture fills the space with soft bedding and cozy decor, making it the perfect winter escape from the snow after a long day of skiing.

Speaking of, fluffy white flakes cascade through the night sky outside, piling up rapidly on the snow-covered ground.

As I pull my eyes from the window and scan the room, my future bride is nowhere to be found.

My bride. The words settle in my chest. To say the past few months have been a whirlwind is an understatement.

I'm no longer her nanny; instead, I'm her partner in everything. On top of my new role as a dad, I've settled into splitting my time between helping Maggie with the financial side of the orchard and working with kids at the community center in Maple Ridge Hollow.

I still get to shape young minds, but I get to focus most of my time and energy on my two favorite girls—Maggie and Lily.

Father and I still have a long way to go, but we're working on our relationship. He kept his promise and became an investor for the orchard, allowing Maggie peace of mind and the ability to expand her business.

True to her word, Maggie paid me back every cent I spent on the festival. What she doesn't know is that I deposited it all into a high-yield savings account for Lily's future.

"There you are, beautiful wife," I say as I lean against the door to the bathroom.

Maggie is surrounded by a mountain of bubbles, soaking in the massive bathtub. "How did bedtime go?" She sips from a glass of champagne before setting it on the platform surrounding the jetted tub.

I snap my fingers. "Out like a light." Kneeling next to the tub, I run my hand under the water, caressing her smooth thigh. "She called me Dad."

"She did?" Water sloshes over the side of the tub when Maggie sits up. "Oh, Viktor, that's amazing!"

When she clutches my forearm, her new ring sparkles in the dim light of the bathroom. A few lit candles flicker along the edge of the tub. She went all out to set the mood in here, so I might as well take advantage. "Are you happy, sweetheart?"

"So happy, Viktor. I never thought I'd be lucky enough to find love again after Roman. You changed everything." Closing the distance between us, she presses her lips to mine.

Every time she kisses me, the monster inside purrs. Even now, his chest rattles until the rumble takes life as an audible noise.

Wrapping my hand around Maggie's slender neck, I hold her mouth to mine and give in to his desires. My tongue lashes against hers. My fangs nip at her plump lips.

When I swing my leg over the side of the tub, the tepid water soaks the thin fabric of my pajama pants, and they stick to my skin.

"Viktor!" Maggie squeaks as I settle between her thighs, not caring that the water is soaking my clothes. I just need her. "What are you doing?"

"I need my wife." I nip and suck at her neck as she relaxes back into the tub, her moans filling the humid air.

Gripping her under the thighs, I lift her soaked body and deposit her on the platform around the tub. It's big enough that she can recline on her elbows, hooded eyes keeping watch on me as I swipe my tongue through her folds.

"Mmmm...the first taste never gets old, sweetheart. Always so slick and ready for me," I growl, pumping a finger into her tight channel.

Maggie's spine arches, and her head falls back on a cry when I suck her clit between my lips.

"You're already so wet, my sweet whore. What were you doing in here? Were you playing with yourself, just hoping I'd find you and finish the job?" Spreading her pussy wide with my thumbs, my eyes catch on a hint of crimson in her back hole.

Thumb landing on the ruby gemstone nestled between her ass cheeks, I press gently. "Naughty slut. You did start without me. What's this?"

Her chest heaves, the skin flushed from the hot water and her arousal. "Merry Christmas, city boy." She moans when I add a second finger to her pussy, curling them against her favorite spot while my thumb plays with the plug in her ass. "Please, Viktor."

"Fuck, you're perfect. Does my wife need to come?" *Wife.* That word does something to me, twisting my insides into a possessive mess. Yes, she's my mate, but once we're married, she'll be mine in every way.

And I'll be hers.

Supple thighs tighten around my head, holding me hostage against her heated skin. "Yes. Please."

"You beg so nicely, Maggie." Leaving the plug alone for now, my fingers curl inside her again, and my tongue lashes at her clit until she's trembling.

But I don't stop.

I can't. Not until she falls over the edge and her cunt strangles my fingers.

The hypnotic clench of her inner muscles has my cock harder than steel in my soaked pants. I need to be inside her. I need to fuck my wife.

Her body goes limp and sated, and I scoop Maggie into my arms, heading to the bed. "Viktor! The water... The resort staff are going to hate us!"

"I don't care." I throw her onto the bed, her perky tits bouncing as her weight settles on the mattress. Mmm... The peaked, rosy nipples call to my fangs until they ache and throb. "I need to be inside you. *Now*."

As I shove the sopping fabric of my shirt over my head, Maggie spreads her legs, exposing her glistening core and plugged ass. The skin is pinkened to perfection.

"Are you desperate, city boy?" Dainty fingers trail between her breasts, down her soft tummy, through the patch of dark-blonde curls until they strum her engorged clit. Like sin incarnate, she teases me with her sopping wet cunt and bejeweled ass as she writhes on the bed.

Fuuuuck. Why does she torture me?

My fingers fumble with the tie on my pants, and I nearly face plant onto the bed in my haste to get them over my feet.

Once I'm free, I prowl over her perfect body. My fingers trace the silver stretch marks on the sides of her breasts before pinching the nipple. "I'm always desperate for you, country girl."

Maggie's eyes darken, and she moans, pushing her flesh into my hand.

Between her breasts, my pocket watch rests against her skin. I run a finger against the chain, a constant reminder of our love and our bond.

Maggie wraps a hand around mine, keeping the watch between us as I push inside her tight cunt. Foreheads tipped together, we groan in unison when the head of my cock hits a spot deep inside her. "Fuck, Viktor. I love the way you stretch me. I'm so full. So close to you."

"Ditto, sweetheart. I'd stay inside you forever if I could." With lazy thrusts, I start the climb toward my peak, a low tingle at the base of my spine.

"Do you need to feed?" Maggie asks, meeting each snap of my hips with one of her own.

She loves when she's impaled on my cock and my fangs are buried in her skin. In fact, she begs for my bite almost every time we make love. I hum, running my nose up the side of her throat. Venturing farther north, my lips graze her ear as I whisper, "Did you not get enough of my bite when I had you screaming my name in the shower this morning?"

The evidence of our quickie still marks her skin. Faint puncture wounds dot her supple breasts, lighting an inferno in my veins.

My thirst for blood may be quenched, but my thirst for my mate never will be.

"It's never enough, Viktor. Please."

As much as I yearn to sink my fangs into her sweet skin and feast on her intoxicating blood, what I really want is to sink my cock balls deep in her ass while she chants my name like a prayer. "Not yet, sweetheart. Give me one orgasm first."

My hand slips between our sweat and water-slicked bodies, searching for that magic button. Finding her clit, I start with soft, slow circles until the walls of her pussy tighten, making it harder to thrust in and out of her.

Her thighs clamp around my hips, and I increase the pressure on her clit. As her inner muscles grip my cock like a vise, I'm forced to hold deep inside her sweet heat while her mouth falls open on a silent scream, eyes pinching shut.

"Good girl. That's one." Slipping free of her pussy, I groan as the tight muscle grips each piercing, trying to pull me back into her body. "So greedy." My fingers connect with her clit, and she moans.

"Now?" Like a kid on Christmas morning, her sea-glass eyes glow when I gently wiggle the plug free from her ass.

"Now, my beautiful whore." Once the plug is removed, I test the waters by sliding a finger into her ass. Warm and tight, the muscles give way as I give a few testing pumps.

She tosses me a bottle of lube, and I use it to coat my cock. "Ready, Maggie?"

Vigorously, her head bobs up and down. She maneuvers so she's propped up on her elbows, eyes glued to my hand as it wraps around my cock again. Pre-cum oozes from the tip, spilling between my fingers when I run my fist up and down the length a few times.

Lining the head up with her puckered hole, I press into her slowly. Warmth overtakes me with each inch her ass swallows. "You were made for me, sweetheart. Weren't you? Your tight ass fits my cock like a glove. It feels fucking amazing."

"Yes, Viktor. Fuck me, please." Her voice cracks on a whine when I bottom out.

Her left hand falls to her clit, the diamond and ruby shimmering in the moonlight with each flick of her wrist.

I'm not going to last long with this goddess spread out on the sheets below me. Back arched, her breasts have my fangs elongating.

Lying back on the bed, her free hand comes up to cup my cheek. "You're beautiful like this, Viktor." The red glow of my eyes reflects back to me when I look deep into hers. Black claws dig into the flesh of her hips when I wrap my fingers around her body.

Most women would be terrified of being fucked by a monster, but not Maggie. Never Maggie. She's seen the real me and never shied away.

Bending down, I plaster my body to hers, lips hovering above hers. "And you're beautiful like this, wife. Taking every piercing into your tight little ass. Swallowing every inch like a good girl."

Her answering moan has my hips pistoning until the familiar buzz takes over my senses. My orgasm is close.

Teetering on the knife's edge, I give Maggie what she's been begging for. With a growl, I bare my fangs and strike where her neck and shoulder meet. Combined with her fingers on her clit and my cock driving in and out of her ass, she shatters. "Viktor! Oh, fuck! Yes, Viktor..."

I retract my fangs and quickly seal the wound with my tongue before slapping a hand over her mouth. "Shhh, sweetheart. You don't want to wake Lily."

Her eyes slam shut, and she lets out another loud moan, muffled by my hand as her ass spasms around my cock. The added friction sets off my own release, and I slam my lips against hers to stifle both of our moans.

"I love you, Maggie," I whisper against her lips once we finally come up for air.

Her mouth curves against mine. "I love you, too."

After a quick clean-up, we climb back into bed. I'm ready to sleep for a solid twenty-four hours after she drained me dry. Maggie nestles against my chest. I tuck one arm behind my head, and the other finds its home around her waist.

She yawns, idly drawing circles on my chest with her finger. "Did Vanessa make it home okay?"

My sister offered to watch the house for us while we're away. She was supposed to head back to the city this evening in order to spend Christmas morning with our parents.

Grabbing my cell phone from the nightstand, the screen lights up with a severe weather alert. Blizzard warning in place for New York City and the surrounding area—including Maple Ridge Hollow. "Looks like there's a bad storm coming in." I hold my phone up to Maggie, and her brow furrows. "I'll give her a call." Before I can pull up her number, another notification comes through. "And our flight is delayed. I guess we're spending Christmas here."

Find out what happens when Viktor's twin sister, Vanessa, gets snowed in with Jean-Luc, the grumpy minotaur. Their story is next in the Monstrous New York universe!

E.M. SAUBER
paranormal
romance author

E.M. Sauber was born and raised in the Midwest. Reading has always been a part of her life. A way to escape when the real world gets to be too much.

She currently lives in Minnesota with her wonderful husband, two children, and two dogs.

When she isn't writing steamy shifter stories, you can find her cuddled on the couch under a fuzzy blanket with her kindle or daydreaming about a new idea for a book.

www.ingramcontent.com/pod-product-compliance
Lightning Source LLC
Chambersburg PA
CBHW070215260626
47160CB00002B/558